OLD MONEY

By Jackie J. Brisendine

ISBN: 978-0-557-67896-9

In memory of George Thomas Reed Jr. (Tommy)

1946 – 1987

JIM

Sometimes going off to war and being sent into combat brings out the best in a man; sometimes it brings out the worst. Jim Vess was most surely the latter. Born of an Italian mother and part Cherokee Indian father, Jim was a handsome man, even though he was slightly on the heavy side. He stood six feet tall, had dark brown eyes, and black curly hair. He sported a barely noticeable scar that ran from the center of his forehead down the bridge of his nose. If anything, the scar complemented him; projecting an aura of toughness that you would expect of a gangster in a forties movie. The fact that he had a thick neck, wide shoulders, and weighed over two hundred and fifty pounds made him even more menacing.

Jim had moved around a lot before the war started, mostly driving the big rigs, hauling produce back up north from Florida. Upon being drafted into the Army, he quickly adapted to military life and would have moved up in rank if it were not for the lack of a formal education. He had limited reading skills, but made up for it with his knack for commanding the respect of his fellow soldiers.

Jim almost seemed to relish going into battle; he fought through Germany, France, Belgium, and parts of North Africa. By the time he ended up back in Germany after the truce was signed, he had earned two battlefield promotions; he was once recommended for a commission, but was rejected due to his limited education.

Volunteering to stay in Europe after he had accumulated the required number of points to go back to the States, he soon got into trouble. Several times, the locals accused him of robbery and theft, but somehow he always managed to get out of it.

Jim's commanding officer quickly had him shipped stateside after he was accused of murder by a German shop owner. The charges were not pursued due to his combat record and the fact that he was sent back to the United States.

****

JERRY

Jerry Pardue was a long-legged, hawk-nosed, blond kid who was drafted into the Army two weeks after the bombing of Pearl Harbor. He was taller than any of his classmates starting in the fourth grade. By the time he was a sophomore in high school, he had reached six feet, four inches tall. When he entered high school he was nicknamed "Big Bird" due to his hawk-nose and skinny legs. He ate like a horse to gain weight, but it never happened. He carried the nickname until he went into the Army.

Jerry was an agreeable young man who made friends easily. After finishing basic training at Ft. Polk, Louisiana, Jerry was sent to Ft. Oglethorpe, Georgia where he worked in the debarkation office. He had learned to type in high school and when the Army found that out, his fate was sealed; he would sit in an office until the war ended.

Feeling guilty for sending so many men off to Europe and the islands of the Pacific but not having to go himself, he became depressed and asked to be transferred to a combat unit. His request was denied more than once; he was told that his services were needed where he was, and to get used to it.

Jerry met a local girl named Glenda, who worked in a drug store in nearby Rossville, Georgia. He and Glenda spent a lot of their free time exploring the nearby Chickamauga Civil War Battlefield. They spent hours walking through the park and studying the many plaques and monuments of the battle.

Jerry and Glenda became good friends, and might have had a deeper relationship, but they knew that he could be sent away at any time. It was a good thing that they remained just good friends.

Three days after the war ended, Jerry was transferred to Ft. Knox, Kentucky.

1

August 2, 1945

Jim Vess and Jerry Pardue jumped onto their 1940 Ford, parked in the alley behind the First National Bank of Evansville, Indiana.

"You're crazy," Jerry said as he leaned over the back seat, pushing the duffel bag down to the floorboard. "You didn't have to shoot that guy, he was just standing in line waiting for the next teller, and it was obvious that they were all scared to the point of wetting their pants."

"I didn't like that smirk on his face; besides they'll think twice about not getting up for ten minutes, like I told them," Jim said without a hint of remorse.

"I hope he's not dead," Jerry added, "robbing a bank is one thing, but killing someone; that's not what I signed up for."

"He'll be OK, I think I got him in the leg, at least that's where I aimed."

Evansville, Indiana is located in the southwestern part of the state on a horseshoe bend of the Ohio River. Jim selected the medium-sized city for several reasons, mostly because of the easy access to the major north-south highway, and the fact that after the bank heist they would be crossing the river into another state. He explained to Jerry that they would be in another police jurisdiction once they crossed the river.

Jerry only nodded, wondering to himself if Jim had ever heard of the highway patrol.

The green Ford headed west, trying not to speed as Jim

searched for the sign pointing to US 41.

He was looking in the rearview mirror when Jerry screamed, "Watch that kid. Damn, you almost hit that colored boy!"

"What the hell is he doing?" asked Jim, still glancing in the mirror.

"He just stepped off the curb, I think he's a paper boy; man, is he pissed; look, he's giving you the finger."

"Screw him," Jim said, turning right and heading south on Highway 41 crossing the two-lane bridge over the Ohio River into Kentucky.

****

Jim and Jerry had been friends since meeting in the Army, where they had spent the last six months together at Ft. Knox, Kentucky, sitting around the barracks waiting to be discharged. They would spend most of the day talking about what they were going to do when they got out of the Army. They both liked the idea of going into charter boat fishing down in Florida, but neither had the money it would take to get started. Jim brought up the idea of how easy it would be to do one bank robbery, and that it would give them more than enough money to buy a boat and the equipment that they needed.

Jerry listened to Jim tell stories about how he had robbed and stole from the Germans after the war was over, and how comfortable he was that they could get away with it.

Jim told Jerry more than once, "Man if you put a gun in their face, what they have is yours."

Jerry was a little frightened by the way Jim talked sometimes, but the idea of buying a boat and starting a business in Florida sounded too good to pass up.

****

No one moved in the bank for several minutes; the customer that was shot screamed in pain as blood darkened his trousers high up on his right thigh.

"Would someone please call the police?" the wounded man asked. "I think I'm going to bleed to death! Does this place not have a security guard for Christ's sake?" the man asked as he started crawling toward the front door.

Tim Ellis, the bank security guard, was still lying on the floor by the front door from when Jim had taken his gun and ordered him to get into a facedown position.

Finally, someone started banging on the front door as the ashen-faced security guard slowly got up and opened the door.

****

Evansville had not had a bank robbery for years; Detective Frank Mumpower and FBI Agent Sam Sanders had their hands full trying to organize what you would call an investigation. The smell of cordite still hung in the air as the two law officers made their way to a conference room on the main floor of the bank. Just before they entered the room, a uniformed patrolman approached Sanders holding a pistol hanging from a pencil that he had stuck through the trigger guard.

"Found this in the alley, sir; pretty sure it belongs to the bank guard."

"More than likely; put it in a bag and give it to Mumpower, we'll dust it for prints," Sanders said, stepping through the door into the conference room.

After interviewing everyone that was in the bank, Mumpower and Sanders briefed Sheriff Stan Wilkey and Police Chief Mike Wilson on how they believed it went down. Sanders picked up a handful of notes, eased half of his butt down on one corner of the long conference table, and addressed the group.

"Two white males, one heavyset about five ten and around two hundred and twenty-five pounds, the other tall, about six two and approximately one hundred and seventy pounds, inconspicuously walked into the bank. The men were dressed casual, they were wearing tan or brown pants, and white or light-colored shirts, each wore brown fedora hats with the brim turned down slightly in the front. The heavyset man walked over to Mr. Ellis, the security guard, he asked the guard to hand him his gun, which he promptly did. The heavy-set man then instructed him to lock the front door and get face down on the floor, which he seemed more than happy to do."

Agent Sanders stopped and looked around the room then returned to his notes.

"The elderly security guard was still in a state of shock, and offered little in the way of help in the investigation. Some time before the bandit took the gun from the guard, both men had pulled handkerchiefs up over their noses, you know the way they do in cowboy movies; no one is sure at what point they did this. After the front door was locked, the tall one went over to the two front windows and closed the blinds. The heavyset bandit announced that they were robbing the bank and for everyone to lie face down on the floor. One of the customers was slow to respond to the order to get on the floor. The heavyset man, who seemed to be the leader, put something over the end of his pistol; which was probably the bag used to carry the money out of the bank, and pulled the trigger.

"Most of the people questioned agreed the sound that the gun made did not sound like a gun but a loud thud. Mr. Smith, the bank customer that was shot, went to the floor without a peep; most thought at first that he was dead. The big man seemed unfazed that he had just shot a man as he threw a green canvas bag, probably a duffle bag on the floor beside Robert McKinney, the head teller. The big man told the teller, 'Fill it up, with nothing less than twenties. Don't try to fool me. I know the Wells Fargo truck just left and I know what he brought you. I'm watching you; if you do not do as I say, so help me I will kill you."

"I'm telling you guys exactly what the teller told me," Sanders said, flipping back through his notes.

"It took the teller less than a minute to fill the bag with the $1000 and $2000 bundles of currency that the armored truck had left just minutes before the bandits entered the bank. The tall slim man walked past the teller cages straight to the back door, the big man followed him halfway, stopped, turned around, and said, "You are being watched, if anyone gets up before ten minutes, they are as good as dead.".' Both men turned and walked out the back door."

Detective Mumpower looked over at the police chief and the sheriff, who were sitting across the table from him. He nodded at Sanders as if to ask, "What else?"."

"Anything I missed?" asked Sanders, looking around the room.

"Do we know how much they took?" Mumpower asked.

"They're still working on that, I'm sure it'll be quite a bit, the armored truck had just made a delivery. It looks like they got most of it. Yeah it's probably going to be a bundle all right," Sanders answered, shaking his head.

The FBI agent stood up rubbing the back of his thigh, which had probably gone to sleep from his awkward position on the corner of the conference table.

"That's it for now, well get back together after lunch over in the sheriff's office. One o'clock sharp."

****

Jim and Jerry drove south on Highway 41, which was the main route to Florida from the Midwest, originating in Chicago and going all the way to Miami.

"I told you it would be a piece of cake, didn't I?" Jim said. "I'll bet they're still lying there on the floor."

"You still shouldn't have used your gun; we would have got the money anyway."

Jim stayed within the speed limit and stopped at all the stop signs and red lights going through the small towns that dotted the highway, as they drove into Kentucky and on southward toward Tennessee.

"How much you think we got?" Jerry asked.

"I don't know, but by the looks of that duffel bag, it's got to be a bunch. We'll find a tourist court somewhere around Nashville, spend the night and count it then."

Jerry squirmed around in his seat," I'm hungry, "the next truck stop you see, how about stopping and get a bite to eat; I gotta piss too."

****

Detective Frank Mumpower and Agent Sanders met in Sheriff Stan Wilkey's office, along with Police Chief Mike Wilson, after interviewing the bank employees and the horrified patrons.

"OK what have we got?" Mumpower asked. "Please don't everybody talk at once. Chief, your people on the street see anything, do we have a getaway car, eyewitness to them leaving, anything at all?"

"Not yet. Detective, so far no one saw them leaving, there was just nobody in that alley that we know of and we are sure that's where they had their car parked," the chief answered like it was an apology.

"Sheriff, do you have any reports of stolen vehicles, jail breaks, or other robberies?"

"Not anything close by, a couple of armed robberies on the west coast and one in Texas," Wilkey answered.

"Agent Sanders, did you get anything from your interviews that would tell us what guns were used."

"We believe the shooter used a German Luger; the slug passed through the bank customer's leg and was taken from the teller counter. The slug appeared to be a seven point sixty-five caliber, know more often as a nine millimeter, which would be consistent for the Luger. We're not sure about the slimmer one; we're pretty certain it was a revolver, probably a thirty-eight."

Mumpower sat there looking around the room waiting for someone to offer something new. There was a faint knock on the door and a pretty blond officer of about twenty years old stuck her head in the door.

"Sheriff, we have someone out here that wants to speak to you, he says he may have something on the robbery."

"Send him in."

The door opened and a skinny Negro boy of around eighteen or twenty years old walked in. He was dressed in a pair of overalls with no shirt, and a newspaper hat fashioned from a previous edition of the Evansville Daily Register. The kid had on tennis shoes that had seen their best days. His right pants leg was rolled up just below the knee, probably to keep it out of the sprocket and chain of a bicycle.

"Have a seat, son, and tell us your name," the sheriff said.

"Andrew Cook," the boy said, looking down at the floor.

"Well, what is it that you have to tell us;" the sheriff asked, grinning at the others in the room as if this was a waste of time.

"I heard on the radio dat the mens who robbed the bank were like slim and shorty, and dat dey had on brown hats and light-colored shirts."

“That’s right,” the sheriff said. “Go on.”

“Well, sir, I sell papers, you know, extras up on 4th and Main.” At the time dey said dat the hold up took place, a green Ford coupe almost run over my ass as I was standing next to the curb holding out a newspaper.”

“Watch your mouth, son, we get the picture,” interrupted the sheriff.

“Sir, he almost came up on the curb, dats when I got a good look at em. I was really pissed; I thought dey did it because I was colored. I didn’t get the tag number, but it was a Kentucky plate. I don’t know if it was them or not, Sheriff, but dey turned south on 41.”

“Is that it?”

“Dat’s all I know, Sheriff,” the boy said, looking back down at the floor; “I just had dis funny feelin about it, and thought you might want to know.”

“OK, son, you did the right thing, we really appreciate you coming in and telling us about what you saw, I’m sure this will be a big help.”

Andrew got up and walked toward the door, never taking his eyes off the floor. He stopped just as he reached the door, turned around, and looked up at the sheriff.

“Sir, I seen in the eyes of dat man driving, I think he is a mean man.” Andrew lowered his head and walked out the door.

“What do you think guys?” the sheriff asked as soon as Andrew had shut the door. “Do you think we should go with it?”

Mumpower was first to speak, “Hell yes, I think it could have been them, besides that’s all we got. I’ll put out an all points, especially south, and to be on the lookout for a green Ford coupe.”

“The FBI will alert the State Police all the way to Florida, and the border crossings into Canada, they may try to flee the country,” Agent Sanders said.

"If anything new comes up, run it through my office, thanks for everything." The sheriff looked at his watch and then back up at the group. "Let's go to work."

****

"There, up on the right, pull in, it looks like there's a restaurant inside, my dad always said the best place to eat on the highway is at truck stops, the truckers know where the good food is," Jerry said, folding the roadmap and putting it back down on the seat.

They had entered into Tennessee at Clarksville, and were within twenty miles of Nashville; it was beginning to get dark and business at the truck stop seemed to be light.

"Reach back there and see if you can fish out one of those bundles of cash, we'll need money to pay for the food and gas; I'm about broke."

Jerry leaned over the seat and released the snap hook that was attached to the shoulder strap of the duffel bag. He smiled as he ran his hand down in the bag and pulled out a bundle of bills with a paper strap around it, imprinted with $2000.00.

"Holy mother of Jesus," Jerry stammered, "look here, Jim, two thousand in twenties, we can buy a whole fleet of boats, there's no telling how much money is in there!"

Sweat began to bead on Jerry's upper lip as he closed up the duffel bag and eased it back down behind his seat.

"Don't get excited, pull off a couple of twenties and put the rest back in the bag. All we need is for somebody to see us flashing around that much cash."

As Jim drove up to the gas pump, the bell alerting the attendant rang, telling him there was a customer. As soon as the car stopped, the attendant was already spraying the windshield and reaching for a paper towel.

"Fill her up?" asked the red-haired young man. He was wearing a military-style hat and a dark-colored shirt with the name "Buddy" embroidered above the pocket.

"Yes, with regular and check the oil."

The pungent odor of scorched oil drifted through the open window as the attendant raised the hood on the slightly overheated Ford.

"She's a little over a quart low," Buddy said, showing Jim the dipstick.

"Go ahead and add a quart; thirty weight."

Jim and Jerry sat quietly; watching the traffic on the highway and observing the truckers kick tires and inspect their rigs before getting back on the highway.

"That will be four dollars and twenty-five cents with the oil," Buddy said with a smile. "Have you guys just been discharged?"

"Why you ask," Jim snapped back, without looking up at the attendant while handing him a twenty-dollar bill.

"I see your duffel bag there in the back, a lot of guys passing through here lately are headed home, a German helmet in one hand and a Jap rifle in the other." Buddy stood smiling waiting for one of the two men to answer the simple question. "I'll be right back with your change," he said, as the bell rang again, triggered this time by the pickup truck that had just pulled up to the pump beside Jim.

The attendant went inside to get change for the twenty, telling the driver of the truck that he would be right back. The boy returned in less than a minute.

"Thanks, and come back," the attendant said, as he handed Jim his change, grabbed the spray bottle, turned, and walked toward the pickup.

Jim pulled the Ford away from the gas pump and drove across the parking lot to the restaurant that was connected by a covered walkway from the service station.

"Here's the key, Jerry, get that damn duffel bag out of the floorboard and put it into the trunk, be sure to lock the car. I'm going to the restroom," Jim said as he slammed the car door.

Jerry entered the restaurant, took a seat in a booth in the corner, and waited for Jim to return from the restroom. He picked up the menu and had just started to read it when Jim slid into the seat across the table from him.

"I could eat a horse," muttered Jerry tiredly, as a slightly overweight blond walked up to the table, pulling a pencil out from under her hair.

"Can I get you some coffee?" inquired the blond.

" Yes Mam please, you want some too, don't you, Jim?"

"Yes, that would be fine," Jim said without looking up.

"You ready to order; or do you want a minute?"

"I'm ready," Jerry barked, "I'll have the special."

"What about you, sweetie?" the girl said, looking down at Jim.

"I'll have the large hamburger with fries, and bring me a coca-cola too."

"Coming up," the waitress said as she turned and walked back toward the kitchen.

Jerry sensed that something was bothering Jim as he had very little to say since they had left Evansville; he seemed to be preoccupied about something. More than once he tried to talk to Jim, but he gave up after several attempts. He had questions about where in Florida they were headed and how they were going to get the money into a checking account to buy the boat and equipment they were going to need to start their business. Jim mumbled something to himself about Jerry worrying too much. He told Jerry that he needed to think and for him to let it rest, that they would talk about it later.

It didn't take long for Jim and Jerry to finish off their meal; neither man said much for fear of being overheard.

As they were eating, a highway patrolman came in and sat at the counter almost across from them. The trooper didn't stay very long; one cup of coffee and he was gone. They were relieved when he left, but it served as an incentive to eat and get back on the road.

Jerry was the first to speak sliding into the front seat of the Ford. "That asshole gave me the creeps; just about killed my appetite." Jim pulled the green Ford back onto the highway and headed south. He waited until he had shifted through the gears and lowered the shifter down into third gear before acknowledging Jerry's comment.

"Are you going to wet your pants every time you see a cop?" You're going to have to understand cops are everywhere. Turn on the radio, Jerry; see if you can pick up the Grand Ole Opry; Nashville is only a few miles down the road. It's WSM, that's 650 on the dial; we should be able to pick it up now."

Jim drove through Nashville being careful to stop at all the traffic lights. The lights of the city began to fade behind them as they made their way out into Murfreesboro, listening to Roy Acuff, Red Foley, and Minnie Pearl sing and tell jokes. It was 10:00 PM and between a commercial for National Life and Accident Insurance Company and returning to hear Eddie Arnold, an announcer came on with a news report.

"AUTHORITIES ARE ON THE LOOKOUT FOR TWO MEN WHO ROBBED THE FIRST NATIONAL BANK IN EVANSVILLE, INDIANA TODAY. THE MEN GOT AWAY WITH AN UNDISCLOSED AMOUNT OF MONEY AFTER SHOOTING AND SERIOUSLY WOUNDING A BANK CUSTOMER. THESE MEN ARE CONSIDERED TO BE ARMED AND DANGEROUS. THEY ARE BELIEVED TO BE

DRIVING A GREEN 1940 OR 41 FORD COUPE AND POSSIBLY HEADED SOUTH."

The radio station returned to the Grand Ole Opry with Eddie Arnold singing, *"Make the world go away."*

"Well, well, well," Jim mumbled, "that's it; we got to get another car. I didn't think anyone saw us come out that bank back door, I don't get it."

They listened to the music while both men replayed in their heads the news bulletin they had just heard on the radio.

"I'll bet somebody saw us go in and park, that's got to be it," Jerry said.

"It don't matter, shut up and let me think." He mumbled something under his breath then hit the steering wheel with both of his palms hard enough to make Jerry flinch.

"We better get this buggy off the highway; the highway patrol will be on the lookout now. Look at the map, see where we're at; we need to find a motel maybe one with cabins we can pull up between."

Jim glanced at Jerry out of the corner of his eye. Manchester is just up the road, should be one around there."

Jerry leaned back in the seat, closed his eyes, and reflected on what had taken place so far.

What the hell have we done? It sounded like a good idea when we were planning it, but now I'm not so sure. I wasn't planning on hurting anybody; I've never hurt anyone in my life. Jim scares me a lot, I thought I knew him but now I just don't know. He didn't have to shoot that man in that bank; hell I think he enjoyed it. Well, I'm in it up to my ass now; I guess I'll just have to ride it out and see what happens. I think I've made up my mind though; when we get down in Florida, I think I'll get Jim to split the money up. He can go his way and I'll go mine. Going into business with him would be the...

"Wake up, asshole; I told you to look for a place to stay. We can sleep later," bellowed Jim.

"I'm awake, I'm awake, I was just resting my eyes." Jerry sat back up straight in the seat, his heart racing from the sudden interruption in his short nap.

They had just come out of a curve in the road when Jerry pointed out through the windshield. "Look up ahead, there on the left."

A red neon sign that read, "VACANCY, ROOMS $3.00," crowded the shoulder of the highway.

Jim slowly swerved off the highway and eased the Ford up to the office, which was a small booth located in front of a row of cabins. The parking spots were between each building, which was just what Jim was looking for.

"I'll go in; you stay in the car." Jim pulled up on the door-handle while at the same time removing the key from the ignition. .

He walked into the little office and up to the counter and looked over at the ugliest little man he had ever seen, sound asleep in a swivel desk chair propped back against the wall. The little man had an almost perfectly round head, no hair, and a nose that looked like it had been chewed on by an angry dog. He wondered if the condition of the little man's nose could have been the result of drinking the whiskey that was bootlegged from the nearby mountains.. He had on short pants and a shirt with the sleeves cut off at the shoulders. It said MANAGER above the pocket.

"Excuse me," Jim said softly.

The little man jumped, almost falling out of his chair as he tried to stand at the same time.

"I'm sorry, I must have dosed off; been kind of quiet around here this evening. I guess you need a cabin, otherwise you wouldn't be here."

"Do you have a room with two beds?"

"Got one with twin beds, will that do?"

"That'll be fine, how much?"

"Three dollars and nine cents with tax; that will be for one night I guess?"

The manager turned around and took down a key from a hook located beside a small window in the back of the office.

"Number four," the little man said, reaching behind him searching for his chair. "You just park between the cabins; if I can help you, let me know."

Jim backed into the parking space between cabins three and four, opened the trunk, and grabbed his small grip along with Jerry's, containing a change of clothes, clean underwear, a toothbrush, and a razor.

They took a bath, shaved, and sat down on the bed; each drinking from the bottle of Jack Daniels that Jim had tucked away in his overnight bag. Jim took a long pull from the Jack Daniels and handed the now mostly empty bottle back to Jerry

"OK, go get the duffel bag and let's see what we've got."

Jerry peeked out the blinds to see if anyone was in the parking lot before going out to get the money. Satisfied that no one was in the parking lot, he went to the car, brought the duffel bag in, and threw it on the bed.

"Lock that door, Jerry, and make sure those blinds are shut well before you dump all that on the bed." Jerry followed Jim's instruction and returned to the bed. He dumped the full contents of the bag of money, spilling it over to the floor on both sides.

"Man, this is more than I ever expected to get," Jerry said. "How much do you think is here?"

"We'll never know if you don't count it." Jim examined a packet of the bills and tossed it back onto the bed.

They started counting, Jerry stacking his up on one side of the bed, Jim on the other. Jerry's heart pounded as the stacks of bills began to grow. All he could utter was, "Damn, damn, damn," as he wiped sweat from his forehead with the back of his hand.

Each bundle had the amount on the paper band that held it together; they were mostly $1000.00 or $2000.00 bundles, several of the bundles were of hundreds, but mainly of the smaller denominations.

"They followed instructions well; I guess shooting that guy made a believer out of somebody," Jerry mumbled, marveling at the stacks of cash growing in front of him.

Jim showed hardly any emotion as he stacked his bundles up and waited for Jerry to add his up.

"Quit admiring it, how much you got over there?" Jim asked.

"120,000.00, how much you got?"

"130,000.00, minus the $40.00 we took out at the restaurant."

"Son… of… a… bitch, that's a quarter of a million dollars!"

Jim didn't reply, he just looked down at the money and shook his head.

"All right, Jerry, let's put the money back into the bag and get some sleep. Let me think how we are going to get rid of our car and get another one."

****

Jim was up before daylight, looking through the blinds when Jerry rose up on one elbow. "See any cars out there we could hotwire?"

"Why you think we should steal a car, Jerry, don't you think we can afford to buy one?"

Jerry thought for a minute. "Hell, I didn't think about that."

"I'm not going to trade for one, I want to get rid of the Ford; put it somewhere so it won't be found. I think I know just the place, get up and get ready, let's get out of here," Jim said.

It was getting light when they pulled onto the highway, heading south, approaching the town of Manchester.

"Look for a used car lot, I know cars are hard to come by, but we might get lucky," said Jim tossing the empty whiskey bottle in the trash and reaching for his small grip.

"Why are there so few cars for sale; you would see car lots everywhere before I went over seas. Christ I haven't seen two since we left Evansville," grumbled Jerry.

"You see Jerry; no cars were manufactured for civilian use during the war years and the thousands of soldiers being discharged made it almost impossible to buy one. To help out until the automobile industry got back on track; the government started releasing military jeeps. They repainted them and fitted them with canvass tops and doors. Most were grabbed up by dealers in the south since they had no heaters, making them very uncomfortable in the colder climate of the north."

Jim had started to say more, when something caught his eye as they were approaching a small fire station.

"Now how's that for timing?"

"Look, the fire station on the right, is that a "for sale" sign on the windshield of that red jeep parked by the door there?

"It sure is, let's pull in."

Two firemen were sitting by the open bay door of the fire station where the front end of a fire truck could be seen partially protruding from the open door.

"How much for the jeep?" inquired Jerry out the window as Jim drove up beside the firemen.

"One twenty-five," one of the men said.

"Will it run," Jerry asked.

"It better, almost like new, got little over a thousand miles on it; want to drive it?"

Jerry looked over at Jim. "What you think?"

"Offer him a hundred."

"A hundred dollars," barked Jerry.

"I'll take one twenty," replied the fireman, standing up and going around to Jim's side of the car.

The fireman was looking at the Ford, checking the tires as he went.

"What you take for this one," he asked, looking straight at Jim.

"It's not for sale." Jim lowered his head so the brim of his hat covered his eyes from the fireman's stare. "We just want a jeep; we've been riding in one for the last four years, kind of got used to it."

After the fireman agreed to leave the license plate on the jeep, Jim gave him the hundred and twenty-five dollars that they had originally asked for.

"Follow me down to the next gas station and we'll fill her up and check the oil," Jim told Jerry as he pulled up beside the jeep.

Jerry followed Jim into the ESSO service station three blocks down from the fire hall.

"I'll stay behind you," Jim said as he paid the attendant for filling up both vehicles and checking the oil. "We will be going up Monteagle Mountain shortly; that jeep should be OK but you never know. I have a plan to get this car off the highway, I'll tell you about it when we get over the mountain."

****

Jerry was born in Lumberton, Mississippi; a small town thirty miles north of the gulf coast towns of Gulfport and Biloxi. He spent his high school summer vacations and the short time between graduation and the war working in the fishing industry along the coast. He had dreamed since he was a young boy of having his own boat and taking tourists out to catch the big fish. Jerry had the knowledge and skills to do just that, the only thing he didn't have was the money; just maybe he could make it happen.

Jim, on the other hand, had spent his childhood in the tough neighborhoods of the steel town of Gary, Indiana, just east of Chicago's south side. He lived with his mother after she divorced his father when he was eight years old. His dad worked in a foundry and showed little interest in the welfare of his son. Jim grew up on the streets and would probably have gone to jail at a young age had the Japs not bombed Pearl Harbor. He went in the Army instead.

Jim cared nothing about fishing; the only boats he saw were the ships on Lake Michigan heading in and out of the docks of Gary. Jim never intended to go into the fishing business with Jerry, maybe he would stay in the bank robbing business. If he did, he probably would have to get another partner. Jerry just didn't seem to be the type.

****

The surplus army jeep followed by the green Ford slowed to a crawl, as they followed behind a transfer truck making its way around hairpin curves that weaved up the western side of Monteagle Mountain. As the truck rounded one of the curves, you could see the driver standing out on the running board with the door open, steering with his right arm, trying to escape the extreme heat given off by the huge gasoline powered engine. When they reached the summit, Jerry motioned for Jim to pull off behind him as the road straightened out and the shoulders widened, giving a place for overheated cars and trucks to get off of the highway.

"I thought we would never make it up here," Jerry groaned, "I'm about to wet my pants!"

Turning and facing the woods, he unzipped his pants and let

go with a stream of urine that would make a cow jealous.

"Come over here when you get through watering the grass. Here is what we're going to do; after we get down this mountain, we will be coming up on the Tennessee River. We cross the river right below Hales Bar Dam. I am going to look for a place on the lakeside of the dam where the water is the deepest. We'll run the Ford off in the lake there, it'll be a long time before they find it if ever. I just hope we get there before some patrolman remembers that a green 1940 Ford is still on his hot sheet."

The jeep led the way, as they drove across the narrow truss bridge that spanned the river a mile south of Hales Bar Dam. Jim stopped just as they got off the bridge at a wide place in the road in front of the post office in Haletown, Tennessee.

"Follow me," scowled Jim through the window as he pulled in front of the jeep.

He followed the highway for about a mile past the dam powerhouse and turned left down a dirt road that led to the river. The river channel was on the east side of the river and was sixty to seventy feet deep close to the dam powerhouse. The two vehicles came to a stop in a cloud of dust on an overlook in a sharp curve that could not be seen from the dirt road from either direction.

Jim got out of the Ford and walked back to Jerry.

"This place looks perfect," Jim said, looking down at the river thirty feet below the road.

He eased the Ford right up to the edge of the cliff, turned the engine off, and got out.

"I'll get our stuff out of the front, you get the duffel bag and put it in the jeep," Jim said, with coldness in his voice.

Jerry raised the trunk, grabbed the handle of the duffel bag and began to pull up when he heard the unmistakable sound of the chamber sliding forward on the German Luger.

"Sorry," Jim said casually, as he squeezed the trigger,

sending the 9mm hollow point slug into the back of Jerry's head, killing him instantly, and doing so without the slightest hint of emotion.

The echo from the .38 returned from across the river at the same time that Jerry fell halfway into the trunk.

Jim pulled the duffel bag out of the trunk and with one hand grabbed Jerry by the belt and with his knee; he eased his body over into the now empty trunk. He loaded the duffel bag and what items they had left in the Ford into the jeep. He opened the door of the Ford, put his foot on the clutch, and put the car out of gear. With a bead of sweat forming on his upper lip he walked back to the rear of the car, leaned onto the back fender and started to push. Jim was a big man and very strong, but the Ford would not bulge an inch.

Wiping the sweat from his face as he walked back up to the front of the car, he jerked open the door and got in.

He started the engine, backed up a few feet, put the Ford in first gear and let out the clutch. The Ford lurched forward as Jim rolled out of the front seat, landing hard on his side and rolling to a stop inches from the cliff. The big man sat on the ground breathing hard, watching; as the green Ford hit the surface of the Tennessee River, grill first. It was as if the car had made a perfect swan dive; there was hardly any splash and very little sound as the car, along with Jerry's body, disappeared into eighty feet of water to the bottom of the Tennessee River.

Before the Ford had completely disappeared Jim got up and ran to the jeep, jumped in and continued on down the road toward the riverbank. He wanted to go down the road to make sure no one had witnessed the shooting; he knew this was the only way back out and had made up his mind. If he met someone, that person or persons would be in for a very bad day.

He drove on for more than a mile not encountering anyone; he could see that the road dead-ended at a boat ramp that was empty at the time. He gave a slight sigh of relief, turned the jeep around and headed back up to the highway.

"Sorry I had to do that, Jerry," he muttered to himself, "if I stuck with you, you would have got us caught sooner or later." Jim smiled as he thought about the money. *I'll have twice as much now.*

The highway followed the river around the base of Raccoon Mountain that led on to Lookout Mountain and into the City of Chattanooga. Jim was glad that he had resolved the issue about Jerry; every time he started to feel any remorse he would just look in the mirror and see the duffel bag lying on the floor in front of the jeep's back seat.

Having driven this highway before the war and had a pretty good idea of where he was headed; he had little need of a road map. He thought maybe he should get off the main road and take some back roads, but decided against it. *Hell, no one's looking for a jeep, besides,* he thought to himself, *I may just get something more comfortable to drive.*

****

Sheriff Stan Wilkey had just returned from lunch and was headed to the small restroom in the rear of his office when a barely audible knock came from the door he had just entered.

"Come in," Wilkey bellowed over his shoulder, just as his hand touched the doorknob on the restroom door.

The door opened as the pretty blond officer entered, wearing a uniform that consisted of a very tight blue skirt and a lighter blue shirt. The policewoman's shirt was heavily starched and neatly pressed, with a badge above the pocket on one side and a silver nametag on the other, which was engraved "BUMSTARK."

The sheriff really needed to take a leak, but decided he could wait; he always seemed to find time for Miss Bumstark.

"I know you just got back from lunch, Sheriff, but we just got a lead on that bank robbery, I thought you would want to know." She closed the door behind her and walked toward the sheriff, who was standing in the rear of the office.

"You're damn right I do, what have you got?" the sheriff asked, feeling the fullness in his bladder increase as he eased over to his desk and sat down.

"Well, it looks like that paper boy, you know, Andrew, he may have been right," Officer Bumstark replied. "We got a call from the sheriff down in Tennessee; Manchester I think it was, a little town south of Nashville. A pair of men fitting the description of our suspects and driving a green 1940 Ford purchased a jeep from a fireman there in Manchester. The fireman heard about the robbery on the radio and got suspicious after remembering that they wanted to leave the tags on the jeep. He didn't get a good look at the big man that was driving the Ford, said that he sort of had his hat pulled down in the front. Anyway, Sheriff, it was a red jeep, you know the war surplus ones the Army is selling, and we have the tag number too." She smiled as she leaned on the corner of the desk looking down at the sheriff.

"Miss Bumstark, why are we making such a big deal out of this, the guy that was shot is going to be OK; how much money did they get anyway?"

"The big deal, Sheriff, is they got off with around a quarter of a million dollars and the bad part is there is a mix up on the serial numbers of the currency."

"What do you mean a mix up?"

"The bank did not record the numbers; it seems that the robbers took the list with the money and Wells Fargo lost the duplicate if they ever had one. This money was being transferred from a bank in Louisville, Kentucky and they left it up to Wells

Fargo to keep track of the serial numbers; it's a big mess, Sheriff, they're working on it but they want to catch the assholes fast."

"All right, I get the message, Miss Bumstark, you don't have to use profanity," the sheriff mused with a sigh. "I think the paper boy was right," the sheriff continued, standing up and looking at the restroom door out of the corner of his eye. "They figure that they got away without anyone getting a description of their vehicle, but they will probably ditch the Ford now. Get out a bulletin for everyone to be on the lookout for the jeep. We already have one on the Ford, hell; somebody should spot a red jeep for Christ's sake."

"I'll get it started," Miss Bumstark said calmly as she turned and headed toward the door with a slight sway in her step. "Sheriff," the blond said, looking over her shoulder as she reached for the door, "you can go pee now."

****

Now where do I go from here? Jim mused as he drove through the city of Chattanooga, up Missionary Ridge, through the Bachman Tubes and into the town of East Ridge, Tennessee. It was late afternoon and he was looking for a place to spend the night, when he spotted the Pines Motel, which had a restaurant out in front of a row of motel rooms. The thing that impressed him the most was a Falstaff Beer sign in the window.

"Hell yeah," he muttered to himself, "a cold beer would taste pretty good, maybe more than one." He eased the four-wheel drive vehicle off the highway and up in front of the office of the motel, making sure he could keep an eye on the jeep while inside.

"Any vacancies?" asked Jim, looking through the stream of smoke just exhaled by a plump but very pretty black-haired woman of about thirty, dressed in a print dress cut low in the front, exposing plenty of cleavage of her ample breasts.

"I sure do, handsome." The woman smiled. She was probably about two-thirds Indian. "Just you honey?" she asked as she blew another stream of smoke that flattened out as it reached the ceiling.

"Yep, just me. I'll only be here one night, how much?"

"Three fifty with tax. My name's Donna, people here call me Donnie. If I can get you anything, I'll be right here," she said still smiling. She tossed Jim the key to the room then put out her cigarette in an over flowing ashtray on the corner of her small desk.

Jim dodged another plume of smoke as he turned and ducked out the door, almost falling down the steps.

The motel was made up of five units in a single row facing the highway, with three rooms per unit. The motel backed up to a pine thicket, hence the name of the motel, with the restaurant located closer to the highway. The motel rooms and the restaurant were both painted white and had red shutters. In this part of the country, this type of restaurant was commonly referred to as a beer joint, Church women liked to call them road houses.

Jim jumped in the jeep and looked down at the key in his hand. "Number four again; it must be my lucky number." He parked outside room number four and killed the engine.

After pushing the duffel bag up under the bed, Jim washed his hands and face, ran a comb through his curly hair, and headed across the parking lot to get that beer he had been waiting for. He walked from the motel across the gravel parking lot littered with beer and soda pop tops into the back door of the restaurant, which upon entering he discovered was no more than a tavern. The interior of the tavern consisted of one long bar that ran the length of building and a few tables scattered around the room. There was a door in the front and one in the rear; both were wide open and had no screens. The two open doors served as sort of a breezeway that created a natural draft, cooling the building dramatically in the summer heat. He walked up to the bar, swung his leg over a bar stool, reached into his pocket pulling out a handful of bills, and put them in front of him on the bar.

"What you having?" the bartender asked, walking up in front of Jim while drying his hands on a towel.

"I'll have a Falstaff; and bring me a cold mug if you have one."

The bartender was a tall slim man, too old to have been in the war, but he had a scar on his upper arm that was definitely the result of a gunshot. Jim looked around the room while waiting for the bartender to return with his beer. Only one other customer was at the bar, a kid who did not look old enough to buy beer, and three men sitting around one of the tables telling war stories.

"That'll be twenty-five cents or do you want to run a tab?" The skinny bartender set the longneck bottle and frosty mug down in front of Jim.

"Let's run a tab, I'm dry as a bone," Jim grasped the cold mug with his meaty hand bringing it slowly up to his lips. He almost drained the entire mug before setting it back on the bar.

Jim sat quietly sipping his beer and going over the recent events in his mind. *Did I leave any loose ends?* He asked himself. *Did I cover my trail well enough?* He saw movement out of the corner of his eye as a pretty redhead with a little too much lipstick eased up beside him on the barstool to his right. He turned slightly on his stool to get a better view her. She was young, probably in her late twenties, wearing very tight shorts, with an even tighter T-shirt.

"With all these empty stools, you chose the one right next to me, so can I offer to buy you a beer," Jim asked with his best flirting smile.

"I chose this stool so I can see out the door, but yes you can buy me a beer," she replied smiling, exposing, white even teeth tinged with red lipstick.

It had been some time since Jim had been with a woman; not because he couldn't, most women found him very attractive with his dark curly hair and olive complexion. He had a way with women; he never had any trouble picking one up, even though, he seemed to go for the ones who appeared to be a little less virtuous.

"My name's Barbara Jo, what's yours."

"It's Jim, Jim Vess, pleased to meet you." He held up his beer mug so as to propose a toast. "I didn't see you drive up; did you come from the motel?"

"No, I live over on McBrien Road, I walked over here; there's a path through the woods behind the motel that goes straight to my backyard."

Jim and the redhead exchanged small talk, all the while Barbara Jo kept an eye on the parking lot through the open back door.

Suddenly, she pulled a napkin from under her beer glass, picked up a pencil that the bartender had left lying on the bar, and hurriedly wrote something on the napkin before handing it to Jim.

"Listen, Jim," the redhead said, "I've got to go now. I don't have a telephone but that's my address on the napkin, come by after a while." She got off the stool, turned and started to go, then turned back to Jim and smiled. "Make it after eight." The redhead walked to the open back door, turned and winked, then ran down the steps.

Jim finished his beer and ordered another one, smiling to himself reflecting on the encounter he just had with the redhead. One of the men setting at a table behind the bar got up and walked over to the bar and stood beside Jim.

"She's hot, but be careful, she has an old man and he tries to keep an eye on her," the man said, looking at Jim in the mirror behind the bar.

Jim started to ask the man something, but he turned and walked on down the breezeway and into the restroom. Jim took another swig of beer, slid off the barstool and headed to the restroom himself. He walked up to the urinal and stood beside the man who had spoken to him at the bar. Just as he was about to speak to the man, a lump formed in his throat; through the window he saw an East Ridge Police car stop behind his jeep.

Jim pissed all over his pants and shoes, trying to get a good look through the four-inch gap under the partially opened window in front of the urinal. "Son of a bitch," he said out loud as he watched the policeman get out of the squad car and walk over to the jeep.

The cop peered inside the jeep, and then walked completely around, stopping at the rear and studying the tag for a few seconds before returning to his car. Jim hurried back into the bar, threw a ten-dollar bill next to his beer mug and walked to the back door. He stopped and peered around the corner of the door before going down the steps, his heart pounding as he watched the cop car pull up to the office of the motel.

Trying not to run, he crossed the parking lot and headed to a row of rooms down from the row he was staying. Jim hoped the cop had not noticed him cross the parking lot and dart between the two cars parked in front of the motel rooms. As soon as he reached the front of the parked cars, he turned and walked down to his row of rooms, before slipping inside.

Sweat was dripping from the tip of his nose as he pulled the duffel bag from under the bed, and grabbed the Luger from the desk drawer, shoving it down the front of his pants. Heart pounding he stood up, and ran both hands through his now very wet hair. "I got to think," he said to himself as he walked over to the window and peeked between the blinds.

The police car was still parked in front of the office; he could see the officer talking to Donna through the open front door. Jim walked to the rear of the motel room where a lone window looked out on the woods behind the motel. He raised the window as high as it would go, picked up the duffel bag and threw it through the screen. The duffel bag landed on the ground four feet below the windowsill, with him right behind it. As soon as he picked up the duffel bag, he spotted the little path that Barbara Jo had taken to get to the tavern. He grabbed the handle of the bag and headed off down the path, wondering to himself how the police knew about the Jeep. Then it hit him like a ton of bricks: the firemen. It had to be the firemen.

Without looking back he hurried down the path cursing his bad luck, weaving in and out between pine trees and poison ivy plants.

Finally, he came out at a clearing and was able to see that the path did indeed come out at a street, the backyards of which bordered the woods. Barbara Jo had said that the path started at her backyard, so the house directly in front of him must be hers. He picked up the duffel bag, walked up to the back door located on the side of the house, and knocked. After knocking three times and getting no answer, he walked to the back of the house. "I've got to do something with this money," he said out loud, looking around.

An idea popped into his head as he spotted the trapdoor that led to the crawl space under the house. He slid open the latch that held the door secure, he threw the duffel bag under the house, and crawled in behind it. Just inside the door he had to move some garden tools that blocked his path. It was dark after he shut the small door behind him, but his eyes adjusted after a few minutes, and he could see fairly well with the light coming in from the vents scattered around the foundation of the house.

Think, think, think, he mumbled to himself.

****

Jim leaned back against the block foundation, closed his eyes and pondered his situation. He opened his eyes and crawled over by the door where he had tossed the garden tools. There lay a rake, a shovel, and a garden hoe. He picked up the tools and crawled back to the center of the house. There was not much room under the house, around four feet from the ground up to the floor, but plenty of room to do what he planned to do.

He had decided to bury the money and come back for it later if he had too. The ground was reasonably soft and he had no problem digging down deep enough to cover the duffel bag. After covering the bag with about six to eight inches of soil, he leaned back up against the wall, breathing heavily, his shirt soaked with sweat.

After a short breather, he decided that he had to be on the move, try to find a car, get out of town, and come back for the money later. If he got caught, he would say that Jerry had taken off with the money, they couldn't prove otherwise and Jerry sure wasn't going to tell them any different.

Slowly pushing the crawl space door open and looking in all directions before crawling out, Jim pulled his bulky body through the small door and stood up.

Walking between the houses toward the street, he reached into his pocket and pulled the napkin out that Barbara Jo had handed him just before leaving the tavern. The only thing that she had written on it was 712 McBrien Rd. After reaching the street, Jim turned and faced the house; beside the front door in black lettering was the number *SEVEN TWELVE.*

Burning the number into his memory he ripped the napkin

into small pieces, turned, and walked up the street back toward Highway 41.

As he walked, it became pretty clear to him that he had a better than good chance of getting caught. Chain smoking, Donna had surely given the police a good description of him and had let the police into the room, Jim speculated. *Maybe I should just turn myself in and blame it all on Jerry,* he thought to himself.

"Hell, I still have the money," he mumbled to himself, "they'll never find Jerry or the car; do a couple of years, come back get the money, yeah it's worth it."

As he walked down the street in what he was sure was the direction to the highway, more than once he almost turned around to go get the duffel bag full of money and try something else. *No, the best plan is to try later, even if I get caught, the money will be safe there, it's the best I can do right now.*

Jim reached the highway, turned south, and started walking in the direction of the motel. He stuck out his thumb when a car came by. "Who knows, I might get a break."

The sign of the motel had just come into view, when an East Ridge Police car pulled off the highway in front of him; the officer got out and walked in his direction.

"Stop right there," the officer said as he put his hand on top of his pistol.

Jim stopped and put up his hands, just as another police car pulled in behind him.

****

"Alright, Mr. Vess, let me get this straight; you say your partner helped you rob the bank, then took off with the money, and left you high and dry, is that right?" East Ridge Detective Bill Wampler asked.

"That's what I said; I've already told you that five times," Jim said calmly, looking around hoping to solicit support from the others who were crowded into the small room.

"I should have never let him drive that Ford, the son of a bitch just took off; I couldn't catch up to him in that jeep. I should have known not to trust that skinny bastard with all that money, hell; I couldn't call the police, could I?"

"You have any idea where he might be heading, any family or friends that you know of that might take him in," asked the detective.

"His family lives down in Mississippi, somewhere around Biloxi I think, I don't know of any friends," Jim said, making an effort to look like he was really trying to help.

"So he just took off with the money and you're sitting around in a beer joint, drinking beer and trying to pick up some whore? You're full of crap, mister, you're the one who shot that man in that bank, and you're going away for a long time..."

****

Jim was arrested, tried and convicted of armed robbery, but he stuck to his story about Jerry running off with the stolen money. The police never found Jerry or the money, but it didn't keep Jim from receiving twenty years to life in prison.

Jim smiled to himself as he looked up at the entrance to Brushy Mountain State Prison at Petros, Tennessee.

"I'll get out one day, and when I do, I'll be a rich man, they won't keep me in here forever."

Two guards stationed at the entrance walked beside the steel gates as they slowly opened to allow the prison bus to enter. The driver eased out the clutch as the bus began to creep up the stone driveway that led to the reception station.

Jim Vess had arrived at his new home.

2

No other period in the history of the United States was more glorious a time to have been an adolescent than the years between World War II and Vietnam. It was a time of true innocence, before everything became political, and children could be themselves without the structured protectiveness that society bestowed on the next generation.

Someone once said, things changed when kids stopped saying, "Yes Mam, no Mam, yes Sir, and no Sir." Many say that the embracing of the child-rearing methods set forth in Dr Benjamin Spock's best selling book was a factor. You could list hundreds of reasons, but for whatever reason, things just changed, and would never be the same again.

Children that were born right after World War II and started school in the early fifties were witness to both a technological and a social revolution before they graduated high school. It was not unusual to come home from school and find the neighbors in the kitchen, admiring a refrigerator that had just been delivered. The ice man would soon have to find another line of work. They thought they had seen it all; radios with picture screens called TVs, air conditioning in houses, as well as in cars, and of course, Elvis.

Even with all the changes taking place, and new inventions coming on every day, children still mostly entertained themselves. Televisions began to appear in the early fifties, but still without air conditioning in most homes, kids took to the outdoors, especially during the summertime.

Most every generation will probably argue that their childhood years were the best time to be alive. Some who grew up in the Great Depression and had to struggle to find something to eat still reflect on those times as the best times of their life. Not everyone will agree that the fifties and sixties were the best time to be a kid, but most agree that it had to be close to the top of the list.

****

June 1, 1956

"Jackie… Jackie… Jackie…Jackie."

Jackie Malone opened his eyes and looked around his small bedroom that he shared with his sister. Judy was still sound asleep in her small twin bed on the other side of the room. She lay facing her window where a cool breeze was generated by a large window fan located in the other bedroom.

Did I just hear my name called or was I dreaming? Jackie thought.

The sun was up and it was already beginning to get warm as he lay still, listening to the sound of the small birds chirping outside his window.

"Jackie… Jackie… Get up."

"Guess that answers my question," Jackie said to himself as he put his head up to the screen of his bedroom window.

"Tommy, is that you?"

"You gonna sleep all day? It's the first day schools out and you lay in there all day, get up!"

"Hold it down a little; Judy's still asleep, I'll be out in a minute."

"Hurry up, and get Judy up too, her friend from next door is out here looking for her."

Jackie slid from his bed, pulled on a pair of blue jeans, walked through the house to the kitchen past his Mom, and headed to the back door.

"Well, it's time you got up; do you want some toast and jelly? I just took some out of the oven with butter the way you like it," his mother said, drying her hands on her apron.

"Sure, I'll take it with me," Jackie replied, reaching for the plate of two pieces of buttered toast.

"Jack, will you slow down, Tommy's been out there for half an hour, he can wait another few minutes," his mother pleaded, trying to put a spoonful of blackberry jam on the plate.

Jackie pushed open the screen door and went on outside without saying a word, with his mother following him, holding out a glass of orange juice for him to grab just before the spring pulled the screen shut.

Jackie had eaten one piece of toast and had started on the second one before he rounded the corner and found Tommy sitting under the elm tree that stood outside his bedroom window.

"Tell Judy, that Kitty, I think that's her name, has gone home, her mother was calling her," said Tommy, shifting his weight on an old washtub he had turned upside down to sit on.

Jackie jumped up on top of the wheelbarrow that was propped up under his window so he could see inside his bedroom.

"I think Kitty must feel you don't want to play with her, she's gone home; get up and see if you can find her, we don't want you following us around all day, now get up," Jackie yelled through the open window.

"I can't believe it, school's out already, what we gonna do?" Jackie asked, downing the last piece of toast and jelly and finishing off the glass of orange juice.

****

Jackie Malone and Tommy Redden had been friends since they met while waiting for the school bus when Jackie was in the second grade and Tommy was starting in the first.

The neighborhood that they lived in, Rankin Park, was built in 1948 and named after the developer who bragged that he could carry off all the leftover lumber in one wheelbarrow when he had finished. The development, just south of the Tennessee and Georgia state line was hastily built to accommodate families of returning servicemen after the war. There were six streets of two-bedroom houses, built almost identical. The streets were named after different cities in Florida. These types of developments sprang up all over the country and were commonly referred to as GI houses.

Rankin Park was a bedroom community of Chattanooga, Tennessee, and in the majority of the families, only the fathers worked. Chattanooga was an industrial city and most of the jobs were of the blue-collar type. The schools were overcrowded, and being in a poor county, the roads in Rankin Park were not paved until the mid-fifties. In the first few years before the roads were paved, the men of the neighborhood got together and filled the potholes themselves; the county just did not have the funding to keep up with the rapid growth.

Crime in that part of the country was almost nonexistent; there was the occasional burglary or assault, and of course the feds would bust up a whiskey still or catch a car full of moonshine now and then, but most people were law-abiding citizens.

There were a variety of places to go and things to do; the neighborhood was in a rural area but close enough to the city to go to a picture show or to a ball game, as Rankin Park was within walking distance of the city bus line that went into Chattanooga.

The girls of the neighborhood had their friends, but spent a lot of time with their mothers learning how to do the things that mothers do, since most of them were housewives and stayed at home.

The boys had so many options of things to do that they sometimes spent half the day trying to decide on what to do. In the summer they could play baseball, go to the creek and fish, or go skinny-dipping, or maybe follow the creek that led to Lake Winnepesaukah; an amusement park that had a huge swimming pool. Whatever they decided to do, it was something that they chose, not what their parents had chosen for them.

****

"Jack, will you come around here a minute?" his mother shouted from the back porch. "How about you and Tommy walking down to the store and getting a carton of cokes before it gets too hot; you don't mind, do you? Get that carton of empties on the back porch, you and Tommy can get a cold drink with the deposit money," his mother shouted before Jackie could answer.

"I guess so, I'll need some money," replied Jackie with a hint of frustration in his voice. Come on, Tommy, let's go, we'll decide what we're gonna do on the way."

"There's a quarter beside the empty bottles; you boys hurry back, I'd like to have one of those cokes, it's already starting to get hot." Mrs. Malone smiled as she talked to the boys through the screen door.

Louie's store was two and a half blocks down Stateline Road and it took Jackie and Tommy almost thirty minutes to walk the distance because they were looking for empty Camel cigarette packs along the side of the road. It was a game they played; whoever found the empty pack got to pull the blue tax stamp from the top to see if the underneath was imprinted with an S or an H. If the empty pack contained an S,_that meant you could slap the other person; if it contained an H, then you could hit with your fist. The boys spotted three packs of Pall Mall's, two packs of Lucky Strikes, two packs of Cool's, one pack of Chesterfields, but only one pack of Camels. Tommy got to the pack first, but the tax stamp had already been pulled off, which meant the pack could not be used to collect a hit or a slap.

Jackie pulled open the screen door to the store, walked in, and heaved the carton of empty coke bottles up on the counter. "Give us nickels, Louie, we're gonna get us something to drink out of the machine here."

Louie set the bottles to the side, opened the drawer and handed Jackie eighteen cents for the deposit on the bottles.

Jackie raised the top to the cold drink cooler, bumping heads with Tommy as he looked down studying caps on the bottles, trying to decide on a Coca Cola or a Dr. Pepper.

"Ouch," Tommy yelled, feeling the side of his head, "you almost knocked my brains out, move your butt over."

The boys downed their drinks, paid for the carton of cokes and walked over to a case of Coca Colas sitting beside the front door.

"I'll pull you far away for a nickel," Tommy said, reaching into his pocket.

"You're on, you pull first."

Tommy reached in the case, pulled a bottle from the corner, set it on the counter, and smiled at Jackie.

"Pull one," Tommy said with confidence; "you never beat me at this."

Jackie pulled a bottle from the other corner of the case and set it on the counter.

"OK, what you got?" Tommy turned his bottle upside down looking at the city name imprinted in the glass on the bottom of the bottle.

"I knew it," Tommy scowled, before Jackie even got his

bottle turned over, “CHATTANOOGA, TN.”

“Read it and weep.” Jackie pushed the bottom of the bottle into Tommy’s face, “ATLANTA, GA.”

Tommy slapped the nickel down on the counter. “Let’s go, the road’s gonna be hot, we should have worn our shoes.”

The boys started back, watching their step, trying not to step in hot tar seeping through the thin patches of gravel in the road.

“I’ll give you your nickel back if you’ll carry this carton of cokes,” Jackie said, holding the nickel out in his hand.

“I’ll carry ‘em for a dime.”

Tommy was trying to stay in the loose gravel on the side of the road to keep from burning his bare feet. He smiled, proud of himself for his getting his nickel back form Jackie with one to boot.

“You’re a real hardnosed businessman, here’s your dime and here are the cokes, now hurry up; I’d like to go down to the creek after we get these cokes home.”

****

JACKIE

Jackie’s dad purchased the house in Rankin Park in 1948, just after his sister Judy was born. Jackie was four years old when they moved there from Dayton, Tennessee, fifty miles to the north, so his dad could be closer to his job as a foreman at a steel plant in Chattanooga. Jackie was not going to be a very tall man, but by the time he was a teenager, he had developed tremendous upper body strength. When he got tall enough to reach the crossbar of the close line post, he would do chin-ups every time he got near it. It wasn’t long before he could do twenty-five or thirty pull-ups without stopping.

Jackie’s dad, Harvey, had grown up during the great

depression and had to quit school at an early age to help feed what was left of his family; his mother had died while giving birth to him and his father passed away a short time later.

Harvey was a quiet man with little or no sense of humor, and at times, he was abusive to Jackie and his mother, but never to Judy.

As he got older, Jackie became fearful of his dad and was constantly worried that he might harm his mother. Harve, as his mother called him, would occasionally come home drunk and verbally abuse and hit his mother. Jackie could never forgive his father for the way he treated his mother, who he loved dearly. However, he forgave his dad for the way he treated him.

Jackie, Judy, and his mother had to walk on eggshells around Harve, but they had learned what it took to piss him off, and for most of the time it was bearable.

****

TOMMY

Tommy Redden lived one street down from Jackie, which bordered Willingham's dairy farm. Tommy lived in an identical house to Jackie, which was built by Mr. Rankin, who no doubt had only one set of blueprints. A year younger than Jackie, Tommy was twenty pounds heaver and two inches taller, but still carried what appeared to be baby fat, mostly around his belly and butt.

Tommy's father did not own an automobile and had to walk the four blocks to catch a bus to take him to work and back. Maxwell Redden worked the second shift in a plant in Chattanooga that made Coca Cola vending machines. Tommy may have been a little embarrassed because they did not have a car, but he was comforted by the fact that he was not alone. It was not unusual to see Mr. Redden, who was an ex-marine, run the four blocks from the bus line, especially on cold winter days; if he were offered a ride he would often refuse, saying that he was trying to keep in shape.

Tommy was proud of his dad, and the people who knew him were too.

****

"Are we gonna fish or just hang out?" Jackie asked Tommy

"Let's take the BB guns," answered Tommy excitedly, "see if we can put those cows on the run, and maybe shoot at some fish."

Jackie ran through the kitchen to his bedroom, returning with his BB gun and three packs of BBs with his mother right on his heels.

"Going to the creek," Jackie shouted without looking back.

"Don't get in that dirty water, be careful with that gun, and make sure you're back by five, when your daddy gets home for supper."

"I will, I will," Jackie said, pushing open the screen door and jumping off the porch, running to catch up with Tommy, who had already reached the edge of the backyard.

The boys headed through the backyards in the direction of Tommy's house: it was the first trip to the creek, school was out, and life couldn't be better. Being outside in the summertime before everyone got air conditioning is something that is never forgotten. It was not just the sounds; wives listening to radio shows while doing their housework, mothers screaming at their kids or animals, or even an occasional squawk of a pet bird could sometimes be heard; it was also the smells.

As you walked between the houses and down the street, you could tell what would be the main course at dinner that evening, or maybe even tell what was not going to be for dinner, nothing smells worse than beans that had run dry of water while on the stove. The smell of summer in Rankin Park was not just food on the stove or the blossoming of the dogwoods early in the summer; the neighborhood had a small problem; septic tanks. Sewers were years away from coming to Rankin Park, and the ground did not perk well, which caused raw sewerage to bubble to the surface from the field lines. Some of the homes had more of a problem than others, but you knew what backyards to stay away from.

****

It took two minutes for Tommy to run through the front door of his house, grab his BB gun, and tear out the back door, pushing extra packs of BBs into the front pocket of his shorts.

“Let’s go to the sycamore, said Tommy.

“No, let’s go to the two logs, Jackie replied.

No one knows how these different places along the creek got their names; Jackie and Tommy could take you to at least six, and all the other boys who played along the creek knew their names as well. Jackie told Ernest Biddle, a new arrival to the neighborhood, that all of the spots on the creek bank were named by the bigger boys. These were the boys who had discovered girls and had decided the creek wasn’t as interesting as it used to be.

“OK, the two logs, Tommy agreed, taking aim at a Blue Jay sitting on the bottom of a maple tree twenty feet away. Tommy pulled the trigger just as the Blue Jay took off, missing the bird by a half a foot.

“I think I winged him,” Tommy said, pulling the lever that cocked the air rifle and forcing another BB into the chamber.

“Bullshit, you missed him a foot, winged him my ass.”

Tommy didn't say anything; he just stopped and took aim at another bird that just landed not ten feet away on the top of a small pine tree.

"Don't shoot that one, that's a Brown Thrasher you know, the Georgia state bird; they'll put your can in jail." Jackie sighed in relief as Tommy lowered the BB gun.

The shallow creek snaked its way north from Lake Winnepesaukah through a dairy farm before winding its way into Tennessee. Five miles further on it merged with another small creek and emptied into the Tennessee River.

They finally arrived at a deep place in the creek that they referred to as the two logs. Why it was called the two logs no one knows; only one log had fallen down years ago and landed in the water next to the bank, where one could walk out on and fish, or dive off of if swimming were the order of the day.

"Let's see how cold the water is." Tommy grumbled about some poison ivy close to the approach to the half submerged log. He jumped onto the log and ran out to the end, sticking his foot ankle deep into the water.

"Wow, no swimming for a while," he yelled, jerking his foot back onto the log.

Tommy scampered back up the log, jumped up on the bank, and then turned to look at Jackie with an expression of shock on his face that looked as if he had seen a ghost.

"I've been stung… I've been stung," Tommy screamed, reaching back and trying to rub the welt that was rapidly turning red in the small of his back.

"Come over here and let's see," Jackie said calmly, walking over to Tommy with a grin on his face as if the whole thing was funny.

"Did you see a bee?"

"That don't look like a bee sting to me, cowboy, you've been hit by a BB," Jackie explained, looking around.

"Are you sure, it feels like a wasp might have got me?"

Just as Jackie was about to say that he was sure that it was a BB, something hit him just above the right elbow that stung so bad, his eyes started to water.

"Get down, get down, somebody is shooting at us," Jackie cried, rubbing his arm.

"Where from?"

"Behind that sycamore next to the foot-log that crosses the creek."

"I see him… .I see him, it's that fat-ass Bud Higgins, see him, his big belly sticking out from behind the tree," cried Tommy."

Bud was two years older than Jackie and weighed twice as much as he did. He was one of those guys that always seemed to know everything and liked to brag about his big adventures, which everyone knew was mostly a bunch of crap.

"Hear him laughing," Tommy whimpered, "he thinks he's really done something, he'll be boasting about this all summer."

"I think it's about time we taught him a lesson," Jackie said. "He probably doesn't know we have our guns with us, I'm going to try to get around behind him, when I start shooting, he'll come around to this side of the tree; when he does, you know what to do. Try not to hit him in the eye; I don't like him but we don't want to put his eye out."

Jackie crawled through some blackberry bushes that led to a small hill so he could keep out of sight until he could get into position to get a clear shot. As he started around the hill, he had an idea; maybe he would just go over the top of the hill and hide behind some of the large rocks that were scattered along the hillside. When he reached the crest of the hill, he could still see Bud standing behind the tree looking around trying to spot where the two boys had gone. Jackie slowly started making his way down the side of the hill, going from rock to rock, making an effort not to make any noise and keep out of sight as much as possible. About a third of the way down, he stopped behind a large boulder that was as big as an automobile. He sat there considering what to do next when he realized that cool air was blowing up his pants leg.

"What the hell," Jackie gasped out loud.

The air was coming out from a hole in the ground that was as big around as a soccer ball; if his foot had been six inches to the left, his whole leg would have gone in up to his balls.

"Damn, we'll check this out later; right now we got business to take care of with that asshole Bud Higgins," His mind still on the hole, he scooted from behind the huge rock.

All he had to do was make it another twenty feet and he would have a clear shot, or at least a chance of hitting that big ass of Bud's.

"There he is," Jackie whispered as he raised the air rifle to his shoulder and took aim at Bud's blue jean-clad butt projecting out from behind the tree.

Jackie squeezed the trigger on the Daisy air rifle and watched as the copper-colored BB made a slight arch and came down square into the side of Bud's big ass.

"Oh… oh… oh," Bud screamed as he ran around to the other side of the tree just in time to catch another BB right above his exposed belly button from Tommy, who had been waiting patiently behind the stump of a tree more than forty yards away.

"Good shot," bellowed Jackie as he watched Bud start screaming incoherently, and throw down his gun. "Why that big sissy, you would think he's been hit with a shotgun blast. Hey, Tommy, you must have hit him in the nuts, look he's putting on a real show."

"I'm going to wet my pants." Tommy was laughing so hard he had to hold his side; tears running down both cheeks.

Still going on with that high pitched wailing; Bud suddenly

made a dash straight to the creek, unbuttoning his jeans as he ran out into the water. Jackie and Tommy ran down to where Bud was rolling around and thrashing about, still trying to get his jeans off in the four-foot-deep water. Jackie raised the BB gun to his shoulder thinking about shooting Bud one more time when he finally understood what Bud was trying to say.

"YELLOW JACKETS… YELLOW JACKETS… YELLOW JACKETS."

The two boys looked at each other not knowing exactly what they should do, they could see them now, and he was covered with them.

Bud finally got his jeans off and you could see the stings beginning to make red welts all over his legs and butt. He had been stung all over his body, but it looked as if there were more welts where his jeans had been.

"What can we do Bud, you want us to go get you some more clothes or something, Jackie asked, trying to keep from laughing?"

The two boys glanced at each other as Bud's teeth began chattering, either from the cold water or the stings. "What's he saying?" mumbled Tommy. "It doesn't matter; I can't understand a word he's saying anyway. Bud's not the most popular kid on the block, but I wouldn't wish this on anybody, it hurt's just to look at him", Jackie mumbled back with a mystified look on his face.

"Come on, Bud, try to get back up here on the bank, you need to get home, that many stings could be dangerous," Jackie insisted.

Bud struggled but he made it out of the creek and back to his house, which was right across the street from where Tommy lived. He walked back up through the cow pasture, between the houses and across the street to his house, butt naked; Bud could have died but it was still hard for Jackie and Tommy to keep from laughing as they presented him to his mother, standing on the front porch with her mouth wide open.

It was days later before Bud ventured to come outside and lie in the hammock that was strung up between two elm trees in the backyard.

"How many are there?" Tommy asked, "Anybody counted them yet?"

"Seventy-two, we think, two of them could be BB shots, you little fart."

"You shot us first," Jackie fired back, "trying to keep from laughing out loud. "Where did they come from, we didn't know what in the world was going on with you?"

"When I moved around the tree, they were on the other side; I must have stepped right in the middle of their nest….. You little punks get on out of here; I don't feel like talking about it any more!"

Jackie and Tommy had started back across the street to Tommy's house when Bud sat up in the hammock picking at one of the bee stings.

"Daddy's buying me a new Daisy Pump, it shoots a lot harder than those little pissy things you guys have; I'll have it payday." Bud eased back down in the hammock still scratching at one of the bee stings.

Bud survived his Yellow Jacket encounter, but by the time he was well enough to spin his side of the famous BB battle, it was too late. The other boys already knew what happened so he finally began to laugh at himself, which no doubt made him a better person later on in life.

****

Shortly after the Civil War, iron ore began to be mined in the hills of north Georgia and southeast Tennessee. As the ore was brought out of the ground, many small foundries began to spring up in this area. The small town of South Pittsburgh, Tennessee adopted its name from the larger and more famous steel city of the north. When the automobile industry started booming in Michigan, the demand for a better grade of ore was needed. The lower grade of ore that was pulled from the mines in the southeast could not meet the demands of the industrial revolution taking place up north. As the foundries began to shut down, the mines were soon to follow.

By the 1920s most of the mines were closed and sealed by the Bureau of Mines. Very few of the people who lived in this part of the country knew that these mines ever existed. Whole communities were built over these shafts, and the people who lived above them had no idea that just a few feet below the foundations of their home lay an abandoned mine, complete with narrow gauge rails and ore carts.

Jackie met Tommy at his house before Tommy got out of bed this time; more often it was the other way around.

"What's up, you got something on your mind; did your daddy get drunk again?" asked Tommy grinning. "Did he whip you or something?"

"No, no, no, not that." "He usually does that on Fridays or Saturdays; there's something I want to tell you. "

"Come on, man, what is it?

"This has to be our secret, just you and me; do you swear not to tell anybody?" Jackie said, as serious as a judge explaining the death sentence to a convicted murderer.

"I swear, I swear, now cut the crap, what is it?"

"I think I've found a cave," muttered Jackie, looking around to make sure no one else had heard him.

"A cave, what kind of cave?"

"Do you remember when I came down that hill right before I shot Bud?"

"I remember, why?" asked Tommy.

"Well, I almost put my leg down in a hole; it was black down there and cool air was coming out. I think we should check it out, maybe try to go down in it if we can." Jackie was having a hard time trying to hold back his excitement.

"You always exaggerate. Jackie; remember the flying saucer that you said landed on Lookout Mountain that turned out to be the sun shining off the hotel up there. OK, come on show me this rabbit hole you found," Tommy said, rubbing his hand across his flattop hair.

The boys had just started to cross the fence behind Tommy's house, which bordered the pasture, when Judy and Kitty appeared out of nowhere.

"Can we go with you down to the creek?" Judy asked. "We want to go wading in the shallow part to see if we can catch some tadpoles."

"You girls better not go now; the cows are at the crossing where you like to play; you don't want to be chased again, do you?" Remember last time when that Jersey Bull got after you and Kitty," Jackie said, looking at Tommy for confirmation.

"Come on, Kitty, they just don't want us around them, I think I hear the ice cream man anyway," Judy said, turning to the sound of a cowbell dangling from the handle of an ice cream cart.

The old man stopped the cart, looked up, squinting from the afternoon sun as the two girls came running in his direction.

"I want a Brown Cow," Kitty said.

"I want a Cherry Popsicle!" Judy struggled to get a foot-hold on top of one of the wheels of the old push-cart. She plopped a nickel down next to the old man's hand after announcing her choice of ice cream.

The old man put the money in his cigar box, placed the box down in the ice cream cart on top of the dry ice that kept the ice cream frozen solid, wiped his brow with a dirty handkerchief, and started off down the street.

"I think he needs a bath," Judy whispered, wrinkling up her nose as she tried to pull the paper from the hard frozen popsicle.

"Well I'll be dipped in peanut butter, that's no rabbit hole," Tommy gasped. "I can feel the cool air too."

"I told you, didn't I? Hand me that flash light," Jackie said smiling.

Jackie put his head down next to the opening, turned the flashlight on and aimed it through the hole.

"See anything? Let me see," Tommy said, trying to wrestle the flashlight away from Jackie.

"Quiet, let me look. I don't see anything; it's too dark down there." Jackie sat up , pulling his head back from the opening

Tommy took the light from Jackie, put his head down in the opening, and pushed the flashlight down beside his head.

"I can see the bottom." It looks flat like a floor maybe twenty feet down; yes it's a cave all right."

"We've got to get down there; but one thing's for sure, we have to make that opening bigger," Tommy said.

"How do you expect to do that?" Jackie propped up against the big rock next to the opening in the hillside.

"Let's go round up some tools, a pick, sledgehammer, pry bar, or anything else we can find; if we can move that smaller rock by the opening, I think we could get through."

The boys worked for two days with an assortment of tools from not only their homes but many of their neighbors as well. The basketball-sized rock that they were trying to remove finally broke loose and fell to the floor of the cave with a muffled thud. Jackie later told Tommy that the rock gave way due to the continuous cussing that it received, not because of any engineering feat they had executed.

"Wow," Jackie shouted, "that bastard was bigger than I thought; did you hear it hit?"

Tommy just fell back on the hillside, dropping his arms down to his side. "Yeah," was all that he could muster.

They spent hours trying to figure out how to get down to the floor of the cave, including a way to get back out. Jackie insisted that the cave would be known only to him and Tommy, which limited their options as far as soliciting outside help was concerned. The most logical solution was to descend down through the opening on a rope; the only drawback was if they could climb back out.

"I know I can climb a rope twenty-five feet, but can you?" Jackie asked Tommy, who was rubbing his flattop again.

"Only one way to find out," Tommy answered, "let's go climb the rope to the swing."

A creek would not be complete if it did not have a rope swing that you could swing out on and drop off into the water. The rope was a two-inch river barge rope, tied fifty feet up in a sycamore tree. No one knew for sure who had climbed the tree to tie the rope onto the limb, but all agreed he must have had some balls.

Jackie was first to climb the rope, he flew half way up with little or no effort and let himself down the same way he would do if he were going down the rope into the cave.

"It's your turn, bubble butt, see what you can do," Jackie teased with a slight grin.

Tommy knew that he lacked the strength that Jackie had, but he made up for it in determination.

"Here goes," Tommy gasped, as he started up the rope.

He made the first ten feet or so without any problem, but started slowing down and could not go another inch after he had reached what they had estimated to be twenty-five feet.

“I’m coming down,” Tommy grunted as he started down the rope. He had descended only about six feet when he let go of the rope and dropped the remaining distance to the creek below.

Jackie laughed as Tommy climbed back up onto the creek bank rubbing the water from the flattop hair that now stuck to his scalp.

“Lose some of that ass and it’ll get easier.” Jackie grinned at Tommy and smiled. “ I think you can make it OK.”

****

The boys planned for days before they finally agreed on what they needed to take down into the cave; they knew that they each would have to have a flashlight, but whatever else they took down could not weigh much or they would have to leave it down there. Jackie decided to go with a smaller size rope; he talked his dad into giving him some that came from his block and tackle he used for topping trees.

After lying to several of their friends they met along the way as to what they were going to do with the rope, Jackie and Tommy finally arrived at the opening in the side of the hill.

“Whew, I didn’t think we were ever going to get here,” said Jackie, moving a dead log and some small rocks they had used to camouflage the cave entrance.

“Do you think Kenneth and that other kid bought your story about what you were going to do with that rope?” Tommy asked, plopping down on the ground beside the big rock that guarded the opening in the hill.

“Who knows, I had to tell them something, roping a cow sounded good to me at the time.” Jackie laughed. “Kenneth doesn’t know a cow from a horse anyway. I think I’m going to tie the rope around that pine tree instead of around the big rock. Jackie uncoiled the rope from around his shoulder and tossed it on the ground. "It'll take too much rope to go around that rock; I want to make sure we have enough to reach the bottom."

After tying the rope around the base of the pine tree, Jackie fed the rope through the opening, listening and hoping to hear the sound of the rope hitting the bottom of the cave.

"Move over," Tommy scowled, "let me shine this light down there, I don't think it reached the bottom."

Tommy squinted, crawling around the opening on his knees trying to see the end of the rope dangling toward the bottom of the cave.

"I see it, I see it," yelled Tommy, "it's about a foot from the bottom, perfect!"

"OK, you got everything?" asked Jackie, looking at Tommy as if asking with his eyes if he wanted to back out.

"I'm ready; all I have is this flashlight, some string and a few matches."

"I'll go first," Jackie said, looking back at Tommy as if to say, "I'm in charge of this mission, just do what I do."

Jackie descended into the opening, scurried down the rope with little effort, pulling his flashlight from his pocket as soon as his feet touched the floor of the cave, and shining it up the rope as Tommy blocked out all the light as he struggled to get into the opening.

"Come on, Tommy, you're making it look harder than it really is, just take it easy."

Tommy was determined to make it to the bottom without letting the rope slide through his hands. After much grunting and sweating, he finally made it, dropping to his knees and not saying a word as he tried to catch his breath.

After a full minute, Tommy stood up, pulled the flashlight from his pocket, slid the switch on, and directed the light back up the rope to the small opening twenty feet above his head.

"I'm doomed; I'll never get out of here." Tommy sighed,

shining the light back down the rope.

"Don't be such a crybaby, you climbed the rope at the swing; you can climb this one, it's not any higher." Jackie laughed, patting Tommy on the shoulder.

"It's cold down here," muttered Tommy, "we should have worn a coat or something."

After standing around the rope for several minutes, it occurred to them that they had come down there to explore the cave, and not stand there looking up the rope at the small opening in the roof.

Jackie and Tommy began probing the darkness with their flashlights around the small room that they had descended into.

"Look over there," Tommy stammered, "is that an opening?"

"It sure is," Jackie said, holding his beam on the black hole in the wall and walking toward it. "Well I'll be; this is not a cave; this is some kind of mine, look at the timbers around the entrance."

"Do you think it's safe to go in there?" stuttered Tommy, shaking from the cold air.

"It looks OK to me, these timbers are solid," replied Jackie, tapping on the wood with his flashlight.

"Go on then," Tommy grunted, as he pushed Jackie in the back with his light.

"Watch it," cried Jackie, "you're getting in too big a hurry, here's another set of pillars and roof supports, and look up ahead on the floor, it's the start of a small railroad of some kind."

Jackie directed the beam of his flashlight down the track, moving it slowly as he and Tommy watched the narrow track disappear around a curve in the tunnel.

"Well, what are you waiting for?" asked Tommy. "Go on, let's see where it goes."

Jackie started walking down the center of the track stepping lightly on the wood crossties as if they might break and send him plummeting into the abyss. He stopped as he came to the curve in the tunnel as Tommy stumbled into his back, almost knocking him off his feet.

"Watch where you're going," Jackie gasped, reaching for the side of the cave to steady himself.

"Sorry, I was following the light, why did you stop?"

"I don't know, guess I was just wondering what we are going to find around this turn; I'm not scared, I just want to be cautious, that's all."

As Jackie led Tommy around the turn in the cave, the lights revealed a long straight tunnel that led to another bend almost out of reach of the flashlight beams. As the boys continued down the rails deeper into the mine, they would occasionally stop and listen, whisper something to each other and continue on. Later, they would laugh as to why they were whispering, as they recounted how brave they were.

"How far do you think we've come?" Tommy asked as he aimed his light back up the mine shaft in the direction of the rope that he hoped was still hanging from the opening.

"Crap, I don't know, maybe a quarter of a mile or so, do you want to go back or something?"

"No, I was just wondering," muttered Tommy.

As they rounded the next turn in the mineshaft, both boys stopped in their tracks as they traversed their lights back and forth at the two openings that came into view. The tunnel had forked with another set of tracks branching off at almost a ninety-degree angle from the one they had just come.

"What now?" inquired Tommy? "How much farther you think we should go?"

"Let's follow the one we're on; it has to stop somewhere."

After several turns, ascending a slight rise in elevation, the shaft came to an abrupt end. The rails they had been following disappeared under what looked to be a massive cave in.

"I guess we know where this one goes." Tommy said indifferently as he looked down at the pile of rocks and dirt that covered the ore cart rails.

"Let's get out of here, we have the rest of the summer to explore; right now I want to make sure you can get your big ass up that rope," Jackie said, looking at Tommy out of the corner of his eye. There was no fooling around as they made their way back in the direction of the entrance. They stopped for a short break at the fork in the shaft and strained to see the end of their flashlight beams as they played them back and forth down the abandoned mineshaft. After the short break, they walked on in silence. Tommy breathed a short sigh of relief as the rope came into view.

Tommy started up first and did well until he got within ten feet of the opening at the top, where he stopped and insisted that he could go no farther.

"Stay where you are," Jackie shouted, as he scurried up the rope placing his shoulder under Tommy's butt and giving him enough reinforcement to advance the remaining ten feet to the opening.

"That wasn't too bad." Tommy stood up and extended a hand to Jackie, hoisting him out of the opening.

"Yeah sure; you're so full of it, if I hadn't been behind you, I would have had to get the fire department to get you out of there!"

"It's easier for you because you're so skinny." Tommy grinned as he sat down and leaned back against the huge boulder that guarded the opening to the mine.

****

Tommy and Jackie spent days reflecting on their trip down into the cave, which they know now was an abandoned mine.

They laid plans as how to keep this discovery a secret for as long as they could, for if it became known to the other boys it wouldn't be long before it got back to their parents, and that would be the end of it. They spent days camouflaging the entrance to the mine, always coming and going from a different direction so as not to leave a trail or path. Luckily, the entrance to the mine was in an area that was mostly ignored because it was on a hillside and overrun with thorny blackberry bushes. They struggled, lugging a large flat rock from the creek bed to cover the opening in the side of the hill, all the while avoiding others who were constantly coming and going, either to hang out at the creek or to take the short cut to Lake Winnepesaukah.

"You need to know something, Tommy," Jackie said quietly as he coiled up the rope and put it into the small depression under the flat stone where they had decided to stow it. "If we were to go down in the mine or cave, whichever you wish to call it, and somehow the rope was removed or for some reason became untied from the tree, we would be trapped with no way to get out. No one, I say no one, knows where we are and it is quite possible we would never be found. Have you thought about that?"

"How could the rope become untied from the tree? If someone untied, it they would surely know that we were down there?"

"You're probably right," muttered Jackie. "I just wanted you to know as far as we know that rope is the only way back out. I think there is something we need to do before we go back down there," said Jackie, looking around and avoiding eye contact with Tommy.

"What's that?" inquired Tommy.

"We need to talk to Lewis first."

****

LEWIS

Lewis Bolt lived right next door to Jackie. Lewis had become sort of a mentor to Jackie and the other boys in the neighborhood. Lewis was an Army Engineer during the war and fought the Japs while building bridges and roads throughout the islands of the Pacific, ahead of the Allied troops that were soon to follow. Jackie and his friends loved to sit and listen to Lewis convey his experiences, knowing that he had added some color and mixed in a few white lies to boot. He enjoyed being around the boys although he also had two younger children of his own.

Jackie would go to Lewis for advice for things that he would not go to his dad for; Lewis always had an answer and never questioned why you were asking. In addition to answering questions and showing the boys of the neighborhood how to build something or improve things that they had screwed up, he would actually go and take a look at their endeavors.

Lewis liked baseball; he often would take Jackie and Tommy to watch the Chattanooga Lookouts play the Atlanta Crackers in a minor league baseball game in Chattanooga.

If the Lookouts were not playing the Atlanta Crackers, you could forget going to the ball game; Lewis was a big Cracker fan and the other visiting teams were of no interest to him.

Lewis Bolt was not a man that stood out in a crowd; when at home he was usually dressed in kaki pants and plaid shirt. He stood six feet tall and had hair that resembled that of the rock and roll singer, Jerry Lee Lewis. You would never guess that Lewis had an engineering degree from Georgia Tech.

Lewis assigned a nickname to just about everyone he knew; it was just his way of remembering who you were.

****

"Jack Daniels and Tomcat Redden; where in the world have you boys been; are you going to summer school or something?" asked Lewis as Jackie and Tommy rounded the corner of the house and headed toward Lewis, sitting in a lawn chair in his front yard.

"No we're not going to summer school," Jackie said. "We both passed, believe it or not, we've just been real busy. Did you hear about Bud Higgins getting in that Yellow Jacket nest?"

"I heard he had so many wasp stings that you couldn't count 'em all, they said that he had been shot by a BB gun too., I guess you boys don't know anything about that, do you?" Lewis grinned as he fished a pack of Lucky Strikes out of his shirt pocket.

"It couldn't happen to a nicer guy," muttered Tommy as he flopped down on the grass in front of Lewis, who was bringing his lighter up to the tip of his cigarette.

They all three laughed hard as they watched Lewis replace his lighter in his watch pocket, it was almost mechanical the routine he went through; sometimes the boys would mimic him when he wasn't watching.

"I could hear Bud's mother cussing out his dad again, Miss Johnson next door had to go back in the house, that woman sure knows some bad words, some I haven't even heard before," said Lewis. "I don't see how that man takes that crap, some day he's gonna snap."

Jackie and Tommy filled Lewis in on what was going on around the neighborhood, with Lewis injecting his humor and comments along the way.

Jackie glanced up at the front door to make sure Lewis' wife wasn't standing behind the screen as she sometimes did, eavesdropping on the conversations Lewis had with the neighborhood boys. Francis was a quiet woman, but quite often she could not contain herself from stepping out on the porch and reminding Lewis of the facts he had distorted in one of the stories that he was telling.

"We got something we want to ask you," Jackie said indifferently as he slapped at an insect on the back of his neck.

"I figured there was something," Lewis replied tiredly, as he reached in his shirt pocket fumbling for his pack of Luckies. "I know the Lookouts are in town, but they are playing New Orleans tonight; the Pelicans are in the cellar, it wouldn't be much of a game."

"No, no, we don't want to go to the game, we're just trying to find out something," explained Tommy, leaning back on one elbow.

"If it's about girls, I can't help you; otherwise, what is it?"

"Do you know if they used to be mines around here?" Jackie asked, looking back up at the screen door.

"Mines, what kind of mines? I know they used to mine coal out of the mountains around here, some of them are still open over in Tennessee, I've never heard of any here in Georgia."

"I don't mean coal, what about gold or something?" asked Jackie sheepishly.

"They had a gold rush down in Dahlonega a long time ago, but not in this area," Lewis said. "All right, boys, let's hear it, what have you found? You know there are caves all over these hills; if you have found one, what makes you think it is a mine?"

"Timbers, and tracks but no evidence of any coal," answered Tommy.

"We trust you, Lewis, we didn't know who to ask about it; we would like to keep it our secret for now, because we haven't finished exploring it yet."

Lewis didn't say anything for a full minute, looking back and forth at the two boys.

"Where is it?" asked Lewis, with a look of concern on his face.

Tommy and Jackie shuffled around glancing at each other before Jackie said, "Down by the creek."

"Let me get this straight," Lewis said as he flipped the remainder of the Lucky at least fifteen yards out into the yard, "you have found a cave down by the creek and you have been in it and it has timbers and overhead supports and a rail system."

"We did," Jackie and Tommy said at the same time.

"How far does this mine go?" asked Lewis with a little skepticism in his voice.

"We followed only one of the tracks, the shaft came to a y-junction, the one that we followed went on for about a half a mile before ending at what must have been a cave-in," Jackie exaggerated.

"A half a mile you say," probed Lewis.

"Well maybe not that far, but it seemed like it, didn't it, Tommy?"

"It was a long way and we only followed that one track, no telling where the other one went," Tommy answered.

Lewis leaned back in his chair with a slight sigh. "Let me do some checking around, I know a man whose family has been around here since the Civil War; if anybody would know, he would. I'll keep this to myself, but on one condition," said Lewis, looking back and forth at the two boys.

"What's that?" inquired Jackie.

"Show me where it is. If you guys fail to show up for supper, I'll at least know where to start looking."

****

The boys decided to wait until they heard back from Lewis before going back down into what they now called their cave. They spent an enormous amount of time planning for their next excursion, they lowered drinking water and other supplies that they felt that they would need down through the small opening that led to the mineshaft.

To keep from arousing suspicion from the other boys in the neighborhood, they would make it a point to join in when sides were being chosen for a sand lot baseball game, or catch the bus to go downtown with a group of guys. They fished, went swimming in the creek, built a tree house, which they did half-assed due to the fact that going back down in the cave was always on their mind.

One afternoon as Jackie started his trek through the neighbor's backyard in the direction of Tommy's house, Ernest Biddle a six-foot tall, skinny fourteen-year-old who everyone called "Gern" came running in his direction. Gern was relatively new to the neighborhood, but everyone seemed to like him; he was growing so fast you could almost see the change from one day to the next. His face started sprouting pimples hourly and he had just been fitted with glasses. In addition to being a very tall skinny boy with pimples and Clark Kent glasses, he was clumsy. Lewis once made the comment, "We need to give that boy plenty of room; he's all feet and hands."

"Wait up, Jackie," Gern said as he jumped a small patch of dark green grass in Mr. Higgins' back yard, which was most likely a rupture in the sewer field line.

"Slow down, Gern, you're about to fall in that soft spot. Don't you know what caused all that green grass growing there, surely you can smell it?" Jackie said, shaking his head.

Gern adjusted his glasses on his nose and looked down at his feet just inches from the dingy water that could be seen between the blades of tall green grass.

"I'm glad I caught up to you," Gern said. "Mr. Shipp said that you could not do a one-handed chin up, that no one could, and that he would give you twenty dollars if you could. We all told him that you could, he just wouldn't believe us, I know you can, I've seen you do it. He's at home and says that the offer is still good, go show him, Jackie, he's such a smart ass, take his twenty dollars."

"I don't have time for that crap, Gern, he's not going to give anybody twenty dollars; old man Shipp is always blowing about how smart he is."

"Come on, Jackie, go show him, make a believer out of him; you still can do it, can't you?" Gern asked as his voice sounded less excited.

"Sure I can. I just did one on the clothesline post as I left the house, but I tell you he's just shooting his mouth off, he won't give up twenty dollars." Jackie said, feeling challenged by the tone in Gern's voice.

"OK," said Gern as he stepped around the green spot in the backyard. "I'll tell him what you said; I wish I could do a chin up with both hands, let alone one."

Jackie knew what Mr. Shipp would do; he would taunt his friends, and he was just that kind of person that pissed you off by showing how smart he was. *Hell I should go up there and show him I could do it, even though I know he would make some goofy excuse as to why he won't give up the twenty dollars.*

"Hey, Gern, I'm going to Tommy's house, I'll get him and we will be up there in a few minutes; tell old man Shipp to get his money ready," Jackie shouted as he started across the street to Tommy's house.

By the time Jackie and Tommy walked the half a block to Mr. Shipp's backyard, at least a dozen neighborhood boys and a couple of girls had gathered around the clothesline post where old man Shipp was holding court.

Jackie and Tommy turned off the street and walked down the driveway leading to the backyard where the small crowd had gathered.

"Here he is, here he is," shouted Gern as he spotted them

coming down the driveway."

"Come over here," snarled old man Shipp, who had been explaining the way the chin-up, had to be performed to collect the prize.

"Listen, Jackie, these boys think you can do a one-handed chin-up, and I know you think that you can, but here is the way you must do it if you are to collect the twenty dollars. You cannot hold one wrist with the other hand, and you must start from a hanging position with your arm fully extended, your feet not touching the ground. Do you understand what I am saying?" Mr. Ship smiled as he looked around the crowd expecting Jackie to object to the conditions.

"Yes sir, I understand, that's the way I practice doing it at home," said Jackie quietly.

You could see old man Shipp's Adam's apple rise and fall as someone in the back of the crowd hollered, "Do it, Jackie, show him you can do it."

Jackie walked over to the clothesline post, which consisted of a three-inch pipe concreted in the ground with an inch and a half pipe welded across the top to form a T. Jackie grabbed the bar, which was slightly above his head, with his right hand, pulled his feet up off the ground and hung for a full five seconds before Tommy screamed, "Pull, Jackie, you can do it." It must have been because of the adrenalin rush from everyone watching, but it looked as easy as pie; Jackie went from a full hanging position to easing his chin over the bar in no more than two seconds. A cheer went up that brought heads peeping out doors for a block away.

"Holy cow; do it again," someone shouted through an open window from the house next door.

Jackie looked in the direction of the house and grinned. Everyone else in the crowd turned and looked at Mr. Shipp.

Old man Shipp reached in his back pocket, removed his

wallet, pulled out a ten and two fives, and with a face as red as a monkey's ass, he dropped the twenty dollars on the ground. Before the noise had died down, the "know it all" Mr. Shipp turned and headed for his back door.

Tommy scooped up the money and handed it out toward Jackie, who was blushing with the attention that everyone was giving him.

"I'm glad he didn't tell me I had to do it with my left hand. I can't even pee left-handed." Jackie laughed as he took the money from Tommy's hand. "I hate to take old man Shipp's money, I know he's an asshole, but it might put him in a bind."

"You know, he asked for it; he's been calling us and you a liar for two weeks now, it's about time somebody shut him up, anyway how long has it been since you had twenty bucks to spend on anything you wanted?"

"I really need this, Tommy; Mama's worried that she can't get me anything for my birthday, she's doing ironing for people to try to get some extra money, I don't like to see her have to do that. Maybe this will help her out."

****

Jackie tried to give his mother the money from doing the one-handed chin-up but she would not take it, not even half of it. She insisted he spend it on anything he wanted; maybe buy that Ritchie Ashburn baseball glove he had tried on while at Sears one Saturday morning.

It was several days before the news got back to Jackie's dad about him taking the twenty dollars from Mr. Shipp; needless to say he didn't think it was as cool as everyone else.

"What the hell you think you're doing, get your ass up there and give that damn money back to that man, I don't want people to think that I'm raising a con artist or something," Jackie's dad said while placing a pinch of Copenhagen tobacco in his cheek.

Jackie didn't know how his dad would react to the chin-up episode, and that's why he had held onto the money to see what his reaction would be.

Jackie just agreed as he looked down at the supper table; he knew not to argue with his father for fear of getting backhanded or even the dreaded whipping with the belt. He looked out of the corner of his eye at his mother, who stood in the doorway at the end of the table with a look of disgust on her face.

Jackie's dad got up from the table putting the round box of Copenhagen in his shirt pocket as he stood up.

"Don't just sit there; get that money back to that old man before I get this belt off. One-handed chin-up my ass," bellowed Jackie's dad as he lowered himself into his recliner chair.

Jackie never looked at his mother as he walked past her, and left. He had a feeling that his dad would react like this, there was just something about him; he was just a hard man.

****

"Where you going?" Gern shouted to Jackie as he passed by his house headed toward Mr. Shipp's.

"Mr. Shipp's, I've got to give the money back," Jackie hollered back, looking down at his feet as he walked up the street.

"What in the world for?" Gern asked, pushing his glasses back up on his nose, intersecting Jackie as he reached his mailbox in front of his house.

"My dad's making me: says I'm a con artist, that I took advantage of him."

"What a bunch of horseshit, does your dad not know the way old man Shipp is?"

"It don't matter, there's no use trying to reason with him,

he's just that way."

With Gern towering above him, Jackie stood on Mr. Shipp's front porch waiting for someone to answer the knock, at the same time hoping that no one would.

Mr. Shipp slowly pushed open the screen door, squinting in the afternoon sun as he looked up at the pimply-faced skinny boy and back down at the much shorter Jackie.

"What you boys want? I'm in no mood for any of your crap; I haven't been feeling well."

"I'm here to give your money back; Daddy says I can't keep it, that I took advantage of you somehow," muttered Jackie.

Mr. Shipp was silent for a few seconds, his Adam's apple bobbed up and down once as the old man swallowed hard.

"Let me tell you something, Jackie; you did something that very few people can do, probably no more than one in a million. I would have bet this house that you could not have done it. You taught me a lesson; the money is yours. Tell your dad you gave it back, I'll vouch for you; go buy yourself something, because you earned it."

Old man Shipp smiled down at Jackie and back up at Gern as he let the screen door close; disappearing back into the house.

Jackie and Gern stood on the porch for a moment before turning around, leaping to the ground and heading back toward the street.

"I never would have thought he would do that. What are you going to do now?" Gern asked, looking down at Jackie as they stood in the middle of the street.

"I guess I'll keep it; here you take five of it, you're the one who set this up anyway," Jackie said, handing Gern one of the five-dollar bills.

Gern's eyes widened as he took the bill from Jackie, trying to control the slight grin creeping across his face.

"Thanks, man, but I didn't do anything, are you sure you

want me to take this, you're the one who earned it."

"Yeah, but don't say anything, remember, I gave him his money back," Jackie said, grinning back up at Gern.

Jackie's dad never said anything more about the money, but he did tell Jackie that he should not tell people that he could do a one-handed chin-up. "Nobody could do that."

****

Jackie and Tommy decided what to do with the fifteen dollars that was left from the one-handed chin-up episode; they would buy things for their cave. The thing that concerned them the most was that someone would discover the entrance, especially with the opening not being covered while they were inside. They ordered a rope ladder through the mail from a solider of fortune magazine. When the rope ladder finally arrived, they spent days securing it to the lip of the opening of the mineshaft. They drove steel rods deep into the ground next to the entrance where they secured the rope ladder that descended to the floor of the cave. The ladder worked perfectly and was much easier to get in and out of the mine, but one problem still remained; how to cover the entrance while they were down below.

"I've got an idea; why don't we go down by the creek and find one of those big flat rocks, you know one of those that's about an inch thick and as big around as a steering wheel on a city bus, they're not that heavy, we could slide it back over the opening from the ladder," Tommy said, as if he had just discovered the cure for polio.

"It might work, but it would have to look natural from the outside, it would have to be big enough to cover the steel rods." Jackie smiled at Tommy, "what would I ever do without your innovative contribution?"

It took less than two hours walking along the edge of the creek before they found it, lying two inches below the water in the shallow cattle crossing.

"Pull that one up, Tommy, see how heavy it is, I know it's big enough," Jackie said, pointing down at the flat rock lying just below the surface of the water.

Tommy bent down and delicately placed the fingers of both hands under the edge of the large flat rock and pulled up. As the two-and-a-half-foot rock broke the surface of the water, a large crawfish darted between his legs, causing him to release the rock, sending a splash of water directly into the face of Jackie, who was down on one knee watching the operation.

"What the hell are you doing, trying to drown me'" Jackie screamed, falling back and trying to keep his balance.

Before Tommy could reply, Jackie fell backwards trying to catch his fall, his left hand landing squarely in the middle of a fresh pile of cow manure. Without saying a word, he yanked his hand up in front of his face and looked through his fingers at Tommy, who holding his side from laughing.

"Kiss my ass," Jackie said sheepishly as he plunged his hand down into the shallow creek, washing brownish green goo from his hand and watching the green-tinted water pass between Tommy's legs.

After both boys regained their composure, Tommy got another grip on the flat rock and easily pulled it up on its edge. Amazingly, the rock was no more than a half-inch to three quarter inches thick and was light enough for Tommy to lift by himself. He placed it on the creek bank beside Jackie, who was still inspecting his hand as if it had been dipped in poison.

"This should be perfect," Jackie said, cleaning the mud from the underside of the flat rock with the hand that he had just cleaned so thoroughly. "This thing weighs hardly anything at all, great idea, Tommy, now let's get this thing back up on the hill."

After hours of digging and cussing, the boys finally positioned the rock over the entrance of the mineshaft so that it fit in with the neighboring landscape. Anyone who might stumble upon it would never guess what purpose it served; besides, the area was covered in blackberry bushes, the only other visitors were likely to be rabbits.

It was always interesting coming and going; they were very careful not to create a path and sometimes it meant crawling through the vines and thickets of the blackberry bushes to get there. They brought things that they felt they would need while down in the cave; milk bottles full of water, Coleman lanterns that were purchased with the chin-up money, sleeping bags, and of course, Playboy magazines that were given to them by the owner of the Sinclair Gas station up on the highway. Before long, they had cleaned out most of their bedroom junk that their parents wanted them to discard, and a few items from the household that Jackie's dad declared had just mysteriously disappeared.

Each visit made it harder to conceal their avenues of approach to the cave entrance, so they decided to give it a break. Jackie and Tommy had perfected ascending and descending the rope ladder; they could easily pull the flat rock across the entrance while perched below on the third rung of the rope ladder. They were eager to explore more of the mines, but first they decided to visit Lewis; maybe he had acquired some information as to the history of the mines. Jackie agreed with Lewis; it would be better if someone else knew where the entrance of the mine was located, just in case something happened and they were trapped down there while exploring.

****

It was almost dark when the boys walked up behind Lewis as he was washing his car. Lewis traded for a new Ford every year and the color was always black, which may explain why he washed it every week.

"Well I'll be, it's the two spelunkers; I was about to get worried about you two boys but Jackie's mother claims that he's coming home every night, so I guess everything is OK." Lewis smiled as he twisted the nozzle of the water hose and rinsed the soap from the now shinny hubcap.

"What's a spelunker?" inquired Tommy, looking puzzled.

"You don't know what a spelunker is? Tell him, Jackie, the boy is one and don't know what it is," said Lewis, looking down at Tommy, who had now flopped down on the grass beside the driveway.

"Uh, uh, I don't know either. What is it, Lewis, is it something that you made up?"

"When you boys get near a dictionary, look it up, that way you will always remember it, and don't ask me to spell it." Lewis laughed as he placed the water hose on the grass and reached for his shirt pocket, searching for his pack of Lucky Strikes.

"I've got a little information about what you may have stumbled into," said Lewis, pushing the cigarette lighter down in his watch pocket as he talked, with the Lucky bobbing up and down between his lips. "Seems that this area was mined extensively for iron ore during the years after the Civil War, but petered out due to the poor quality they produced. The Bureau of Mines reclaimed them in the 1920s; very few people are still around that remember where they were, but they did exist."

"Do you think it's safe to be going down inside the tunnels?" asked Jackie almost whispering.

"Probably not, but I know you're going to do it anyway, just be careful; you know you'll have to tell the authorities sometime, but right now I'll keep your secret, providing you show me where the entrance is."

"When can you go?"

"We're ready to go deeper but I would like for you to take a look and tell us what you think first," Jackie said, as he watched Tommy nod his head in agreement.

"It's too late today, what about tomorrow afternoon after I get off from work?" asked Lewis as he flipped away the butt of his Lucky and returned to the task of washing the hubcaps on his black Ford Victoria.

"We'll be here when you get home," Tommy said, jumping to his feet.

"Come on, Lewis, what's a spelunker," Tommy asked, as he dodged the spray from Lewis' hose that he had intentionally aimed in his direction.

"Look it up; don't they teach you boys anything in school these days?" grunted Lewis, bending over to pull a kink out of the water hose that had suddenly stopped spraying.

"See you boys tomorrow," shouted Lewis as Jackie and Tommy disappeared around the corner of the house into the almost totally dark summer evening.

"Spelunker, you think that's some kind of made-up word he came up with, or is it for real?" Tommy asked as the two boys stood facing each other in the middle of Jackie's back yard.

"I don't know," Jackie answered, as he turned around and headed in the direction of his back door.

"Hey, Tommy," Jackie shouted back over his shoulder, "he said that you were one, so I guess I'm one too!"

The blinking of hundreds of fireflies greeted the evening as the sun disappeared behind Lookout Mountain. Neither Jackie nor Tommy noticed the flicker of the bugs or the oncoming darkness; they were in deep thought about their visit with Lewis.

****

Jackie greeted his mother with a peck on the cheek as he entered the kitchen. He pulled open the refrigerator, grasped the handle of the ceramic water pitcher that was always full and loaded down with ice. He turned the water pitcher up and began to gulp down the cold water, paying no attention to his mother pleading with him to get a glass.

"I'm sorry, I forgot." He grinned, sliding the pitcher back beside the freezer compartment inside the refrigerator.

"You better hurry if you plan to get your bath before *Dragnet* comes on, it's fifteen till nine now." If it were not for *Dragnet* and *Ozzie and Harriet* you and Tommy would probably stay out all night."

"I'll make it," he shouted above the water splashing into the bathtub in the small bathroom.

Jackie finished his bath, darted into the living room, and plopped down on the sofa just as Sgt. Joe Friday was telling what the weather was like in Los Angeles.

TV had taken the place of the radio and also had changed the habits of most American families during the evening hours; Jackie and his generation would be the last to remember what it was like before the invention of the television.

Jackie had trouble concentrating on TV; even his favorite show could not hold his attention, which was the case of most anything since discovering the mine. It was his and Tommy's big adventure and not even TV shows could pry them away from thinking about it, at least for now.

****

Jackie was up early and out the back door before his mother could catch up to him and insist he eat something before going to do whatever he was into these days. As he approached Tommy's house, he glanced up the street to see Mr. Redden on his way to catch the bus that would carry him to his job downtown. Just as he had crossed the street and was about to enter Tommy's driveway, something caught his eye in the distance just beyond where Mr. Redden was walking. It was a house and it was moving down Stateline Road.

"What in the crap, how could that be; a house moving down the road?" Jackie mumbled to himself as the house disappeared behind the house at the end of the street.

Shaking his head, he walked up the driveway and stepped up on Tommy's back porch. As he reached for the handle of the screen door, the door pushed open and Linda, Tommy's sister, stepped out on the porch.

"He'll be out in a minute, Mother's making him brush his teeth," Linda said, as she stood toe-to-toe with Jackie, making him blush as her rather substantial breasts came within a quarter of an inch of brushing his bare chest.

Jackie had a secret crush on Linda, but he knew it would never go anywhere because she was two years older than he, and not to mention that she was the head majorette at the high school. She knew that she was a knockout, and she liked to flirt, especially with Jackie, it seemed.

Linda broke eye contact with Jackie as Tommy kicked open the screen door, popping her in the rear, making her jerk forward just enough to lightly push her breasts onto Jackie, who was now back peddling and almost falling off the porch.

"Watch where you're going," Linda snapped as she turned away from Jackie, who's face was now the color of an over-ripe tomato.

"Get your big butt out of the way," Tommy muttered as he eased the screen door the rest of the way open with his foot; one hand held a glass of milk and the other a rather large biscuit wrapped in a napkin.

Linda glimpsed back over shoulder and smiled slightly at

Jackie as she closed the screen door behind her and disappeared into the kitchen.

"You're not going to guess what I just saw," Jackie almost shouted, as Tommy took an enormous bite of his biscuit and chased it with a swig of milk.

"As red as your face is, it sure excited the hell out of you," Tommy said grinning.

"I just saw a house; I mean a whole house going down Stateline Road."

"They're moving them from East Ridge, the freeway is going right through the middle of it; a lot of them are being put back on foundations right here in Rankin Park."

"How do you know about everything, I haven't heard about a freeway coming through here?" Jackie asked.

"I heard Mom and Dad talking about it, it's gonna be like it is in California all over the whole country; divided four lane highways and cloverleaves everywhere. It's Eisenhower's deal, you need to pay attention to what's going on," Tommy said with a hint of arrogance because he knew something that Jackie didn't.

"OK, OK, know it all, come on let's go, we got some things to do before Lewis gets home. Hey, Tommy, I think we should go down to the creek and see what's going on, you know be seen and let everybody know we're still alive."

"Yeah, I want to see where that big sycamore fell across the creek after the storm the other night. Linda said she heard people were diving off of it, that it was twenty-five feet high over the water."

The two boys climbed over the wire fence that separated Tommy's back yard from the cow pasture and headed down the dirt path leading to the creek.

****

It was not hard to find the huge sycamore tree that had blown down and fell across the creek at one of its deepest spots. At least half a dozen boys and nearly as many girls were climbing up the slick bark of one of the large limbs that led up to the tree trunk extending across the creek. The fat trunk of the tree was preciously balanced at least twenty feet above the water on four or five of the huge limbs that had broken off and plunged into the creek and creek bank.

You could tell by watching who was afraid of heights and who wasn't; some just walked the natural bridge made by the giant tree trunk to the center of the creek and dived off, others scooted across with their legs wrapped as tightly around the trunk as they could.

"I wonder how deep the water is where they are diving," Jackie asked more to himself than to anyone else, as he and Tommy stood watching the action around the fallen sycamore tree.

Tommy started to mumble something about the water when a scream that could be heard in downtown Chattanooga came from one of the girls that had just jumped from the fallen tree, as she came scrambling up from the creek.

Everyone in line waiting their turn to climb up onto the tree looked in the direction of the now frantic girl, who was jumping up and down and slapping at something on the back of her thigh.

Jackie and Tommy were the first ones to reach her; both boys tried to grab her arms but could not seem to secure a grip due to her jumping and slapping at her leg.

"Hold still for crying out loud," Jackie said calmly, trying to see what she was so excited about.

The poor girl's eyes were almost popping out of their sockets and her face was an expression of pure fear as she looked into Jackie's eyes and tried to free herself from the death grip he had on her wrists.

As she struggled with Jackie, Tommy was down on his knees examining the small dark spot on her leg that was causing her such distress.

"It's just a leach, it's just a leach," Tommy said as calmly as he could. "You would thing you were bitten by a copperhead."

"Get it off, get it off," she screamed as tears ran down her face and began to drip onto Tommy's head, as he tried to pull the leach free from her leg.

"Has anyone got a cigarette?" Jackie inquired of the crowd that had circled around the now slightly calmer girl. Come on, boys and girls, I know some of you smoke, you know who you are; light one up and give it to me."

It wasn't long before cigarettes were being pushed at Jackie from all directions; as he watched the leach begin to grow in size.

"OK, OK, I just need one; do all of you smoke these days?" Jackie said, grinning as he put the tip of the cigarette as close to the leach without burning the girl's leg. The rest of you guys should be checking each other out, see if anyone else has any on them. Be sure to check under your bathing suits too."

"I got one on me," a boy screamed just as the small bloodsucker dropped from the girl, leaving a thin streak of blood down the side of her leg as it landed beside her foot.

"Get one of those cigarettes over here, the bastard's right above the crack of my ass, I can't reach it, how about some help, somebody," cried Emory, who had earned the nicknamed "Howdy Doody" because of his resemblance to the puppet on the Saturday morning TV show.

Some of the older boys knew that they were leaches in the creek, and it was no big deal to them; it was just something you had to put up with if you swam in the creek. It was a different story for some of the others, especially the girls; some of them accepted it, but for others it would be the last time they went swimming in the creek.

****

Jackie and Tommy finally broke free of the others who were engaged in different activities around the creek and made their way up to the entrance of their cave so they could prepare for Lewis' visit later that day. Tommy slid the large flat rock from over the opening and peered down into the mineshaft.

"Look's just like we left it," Tommy said as he lowered himself down into the hole, planting both feet on the third rung of the rope ladder and looking back up at Jackie.

Tommy reached the floor of the mineshaft, grabbed a flashlight and was holding the beam on Jackie as he pulled the flat rock back over the opening before continuing down the ladder.

"It's been a while since we've been down here, I can't wait until we explore the rest of this place, no telling what we'll find down those other shafts," Tommy said excitedly.

"I can't wait either, but I want someone to know where we are just in case something happens and that someone is Lewis."

"Do you think Lewis will come down here?" asked Tommy, watching the mantle in the Coleman lantern grow brighter as he withdrew the match from the small hole at the base of the lantern globe.

"He might, you never know about Lewis, he climbed up in that tree house we had; remember."

"That's right, he did, we tried to stop him but he came on up anyway, and that sucker was a way up there," said Tommy, as he held the lantern above his head looking around the mineshaft as if he had lost something.

"Let's tidy this place up in case he does decide to come down and look around; hide those dirty magazines, he'll never let us hear the last of it if he finds them." Jackie said smiling.

It took a while for the two boys to arrange the mountain of junk that they had accumulated into some kind of order.

Tommy finally sat down and leaned back against one of the timbers that guarded the entrance into the dark tunnel behind him.

"Where did we get all this stuff," Jackie said tiredly, turning an empty Coca Cola case up on its end and sitting down.

"We would have more, but some of our stuff just wouldn't fit through the door up there," Tommy said, pointing up at the roof.

"You know what, Tommy, we're going to have to give this place up sometime, you know that, don't you?"

"Yeah I know, but not now, we got a lot of exploring to do first."

"Let's go back up," Jackie muttered, "we need to fix up the entrance. I want Lewis' opinion on how it looks: he may have an idea or two on how to conceal it better."

****

Lewis seemed to be as excited to see their discovery as they were for him to see it. It was Tommy, Jackie, and Lewis in the rear as they made their way through the backyards, across the fence behind Tommy's house, and out into the cow pasture leading to the creek and eventually up the hill to the mine entrance.

"I'm surprised we are the only ones around here; where's the mob that hangs out down here?" asked Lewis, keeping an eye on a Chicken Hawk that kept circling overhead.

"Its supper time, everyone's gone home to eat," replied Tommy, hoping he wasn't in trouble for missing his favorite meal.

Jackie stopped at a spot where he could survey the creek for a quarter of a mile in both directions and view most of the pasture that sprawled out at the base of the small hill where the mine entrance was located. After he was satisfied that they were not being observed by anyone who may have decided to skip their dinner and linger down by the creek, he ducked under an overhanging blackberry vine and began to make his way up the hill.

"Wait up, Jackie; I know there has to be a better way up this hill than going through these damn thorns." Lewis gasped as he wiped the sweat from his forehead with the back of his hand. "Are you boys trying to kill me, or are you just screwing with me?"

"Sorry about that, Lewis, we just try to make our approach the most difficult so the easy way will be undisturbed, you know what I mean; not leave a path," Jackie explained, as if Lewis should know that.

"If you say so," Lewis replied, "but I have this feeling you boys are messing with me."

Lewis almost ran over Tommy as both boys stopped suddenly and turned to look over at Lewis as if he were someone who had been following them and they had just acknowledged that he had caught up with them.

"Well, what are you looking at, go on?" Lewis muttered, as he stepped up on a flat rock between the two boys, looking around as he tried to anticipate the direction they would be headed.

"We're here." Tommy grinned as he watched the confusion wash over Lewis' face.

"We're here? What in the hell do you mean, we're here. Jackie you better not be pulling my leg about all this; I want to see a cave or mine or whatever it is pretty quick or I'm gonna get pissed."

"Look down between those wingtips; you're standing on it," Jackie said, smiling at Lewis whose face began to turn the color of a spanked baby's butt.

Lewis looked down and then back up at the two boys, who grinned up at him as he stood on the huge flat rock that covered the entrance to the mineshaft.

It was a full minute before anyone said anything. Lewis stepped off the rock, took a step back, and looked down at the rock then back up at Jackie.

"You're telling me that the entrance is under this big rock?" Lewis inquired tiredly.

Without answering, Jackie went down on one knee, grabbed the rock with both hands and slid it from over the hole as if he were removing a manhole cover from a sewer.

"Well I'll be damned!" Lewis was, leaning over and peering down into the dark opening, which he now realized was the entrance to the mineshaft.

"You still think we're pulling your leg?" asked Tommy as he ran a hand through his flattop, bringing it down in one motion and wiping the sweat on the back of his jeans.

"What do you think about our camouflage, would you suspect this would be an entrance to a cave?" asked Jackie as he began to lower himself into the opening.

"Real good, I mean real good." Lewis slowly shook his head as he watched Jackie descend the rope ladder into the darkness of the mineshaft.

It took only a few seconds before Jackie reached the floor, grabbed a flashlight, and aimed the beam back up to the entrance where Tommy and Lewis had not moved, still leaning over and peering down into the shaft.

"Well, Lewis, are you going down or not?" Tommy asked, looking up at Lewis, who had not said a word since Jackie had gone down to the mineshaft.

Lewis just stood there, looking down at Jackie as he put a match to one of the Coleman lanterns that began to grow brighter, illuminating the floor of the shaft.

"What kind of rig have you boys fixed up to get down there? Are you sure it's secured good enough to hold your weight? I mean are you sure it will hold me?" asked Lewis as he examined the rope ladder that was affixed to the Steel rods that had been driven into the lip of the entrance.

"The rope ladder is Navy surplus, those rods are two feet into the side of the entrance; both of us have been on it at the same time," Jackie answered confidently.

"You don't have to come down here if you don't want to, we just wanted you to know where it was in case, you know, something happened," said Jackie, shining the flashlight up and down the rope ladder.

"What the hell," Lewis mumbled to himself as he walked around the entrance trying to determine the easiest method of getting down into the hole and onto the rope ladder.

After several attempts from different angles, he opted to take the same approach that Jackie had taken.

"I'm going first; Tommy, you stay up here, if this rope breaks, somebody's got to go for help," Lewis said, lowering himself down into the entrance and planting his feet on the second rung of the rope ladder.

Lewis climbed quietly down into the shaft as if he had done it a hundred times before, stepping from the ladder and onto the floor of the shaft. He looked over at Jackie as if to say, "Piece of cake."

"It's a mineshaft all right, one of the entrances is right here, you can see where the cart tracks go right up to the wall over there," said Lewis, pointing to the uneven pile of rocks and dirt opposite the dark entranceway that led into the hillside. "When these mines were closed, they dynamited all the entrances; you boys just happened to stumble across a spot that was not sealed off like it should be. Was the hole up there that large when you found it?"

"No, it was no bigger than a softball, it took us forever to get it as big as it is now, we had to remove a huge rock or we would never have been able to get down here."

"Have you spotted any bats or any other animals down here?"

"No, but we've only been down that one shaft there; another shaft splits off from this one, we planned to follow it and see where it goes, but that's when we decided to talk to you about it first."

"What's going on down there, I'm getting tired of sitting up here," Tommy shouted down to Lewis and Jackie, who had wandered a few yards down the tracks that led into the shaft.

They walked back out of the shaft into the opening where Tommy could see them.

"Keep your shorts on, we're coming back up," said Lewis, as he handed a flashlight back to Jackie and stepped onto the first rung of the rope ladder.

It was beginning to get dark as they secured the entrance and began to descend the hill that led back in the direction of the creek.

"I'm sure you guys want me say to go ahead, do your exploring and see where it goes, but I'm not going to say that; I think it could be very dangerous," Lewis said, breathing heavily as they reached the base of the hill. "Hey guys, I know you're going to do it anyway, but you need to be very careful, watch out for animals or snakes. I don't think there will be any large animals since the hole was so small; probably rats or whatever. The only problem is that there may be another entrance, although I doubt it, no bats though; that's funny."

It was quiet for a few minutes before anything was said, Jackie and Tommy lost in thought as to what Lewis had just told them.

"That entrance you boys have devised is good, you have done an excellent job of disguising the entrance, but I hope you understand that more than likely that is the only way out, do you understand what I am saying?"

No one said anything.

"Damn it, I said do you understand?" shouted Lewis.

"We understand," the boys said in unison. "We get it, Lewis."

"I don't know what I'm thinking," mumbled Lewis. "Hell, I ought to call the sheriff before somebody gets hurt."

Tommy said goodbye as he ran up the steps of his back porch and entered the house. The screen door slammed shut behind him with a bang, which was a familiar sound throughout the neighborhood.

Lewis and Jackie walked on in silence for a few minutes, Lewis breathing heavily from too many packs of unfiltered Lucky Strikes.

"I know you're concerned, but we'll be careful, I promise; just let us have a little more fun before someone discovers it; and you know when they do, it will be closed up again for good."

"Oh, I'm not going to say anything right now, but if something happens to you boys, how would you think I would feel."

"Nothing's going to happen," Jackie said quietly, "nothing's going to happen."

As Jackie and Lewis reached the willow tree that sat on the property line between Jackie's backyard and the backyard of the street behind him, which happened to belong to Roy Higgins, they heard a screen door slam as Mr. Higgins stepped out on his back porch.

"Where in the hell have you been? You know what time we eat around here, you sorry asshole. I know where you've been, that's right, go on outside you chicken-shit, you can't stand here and look me in the eye, can you?"

Lewis and Jackie stopped and looked at each other as Mrs. Higgins started on Bud's dad again.

"You think I don't know what's going on, I wasn't born yesterday, now get your ass in here and eat before I throw it in the garbage."

Bud's dad didn't say a word as he stood looking off into space as if he were waiting for someone to drop down from the sky and deliver him from the tirade of verbal abuse that he was enduring.

"I don't see how he takes it," Jackie said, "if that was my dad, he would have backhanded her so hard her eyes would be permanently crossed."

"The sad part of this, Jackie, is that I know people who know this man; he is a good man, and nobody understands why he keeps on taking this off of her."

Mr. Higgins could be seen through the screen door as he walked back into the house, his slim six-foot-three-inch frame towering over his petite five-foot-one, blond wife as she stood with her hands on her hips at the end of the kitchen table.

"Bud, get your big ass in here and get started on these dishes, your dad's finally about to finish eating," Mrs. Higgins said, her shrill voice becoming barely audible as she went deeper into the house.

Lewis started fishing in his shirt pocket for a Lucky as the two parted company, each heading off in the direction of their respective houses.

As Jackie got closer to the small back porch of his house, he could see the outline of someone sitting on the top step of the porch. It was almost dark now and fireflies were getting higher and higher into the early evening sky. As he got closer he could tell that it was his mother.

He had a wave of dread that began to creep into his mind as he got closer; had his dad done something to his mother?

"Hey, Mom, you OK, what are you doing sitting out here, is everything OK?"

"I'm OK, Jack, your daddy came home late, he's been drinking, and I just need to get away from him when he's that way. I think he's gone to bed now, I hope so."

"Did he hit you or anything?"

"No, he was just cussing about his job, you know how he is,

he knocked the lamp over as he came in the door, almost fell on his butt right there in the living room. He blamed it on me, of course, said the table was too close to the door." Jackie just stood at the foot of the steps looking down at his feet, not knowing what to say, when his mother spoke again. "Did you hear Bud's mother chewing out Mr. Higgins again?"

"Yeah, it wouldn't do for her to talk to Daddy that way, would it."

"No it wouldn't, he'd kill her, he really would, Jackie."

Jackie knew that something else was bothering his mother; he could tell that she had something on her mind for a while, maybe now was the time to get it out in the open.

"Mom, something's bothering you and has been for a while, do you want to talk about it? You're not sick or anything, are you?"

"No, nothing like that; Jack, you're getting older now, I have tried to talk to your dad, but he keeps putting off what needs to be done. I don't know what to do."

"What are you talking about?" Jackie asked, almost laughing.

"Jack, you are too old to be sharing a bedroom with your sister, you're a teenager and your sister is not far behind you. It's time you each had your own room. I don't have the money to add a room and your daddy just ignores the situation. I told him that I would get a job if he couldn't get the money, but he just mumbled something to himself, saying that I was not going to work, my place is at home."

Jackie stepped up on the porch and sat down beside his mother, trying to think of what to say.

"I, I, never thought about that," Jackie said sheepishly, "I guess that's why Mr. Redden added a room on the back of his house a couple of years ago."

"Jack, I'm taking in washing and doing ironing for the neighbors to try to make some money to get the material; your daddy doesn't know about me doing that, so don't say anything about it. Uncle Clifford said that he would build it if I could come up with the materials, I just don't know what to do."

"Try not to worry, Mom; I'll get a job when school's out next year; we'll get it done, maybe Daddy will have a change of heart before then."

"Maybe so," Jackie's mother said as she stood up and turned to face Jackie, who was now standing facing her on the porch steps. After giving her son a quick hug, his mother pulled open the screen door and walked into the house.

Jackie followed her into the kitchen, walking softly for fear of waking his dad. He stepped past the small bathroom across the hall from his mom and dad's bedroom. He eased the door open and crept into his and Judy's bedroom.

Judy was not asleep; he could see that her eyes were open even in the dim light that entered the room as he pushed open the door. He noticed something else too; she had been crying.

"You OK?" he asked as he slipped off his jeans and quietly got into his bed, pulling the sheet up to his chest.

"Daddy's been drinking; he says bad things to Mama. Why does he have to be like that, she's good to him? Sometimes I just hate him."

"I know, I know, it's worse when he's drinking. Everything will be all right in the morning, you'll see."

"I heard Mrs. Higgins screaming at Mr. Higgins again, she's just like Daddy," Judy said as she wiped her face with the end of her pillowcase.

"Maybe they need to get together; it would be a hell of a fight," whispered Jackie as he tried to cheer up his sister. "What are you girls up to, I haven't seen you down at the creek lately."

"Not much, we've been watching them move the houses down on Prater Road. It's fun to watch, I didn't know you could move a whole house like that."

"Yeah, they're getting ready to put the new freeway in, it's going to be something."

Jackie started to say something else but stopped; Judy had shut her eyes, he knew it didn't take long for her to go to sleep once her eyes closed.

As Jackie lay there listening to the crickets and cicadas play their summer music, he reflected on what his mother had said earlier. He and the other boys knew about sex, they even considered themselves experts on the subject, although none of them had ever seen a nude girl, much less engaged in anything beyond looking at a Playboy magazine. He understood what his mother was telling him, though he had never given it a thought that he and Judy were of a different sex and sharing the same bedroom would be viewed as something that you just didn't do.

He always said his prayers before he went to sleep, most of the time it was one of two that his mother had taught him. Tonight, he said a special prayer; he prayed for his mother and that she would somehow find a way to have another room built onto the house or that his dad would wake up and see what needed to be done. It wasn't long before his prayers had turned into dreams as he drifted off to sleep; the last thing he remembered was asking God to stop the Russians from dropping an Atomic bomb on everyone while he slept.

****

The day had arrived; today would be the day that the great cave exploration would take place. Tommy was waiting on his back porch as Jackie crossed the street in front of his house and headed down his driveway; both boys were excited.

Tommy's mother opened the screen door and dropped the drain hose to the washing machine on the porch just as Jackie walked up.

"Watch out, boys," she said as soapy water began to gush from the rubber hose. "What's up with you two? Tommy's about to wet his pants, he's been waiting for you before the sun came up."

Not a word was said as they stepped around the puddle of soapy water that had run off the end of the driveway into the grass. This was no time for conversation; they were on a mission. They both tried to cross the fence to the pasture at the same time, causing the top strand of barbed wire to pull loose from the post, which would make it easier to cross in the future. They paid little attention to what was taking place along the creek as they made their way along the bank, trying to determine which approach they would take to the entrance to the mine.

"Wait just a damn minute, stay right there, I'll come over there and kick your ass!"

"Oh no, you know who that is?" Tommy whispered.

"Which one; I see three of them?"

"The big blond-headed boy, that's Sonny Farr. He's that "Tush Hog" from East Ridge. He's the one who beat up that constable down at Louie's store. You know, he hurt him real bad, put him in the hospital,"

Sonny Farr was from across Stateline Road, in Tennessee. He was big for his age and had a reputation for fighting; his trademark was that he liked to sucker punch. Sonny liked to show off in front of his buddies; he always had two or three by his side egging him on. The thing that stood out about Sonny was his hair. He had thick blond hair; it was flat on top but long on the sides, which he combed back overlapping in the back to form what looked like a duck's butt. Some called this hairstyle flattop with fenders.

"Which one of you said, the boy in ducks is a queer," the big blond-headed boy said as he looked across the creek at Tommy and Jackie.

"It was the short one, Sonny, I heard him; he called you a queer," a tall freckle-faced boy said as he spat a stream of tobacco juice into the creek.

"Don't move, I'm coming over there, we'll see who's a queer, you little bastard," said the Tush Hog, as he looked up and down the creek for the easiest way to get across.

"Are you thinking what I'm thinking?" Tommy asked as both boys took off at the same time.

It took the Tush Hog and his two instigators several minutes before they found a place in the creek that was shallow enough to cross without having to swim.

Tommy followed Jackie up the side of the hill, taking the shortest route to the entrance of the mineshaft.

Jackie reached the entrance a good thirty yards ahead of Tommy, he had the flat rock slid away and was waiting for him to get down the ladder as soon as he got there.

"Hurry up," said Jackie calmly, as he looked around to see if Tush had been able to catch up to them.

Satisfied that they were still down the hill, Jackie slid down into the entrance, pulling the huge flat rock over the hole above his head. He quickly scurried down the rope ladder and stood beside Tommy, who already held a flashlight in each hand.

"If Lewis didn't see it, I doubt if these dumb asses will either," whispered Jackie, listening for any sound from above.

"I hear 'em," Tommy said, "they're coming up the hill. He sure is going to make a mess out of you if he finds us; listen to him, they're getting closer."

Tommy ran a hand through his flattop as he and Jackie stood at the bottom of the mineshaft listening to the cussing and bitching that was going on up above.

"Where in the hell did they go, are you sure they came up here, you blind son of a bitch? I ought to whip your ass," Tush said to the freckle-faced boy who stood almost on the entrance looking around, scratching his ass.

The other instigator had never said a word; he just seemed to be along for the ride, always smiling at the big blond-headed boy. This kid seemed to serve the purpose of an audience for Tush to play to.

"Let's get out of these damn blackberry bushes," said Tush. "We'll have chiggers all over our balls. If I ever catch that little bastard out, he'll wish I was a queer."

Hearing this, the two instigators looked at each other and smiled; it was going to be fun watching when their hero caught up to this kid.

"We'll find him, Sonny, I think I heard him say something about your mother too," Freckle-face said as he watched the back of his hero's neck turn red.

Tommy and Jackie stood grinning at each other, the voices growing fainter as Tush and his entourage worked their way around the bushes; occasionally a burst of profanity could be heard as they became entangled in the vines and blackberry bushes that covered the hillside.

"What are you going to do if you meet up with that asshole again?" asked Tommy. "He'll kill you, he's mad as hell."

"I'll worry about that when it happens, he'll meet somebody tougher than him someday. Maybe it will be before I see him again."

"I hope he does," said Tommy. "I hope so."

The two boys talked for a few minutes, happy that they had succeeded in eluding the bullies, but more happy that they had not compromised the existence of their cave.

"Well, we're down here, let's get to doing what we came to do," said Tommy.

"You got it, get those lanterns lit, I'll get the rest of the stuff, we're going exploring."

****

It was time for Mr. Redden to make his daily trek to the bus stop, Mrs. Redden handed him his lunchbox as he stood on his front porch looking up at the sky.

"Think it's going to rain?" he asked. "Get me that umbrella, will you, honey, just in case."

Mrs. Redden stepped back into the house for a second, reappearing with the umbrella in her hand.

"Honey, you really need to think about getting a car, we're one of the few who still don't have one," she said tiredly, handing her husband the umbrella.

"I know, I know, we will, I just need to get a few more things paid off, we're still paying on Linda's room you know."

"It just hurts to see you have to walk everywhere; I heard they may stop delivering groceries, what will we do then?"

Mr. Redden walked down the sidewalk to the driveway and turned back toward his wife standing on the porch.

"We'll see," he said, "don't worry, things will work out, they always do."

"Something else, Max, you need to talk to Tommy, him and Jackie are acting kind of strange, I think they're up to something. See if you can figure out what they're up to, he won't talk to me."

"He's OK, he's just growing up, see if there are any girls playing down at that creek."

They both smiled as he turned and headed up the street.

****

"We should be getting close to where that other shaft veers off to the left," said Tommy as he walked between the rails on the floor of the mineshaft.

"It's around that next bend, I think," Jackie said, holding a lantern in one hand and a flashlight in another.

"You're right; I see it up there now, just like you said."

They stopped and looked at each other before proceeding into the yet to be explored mineshaft. They walked up and down slight rises and drops in elevation, around bends in the tunnel, stopping occasionally to get a drink of water or to listen for sounds that they were sure came from up ahead. After each time they stopped and listened, trying to control their breathing, the only sound that could be heard was the pulse in their head. They walked for over an hour without hearing or seeing anything out of the ordinary; a few places in the low sections of the shaft, water could be seen standing between the wooden crossties below the tracks. No evidence of any animals or bats was observed, only a few spider webs clung to the timbers and cross beams. It was almost as if the miners had just left for the day and would be back tomorrow to continue their work.

"I see something up ahead," Jackie said, as he stopped and trained his flashlight on something that looked to be red fifty feet further down the shaft.

"What the crap is that?" asked Tommy. "A car or something?"

As the boys got closer, it became clear that it was not a car but an ore cart, and it was not just one, four more were in front of it just around the bend in the shaft.

"Well I'll be damned," Jackie muttered. "I guess they decided it was easier just to leave them down here rather than moving them out of here."

"Yeah, and look up ahead, the shaft ends just like the other ones do, this place has been sealed up; no one has been down here since it was closed a long time ago."

"We've not seen any light coming in from anywhere, that explains why no bats or animals have been down here," Jackie said.

A lot of energy was expended trying to disengage the end ore cart from the others only to discover that they were not connected at all. The reason they were unable to move them was simple: they were heavy, weighing over five hundred pounds apiece.

"How did they move these things; especially when they were full of ore?" Tommy asked quietly.

"I think I saw the answer in the back of that end cart there."

"What was it?"

"A couple of harnesses, you know, the thing they put on horses to pull carts and things; these were probably used on mules though," Jackie said, as he wiped the dust from something that had been written on the side of one of the carts.

"Dinky."

Jackie looked over at Tommy.

"I wonder if that was the name of the mule or the name of the cart."

After spending a good amount of time looking for anything that might have been discarded by the men who worked in the mine years ago, Tommy picked up a piece of paper that had been rolled up in a wad and was lying under one of the cart wheels beside the track. He carefully unrolled the flimsy brown paper as Jackie held his flashlight so Tommy could see it more clearly.

"What does it say?" asked Jackie.

"Twist Chewing Tobacco. What did you expect?" Tommy laughed. "A treasure map or something?"

"I don't know, it's kind of disappointing, all this time waiting to explore the rest of this place and this is all we've found," replied Jackie.

"Well, we've got the best damn hideout that anybody ever had; let's go back to our living room."

Very little was said as the two boys made their way back to the entrance, which they referred to as their living room. The room directly below the opening was larger than the other shafts. It became the place where they stored the junk and other items, which included a World War II jungle hammock Jackie had erected between one of the timbers and cross beams. Tommy had tried to bring an aluminum lawn chair down, but couldn't get it through the entrance; he settled for a folding campstool instead.

"What next?" asked Jackie tiredly as he sat down in the middle of the hammock and looked over at Tommy.

"You think we could somehow get one of those carts moving, or maybe make us some kind of buggy; that would be one more ride if we could? I'll bet that shaft went for at least half a mile or more, that would be better than the roller coaster at Lake Winnie," said Tommy, unfolding his campstool.

"I don't know we'll come up with something. Do you think that Tush Hog has moved on yet?"

"I'm not sure if he hasn't you better get ready to get your ass whipped." Tommy grinned.

"I think I can outrun him; what about you?"

Tommy sat silent for a few seconds before standing up and walking over to the rope ladder.

"Let's go, I'm getting hungry," said Tommy, turning the flame down on the lantern as he put one foot on the bottom rung of the rope ladder.

"I think we'll keep it a secret for as long as we can," Tommy said to Jackie as they made their way down the hillside and headed toward home.

"Yeah, it's a place to go; we might bring others that we can trust down though, maybe Gern or somebody."

Jackie said bye to Tommy as he jumped onto his back porch and disappeared into the kitchen. Jackie could hear the TV playing through the open window as he walked down the driveway beside the house. It was Dinah Shore singing. *"See the USA in your Chevrolet"* He thought about Mr. Redden walking to the bus stop every day. It would be nice if he had a Chevrolet.

3

Summer was speeding along; before you know it school would be starting again. Jackie knew that this would be the last summer that he would spend being a kid. The next summer he would be working; Tommy may not, but he knew he would. It was nice that they had such a great hideout and it was fun trying to fashion a roller coaster out of a wagon, but the speed that they had anticipated had yet to be achieved. It was more work pushing it than it was worth.

It seemed that the action around the creek had decreased, some days it was just Jackie, Tommy, and the cows. There was a summer storm that caused the creek to overflow its banks, which brought back the interest for a day or two, but as the water receded so did the kids.

"I know where everybody is," Tommy said excitedly as he met Jackie in the middle of the street in front of his house.

"Let me guess, a flying saucer picked 'em all up"

"No, it's the freeway."

"What about the freeway?"

"Linda's been going over with her boyfriend to watch; they're moving houses, dynamiting, and everything."

"I've been thinking about going over to the golf course in Brainerd; do some caddying if they'll let me," Jackie said. "You want to go? We'll have to cross where they're working on the freeway, maybe we can stop and watch for a while."

"Sounds good to me, it's a pretty good walk though."

"It'll be good for you, Jackie said with slight grin on his face. "It just might walk some of that lard off that ass."

"Screw you; I can out-walk your butt. I got to tell Mama

where we're going," said Tommy as he turned and ran into the house.

The Interstate Highway System, envisioned by President Dwight Eisenhower was modeled after the Autobahn in Germany. When completed, it was said to be possible to travel from coast to coast without stopping for a single traffic light. It would be a massive undertaking that would forever be under construction.

Preparation for the construction was now underway, property procured, houses and business either demolished or, in some cases, moved to other locations. Interstate 75 from the Midwest was to run south from Knoxville through Chattanooga and on to Atlanta. One mile north of the Tennessee and Georgia Stateline, Interstate 24 would branch off and go west through Chattanooga and onward to Nashville. It was this freeway that would parallel US 41 as it tracked northward.

"I need to go by my house," said Jackie. "I need to let my mom know where we're going, I think I'll take my putter too."

Tommy waited outside while Jackie ran in the back door and right back out carrying an old Bull's Eye putter and two very used golf balls.

"I thought you were going to caddy not play," questioned Tommy as he grabbed the putter from Jackie's hand and assumed a putting stance over an imaginary golf ball.

"I hope to caddy, but if not, I'll do some putting on the practice green."

"I'm not going to try to caddy," said Tommy, "I'm gonna look for lost balls. I bet I'll make more money than you do caddying."

It was a while since Jackie and Tommy had gone in a direction other than that of the cow pasture behind Tommy's house. They had traveled no more than a block when Tommy ran a few feet ahead of Jackie and scooped up an empty Camel pack.

Jackie leaned in almost touching heads with Tommy as he very carefully peeled the blue tax stamp from across the top of the crumpled pack.

"It's an H," said Tommy with a grin from ear to ear.

Jackie turned sideways so Tommy would have a good target on the side of his shoulder.

"Ready," asked Tommy, as he let loose with a pretty good punch, enough to hurt a little, but not as hard as he could have.

"Ouch," screamed Jackie, pretending that it hurt a lot more than it did.

"Next time I won't be as easy on you, I'll put a real frog on that arm."

"Yeah, yeah, yeah," said Jackie as they started on down the street, both sets of eyes glued to the ground.

It was beginning to get hot as the sun rose higher in the sky; the search for empty Camel packs began to get old. Jackie decided to use the putter for a walking stick as they crossed the wooden bridge a block before reaching the main highway.

"Well, well, look what we got here, if it isn't that little skinny son of a bitch that called me a queer."

Both boys turned around at the same time to see Tush and his freckle-faced sidekick scrambling up the steep embankment beside the bridge.

"Oh shit," Tommy said under his breath, "no use running."

Jackie stood his ground as Sonny the Tush Hog walked right up in front of him, stopping a foot away, spreading his legs apart, and folding his arms across his chest. Tommy had backed away, but Freckle-face began to creep toward him smiling.

That's the ugliest set of tobacco stained teeth I've ever seen, Tommy thought to himself.

Tush looked down at Jackie trying to decide what to do next; that indecision would cost him his reputation.

Without breaking eye contact, Jackie brought the Bull's Eye

putter up between Tush's slightly parted legs. The sound that it made when the bronze putter head sank three inches into the scrotum of the now bug-eyed Tush Hog would be a sound all four boys would never forget. Tush sank to his knees unable to make a sound; he rolled over on his side holding his crushed nut sack with both hands. Jackie stepped over the now screaming Tush, took hold of the putter in both hands and slowly walked toward the freckle-faced sidekick. Tush's skinny friend must have swallowed his chew because his face was not only white as milk, his freckles stood out like corn flakes. Jackie had not said a word. Tommy stood with his mouth open watching the big bully drawn up in a fetal position beside the road, crying like a newborn baby.

"Do you know where he lives?" Jackie asked Freckle-face as he walked toward him, now holding the golf club in one hand.

"Yes sir."

Tommy almost wet his pants when he heard the tall freckle-faced boy call Jackie sir.

"See if you can get his crybaby ass up and walk him home. Don't just stand there, get him up, get him out of here."

Tommy had never witnessed this kind of reaction from Jackie; it was almost like he had become someone else. *"Well,* he thought, *maybe I'll start calling him sir.*

Freckle-face got down on both knees as he tried to pull the much larger boy's arms away from the death grip he had on his rapidly swelling scrotum.

"Get away from me, asshole, go get my daddy, I'm ruined for life," Tush gasped, as tears washed down the side of his face.

Tommy leaned over trying to assist Freckle-face as he pleaded with his fallen hero to quit crying and get up.

"It's no use," said Tommy, looking up at Jackie, who was watching a car slowing down and pulling over to the side of the road.

The car stopped on the other side of the road across from the still whimpering blond-headed boy lying in a fetal position.

"What's going on here, is somebody hurt?" asked a bald, pear-shaped man as he closed his car door and started walking across the road.

"Yeah, looks like something might have hit him in the balls; he keeps holding them," said Jackie looking straight at Freckle-face still on his knees beside Tush.

"I know this boy; he's the one that hit Mr. Robinson, the constable, put him in the hospital. This couldn't happen to a nicer guy," said the pear-shaped man.

"Can you take him home?" asked Jackie.

"I'll take the big crybaby to the sheriff's office, I know this is him. I'm sure they'll want to ask him some questions, help me get him in the car."

It wasn't easy and it was almost comical, but they finally succeeded in getting Tush in the backseat of the out of breath, pear-shaped man's, Nash rambler.

"Sir," Jackie said quietly. "Do you mind taking that tall skinny boy with you; they might want to ask him some questions too?"

Freckle-face had started walking off up the street after they had deposited Tush in the backseat of the rambler. As soon as he heard Jackie ask the man about taking him too, he scrambled down the embankment beside the bridge and took off down a trail that ran along the creek bank.

"I guess he felt that he didn't have anything to tell the sheriff that might help," Tommy said, as the rambler pulled away with Tush in the backseat, still clutching his balls.

"You know what, Tommy, I don't think we'll have to worry about that butt hole any more, the next time you see him he may be a queer."

"Can you believe it, Jackie; his skinny sidekick called you "sir?"

"Yeah, he's a real tough guy, chewing tobacco and spitting everywhere, did you see his eyes when his hero folded up and hit the ground?"

"I sure did, he turned white as a sheet, but I guess I did too."

"Come on," said Jackie, "let's get out of here."

****

It was getting hotter as the morning turned into afternoon, the peanuts and cokes from the service station had hit the spot, but it was lunchtime and Tommy didn't need a watch to tell him. They could hear the bulldozers and earthmoving equipment long before you could see what was going on ahead of them. Ominous clouds of red dust rose above the trees and the smell of diesel fuel hung in the still summer air.

"Man, would you look at that, I see what the big fuss is all about now," muttered Jackie as he and Tommy stood under a huge oak tree observing the action taking place before them.

It was a massive undertaking; dump trucks going in every direction, earthmovers and bulldozers running back and forth, houses being loaded onto trailers; the freeway system was on the march and whatever was in its path would either be moved or demolished.

"I don't think we can make it across without getting run over," said Tommy. "It looks like a war zone out there."

"If you're planning on getting to the golf course, you'll get across; the only street still open is two miles north of here," Jackie said, pointing toward Missionary Ridge. "I think if we time it just right, we can run across, it's only a couple hundred yards or so."

"The bulldozers don't scare me, they're slow, it's those damn scraper pans; look how fast they're going," Tommy said, running a hand through his flattop.

"You want to go on to the golf course or would you rather just stay here and watch what's going on?" asked Jackie, leaning on his golf club like it was a walking stick.

"Let's go down a little closer, I'd like to watch 'em get that house on that trailer, it looks like there is a lot of head-scratching going on down there. I think they have more house than they do trailer."

"OK, come on," Jackie said, "follow me, I want to get a little closer too, maybe there's something we can do to help; they might even pay us."

"Are you crazy, if we get too close, they'll run our asses off; pay us, are you crazy?"

As they got closer, it was apparent that a disagreement had taken place between the haulers and the loaders. It became clear that the house perched precariously on the flatbed trailer was a son of a bitch, and both crews were testifying to that fact.

"I don't think houses were made to be hauled around on trailers," said Jackie, slowly walking closer to the work crews as they stood around waiting for orders to do something.

Jackie turned around to say something to Tommy, but he was not standing behind him as he had thought. Lying in the red dirt twenty yards behind him, Tommy was trying to free his foot from something protruding out of the ground.

"What in hell are you doing?" Jackie grinned as he walked back to his friend who was spitting dirt and blood in front of him.

"Caught my foot in this stupid ass strap or whatever it is," sputtered Tommy, spitting dirt again.

"I see you put your dobber in the dirt, let me see how bad is it, all your teeth there?"

"I'm OK, just bit my lip."

"What's that you caught your foot on? You got to watch yourself, there's junk everywhere out here."

"It looks like a shoulder strap or something; I've been trying to pull it up, but it won't budge," Tommy grunted, pulling on the strap with both hands.

"Let me see," Jackie said, grabbing hold on the strap beside Tommy.

"Damn, we'll have to dig that bastard out, it won't budge," Jackie said with a sigh as he turned the strap loose.

"Go see if you can borrow a shovel from those guys over there, all they seem to be doing is leaning on them," said Tommy, standing up and brushing the dirt from his jeans and T-shirt.

Jackie walked over to three Negro men standing back from the argument going on around the house-moving fiasco. All three men were leaning on shovels as if that was what they were made for.

"Mind if I borrow one of those shovels for a minute, I'm just gonna take it over there to where my buddy is, it'll only take a minute," asked Jackie as he approached the three Negroes

"Here take mine," said the overweight black man with a dirty T-shirt that was about eight inches short of covering his huge belly. Dey can't make up der mind what to do, but long as we get paid, dat's fine with me."

Jackie trotted back over to where Tommy had already started trying to uncover what was connected to the strap that had ensnarled his foot.

"Move over let's see what we've got here." Jackie put his foot on top on the long-handled shovel and stepped down with all his weight.

The shovel slipped easily into ground beside the olive-colored strap. It took only five good shovels before the brown canvas duffel bag came into view.

"It's an Army duffel bag," Tommy said excitedly, as he swiped at the thin layer of dirt that the shovel had missed.

"See if you can pull it out now." Jackie tossed the shovel down and reached around Tommy, who was pulling with both hands on the strap.

"It's coming, it's coming," screamed Tommy, as the bag slowly stood upright in the shallow hole that it had been resting in.

"I'm going to take the shovel back, carry it up under that tree, and watch out, try not to get run over out here." Jackie smiled as he headed in the direction of the three men still standing and watching.

Tommy wrestled the dusty duffel bag onto his shoulder and staggered back to the tree where they had previously stood and watched the action unfolding before them.

****

It was his third trip, and he feared this time would be no different than the last two. Jim was up for parole again, and no matter how contrite he was, or how much he stayed out of trouble, the board always came back to the same conclusion. "Jim, you shot an innocent man, and you may have killed a man in Germany, you don't need to be out on the street." They always said the same thing, "Sorry, Jim, not this time."

He had tried desperately to keep in contact with Barbara Jo, the girl he had met in the tavern; it took some doing, but he finally obtained her last name. He learned that her last name was Stephenson; he wrote to her several times, but never received an answer. The last few letters that he wrote were returned to him with an endorsement from the Post Office: "MOVED LEFT NO FORWARDING ADDRESS." The thing that worried him the most was that someone new would move into the house and discover the money that he had buried. He could do nothing but wait and hope; someday they would have to let him out.

"Rise and shine, Big Jim, you're on stage in thirty minutes," said the slightly overweight guard standing in front of Jim's cell.

"Don't stand so close, that button might fly off your shirt and put my eye out," Jim joked as he stared at the guard's midsection.

"Well, you're in a good mood, but I hate to pop your balloon; the word is you're not going anywhere."

"Is that right, I guess you know everybody on the board, don't you?"

"No not all of them, just the one that counts." The guard smiled as he put the key in the lock and slid the door open. He stood to the side waiting for Jim to join him on the catwalk outside his cell. The guard slid the cell door closed and motioned for Jim to walk in front of him down the corridor.

Jim was not a threat; he had been a model prisoner, and had made friends with most of the guards. Many times, the guards would solicit his help to quell disputes among other prisoners; he had earned their respect, nobody screwed with Big Jim. It was a walk that he had taken twice before, he knew the drill.

****

Eddy Walker always had a smile on his face whenever he met a stranger; if he stopped to talk, you could count on ten minutes no matter what. In the Sunday morning paper in the comic section, you would find *Smiling Jack;* one of the characters was *BO Plenty.* Eddy Walker was *BO Plenty*; skinny with an Adam's apple that protruded out to the point that you could not help but focus your attention on it. The thing that separated him from the comic character became apparent once he decided to get down to business. Eddy Walker was a special agent with the Tennessee Bureau of Investigation.

"I'm not here to change anybody's opinion as to whether to

send Mr. Vess back out on the street; what I'm here for is to make you aware of something that you may not already be aware of," said Agent Walker as he stood before the seven-man parole board assembled at Petros State Prison.

"Gentleman, this is the third time that the state of Tennessee has had to make a decision as to whether Mr. Vess should be released or should be denied parole once again. I know that he has served eleven years of a life sentence. What I am asking you to do is to consider this; he robbed a bank and got away with a quarter of a million dollars, his accomplice supposedly took off with the money and left Mr. Vess to take the rap. The problem that we have is that we have never been able to track down his accomplice or the money. It has become more complex since the money that was taken could not be traced due to a mix up with the bank and the armored truck company. What makes it even stranger is that Mr. Vess has not tried to contact his buddy, or as far as we can tell, his accomplice has not tried to contact him. I don't want to take away from the fact that he shot a man and possibly killed a German civilian right after the war."

"What I want you to consider is Mr. Vess is in this prison because he does not have a family or a home town; his home was the Army, and the state of Tennessee should have turned him over to the Feds when they caught him, but they didn't. The TBI would like to watch him for a while if you decide to parole him; we know he can't leave the state, but it would be interesting to see what happens."

The parole board consisted of the same seven men that had been on the board the last time that Jim came before them.

"I would like to ask a question," said one of the board members, who stood up as if Agent Walker was the president or something.

"Sure, what is it?"

"What makes you think he'll try to contact his accomplice if he hasn't done it by now?"

"He may not; we just think that he has served his time, he has been a model prisoner; like I said, it's up to you; we would just like to watch him for a while."

"Anything else?"

"Yes sir, I'd like to know if you think this man is a threat to the citizens of Tennessee, I'm not worried about the money or where it is, I just want to know if you think he's a threat?" asked a skinny short man with a mustache that drooped on one side.

"No, I don't think he's dangerous."

"Anything else?"

Agent Walker thanked the board for their time, executed a left face, and walked out of the room.

****

Jim walked into the small room where the all-male parole board sat behind a single row of folding tables. Jim looked straight into the faces of each of the members as he sat down in the single chair in front of the panel.

"Mr. Vess, everyone here on this board are the same folks that were here the last time you came before us," said Charlie Nave, the board spokesman. "We know who you are, we know what you did; just tell us why we should rule different than we did the last time."

Jim cleared his throat. "Well, gentleman, nothing has changed except that I've been here longer and I'm getting older."

"We're all getting older, Jim; what we want to know is do you feel that you have been punished enough for robbing a bank and shooting a man in the process?"

"Yes sir, I do. I told you before, I made a mistake, and it was a long time ago; I've thought about it a lot."

"Have you still not heard from your accomplice, Jerry Pardue? Do you still think he took the money and skipped the country?"

"No sir; I have not heard from him; knowing him he's probably spent that money a long time ago. I told you before; I'll bet he's down in Mexico sipping tequila."

"Jim, you have done all the right things in the past eleven years, we know your sentence is twenty years to life; if we decide to parole you, what do you plan to do? What kind of work can you do, tell us what you would do?" asked Mr. Nave.

"I don't know for sure, I'd like to go down to Chattanooga, they have some foundries down there, and I have done that kind of work before, maybe I could get back into that."

No one else said anything or asked any questions; Jim just sat there looking down at the floor, occasionally looking up at the board members, who had a hard time looking at him.

"Do any of you have any other questions?" asked the assistant warden sitting at a desk beside the door, pretending to write into a notebook that was spread open in front of him.

"Mr. Vess, do you have anything to add?"

"No, sir, I don't," Jim muttered.

4

"Well, open the son of a bitch; let's see what's in there," said Jackie as he reached the shade of the huge oak tree only moments after Tommy had sat the dusty duffel bag down.

Tommy threw the bag down, leaned back against the trunk of the big oak tree, pulling at his lower lip that had begun to swell.

"You open the bastard. Look at my lip, I think all of my bottom teeth are loose," whimpered Tommy.

"You look like my daddy with a chew of Copenhagen behind his lip, quit your whining; you still have all your teeth. What if the Tush had got a hold of you, it could have been a lot worse." Jackie smiled as he fiddled with the snap hook on top of the duffel bag.

Tommy was still massaging his lip when Jackie finally opened the duffel bag and peered inside.

"Holy …"

Tommy quit pulling on his lip, got on his knees, and waddled over to Jackie, who was still peering down into the dusty duffel bag.

"What's so holy, you look like Mr. Shipp when he saw you do that one-handed chin-up."

Tommy pulled the duffel bag open farther so both boys could get a better look at what Jackie was still staring at.

"It can't be real," Jackie said, reaching into the dusty duffel bag and extracting a packet of twenty-dollar bills.

"They look real to me, look, this one says $2000.00."

Nothing was said as the boys reached into the duffel bag, pulling out a bundle or two then reaching back in and pulling out another, time stood still as both boys were lost in their own thoughts.

"Close it back up and put the hook back in place, let's get this out of here, we'll take it to the cave," Jackie said calmly as he placed a bundle of twenties back into the bag, looking around to see if anyone was watching them.

Tommy stood up, put the shoulder strap over his shoulder and headed back in the direction of the street from which they had come.

"Tommy, when we get back to the bridge where we had the run in with the Tush, let's take the creek back to the cave, the less we're seen with this bag, the better." As they left behind the freeway construction, the sounds of machinery, and the smell of diesel fuel slowly evaporated.

"Its real money, it really is, it's a lot of it too," stammered Tommy, his breathing becoming labored as he shifted the duffel bag from shoulder to shoulder as they trudged down the street.

"It looks real, it sure looks real," Jackie agreed. "When you get tired, let me know, I'll carry it for a while, you look like you're on a mission or something, slow down a little." Jackie was almost laughing out loud as he watched his friend marching along beside him with the army duffel bag over his shoulder.

No one paid much attention as they crossed the main highway; Harold, the Sinclair service station owner walked to the door and waved at the boys as they passed by, he shook his head and walked back inside.

"Will you slow the hell down, you're almost running, Tommy, people will think you just robbed a bank. Sit the damn bag down, I'll carry it for a while, you're going to bust a gut." Jackie pulled the strap from Tommy's shoulder and slid it over his own.

"There's a name stenciled on that bag, Tommy, I guess maybe we'll have some place to start in trying to find out where this came from." He adjusted the strap on his shoulder and headed down the street in the direction of the bridge.

"I see the name Tommy replied back." "You can't read it though; something has torn a hole through the first part of the name."

"Yeah I saw that, what does it look like to you?"

"It looks like, J. RDUE; it could be anybody, who knows?"

They were back at the bridge where the showdown between Tush and Jackie had taken place. It had been no more than a couple of hours since the incident had occurred, but to Jackie and Tommy it seemed ages ago.

The two boys slithered down the embankment beside the bridge that led to the path that ran alongside the creek.

"I'd rather not have too many people seeing us carrying this bag and asking questions before we find out what the hell we've got here." Jackie started to say something else but stopped when he stumbled over a root snaking across the narrow path.

The boys took turns carrying the duffel bag as they made their way along the path bordering the north side of the creek. It was a longer route than taking the road, but Jackie was right; they had encountered no one as they rounded a bend in the creek and crossed the Stateline from Tennessee into Georgia.

"Oh my God, look up ahead: it's Bo Goins and his cross-eyed son Cheese," said Tommy tiredly.

It was hard to believe that people like this still existed, but they did and they were in the direct path of the two boys who were trying to make their way back to the seclusion and safety of the mineshaft.

Bo Goins was a small, very ugly troll of a man who squatted in a patch of woods that belonged to Willingham's Dairy Farm. He had become sort of a living legend to the people who lived in and around Rankin Park. The shack of a house that Bo lived in along with his son did not have electricity or running water. A well could be seen beside the shack and it was assumed that was where his water came from. It was obvious that Bo Goins and his son Cheese were a few bricks short of a full load.

It was disturbing to watch the ugly little man push his old wooden cart up and down the street with his load of rags and junk. Occasionally, someone would stop him and try to get a little information about him; occasionally they would offer him food or even money, but Bo would just shake his head, mumble incoherently, lower his head, and trudge on down the road. Once a truant officer approached the shack to investigate why Cheese was not in school, but was turned away at gunpoint. Cheese could not be more than twelve or thirteen years old and no one knew when he dropped out of school if in fact he ever attended school at all.

Most people avoided contact with Bo and his son; both were disgusting to look at with their rotting teeth, shaggy hair, and dirty faces, but the main reason was the atrocious smell one had to endure. Bo Goins and Cheese mostly kept to themselves although they were accused of petty theft around the neighborhood, taking clothes from clotheslines and going through garbage cans, for the most part taking things of little or no value.

"Where you boys going with my duffel bag?" yelled Bo from across the creek, keeping pace with them as they walked on without answering.

"Ye hear what me daddy ask you?" bellowed Cheese, standing on the first limb of a sycamore tree that hung out over the creek.

"It's not yours," said Tommy.

"It sure looks like it," squawked Bo, "where'd you get it?"

Tommy and Jackie remained silent as they moved on up the creek, Bo stalking them from the opposite bank.

"You want me to go over there and get it, Daddy?" asked

Cheese as he dropped down from the sycamore and joined his dad.

Jackie stopped, set the duffel bag down in front of him, turned and faced Bo and his son who had also stopped on the far creek bank.

"This bag belongs to Mr. Willingham, you know, the man who owns that shack you stay in. Do you want us to tell him that you took it?"

"What's in it?" Bo had a wide grin displaying maybe three stained teeth that had not completely rotted away.

"Some newspapers, we're taking them to Mr. Willingham's son, Johnny."

Bo stood still looking up and down the creek. He raised a dirty hand to his chin, rubbing the stubble of a beard as if he were a lawyer in the midst of a trial.

"Come on, Cheese, let's go." "Newspapers don't have enough pictures in 'em for you."

Bo rammed both hands into the pockets of his overalls as he watched Cheese pick up a small rock from the creek bank. Cheese took a wind up like a major league baseball pitcher and side-armed the rock across the creek, hitting the duffel bag square in the center. Tommy and Jackie looked at each other as they tried to comprehend what possessed Cheese to throw the rock at them.

"Do you think he was trying to hit the duffel bag; is he that good or do you think he was just lucky?" asked Tommy, as both boys watched the two trolls disappear into the woods across the creek.

****

Agent Walker entered the room moments after Jim had been led away; he sat down in the chair that Jim had just vacated. The

TBI agent crossed his arms and leaned back in the chair causing the two front legs to rise six inches off the floor.

"What's the verdict?" Walker asked calmly.

"Don't rush us, sir; we've not had a chance to discuss it yet," said Nave. "Give us a little while, come back in an hour. I for one have some things to discuss with the others here."

"Sure, sure," Walker said, letting the two front legs of the chair ease back down onto the floor. "Take all the time you want."

Agent Walker stood up slowly and turned in the direction of the door, his Adam's apple rising and falling like an elevator as he ambled across the room.

"Gentleman, I don't know about you, but I think that Jim Vess knows where his partner is. I think as soon as we turn him loose, he'll go to him. I think watching him would be useless, no one has heard hide nor hair of him in eleven years. Hell, his family hasn't a clue. I'll agree if he's made contact with Jim, then everyone has missed it. Nothing has been in his letters or in his phone calls, but he knows, I'm sure of it."

"What do you want to do, Charlie; keep him in here forever?" asked one of the board members.

"I say offer him a deal, see how he reacts. Give him a full pardon if he rats on his partner; tell him that we think that Jerry Pardue has spent the money anyway."

"It's worth a try," said one of the other members, who had been smoking one cigarette after the other.

"OK gentleman, I'll talk to Walker and the warden, run it by them. If it don't work, we'll have to let him out next time; you know that don't you?" replied Nave tiredly.

It was afternoon before Charlie Nave met with Agent Walker; the other board members were excused. It was obvious that seven men didn't need to be present to discuss the proposed deal with the TBI agent.

"Let me get this straight, Charlie, you think that Vess will rat out his partner if you offer him a full pardon?" asked Walker.

"Yes, sir, we felt that it might be worth a try."

"We're almost sure that he doesn't have any idea where Jerry Pardue is; absolutely no contact with him has been made. It's like he just vanished from the face of the Earth, we're even sure he hasn't contacted his own parents, who by the way have tried in vain to find him."

"What about the money, do you think it's still out there somewhere?"

"Vess is probably correct; the bastard's probably in South America somewhere living like a king."

"I still think it's worth a try," said Nave, "we're going to have to let him out on parole soon anyway."

"What if he tells us to go to hell, what are you going to do then?" asked Walker, sitting down on the corner of one of the tables.

"Tell him we'll see him next year." Nave shrugged with a slight grin.

****

The two boys made their way along the creek; finally coming to the cattle crossing that was only a few inches deep, which would make it easier to wade across. Jackie pulled the duffel bag from Tommy's shoulder as they stepped into the shallow creek bed, fearing Tommy might lose his balance and drop the bag containing what looked to be a small fortune in cash.

The boys reached the other side of the creek, both giving a sigh of relief as they made their way up the slight incline and onto the path that led in the direction of the mineshaft.

"Why did you tell Bo we had newspapers in the duffel bag?" inquired Tommy, as he followed Jackie down the path that skirted the creek bank.

"If you couldn't read or write, what would be the last thing you would want?"

"Do you think they would try to take the bag away from us?" asked Tommy.

"I don't think they wanted what was in the bag as much as they just wanted the bag itself. The stuff that they haul around in that old cart isn't worth anything; you've heard about some of the stuff that they have stolen; most people are glad they took it."

"Do you think Bo is dangerous?"

"I've been told that he's shot at people that got too close to his shack; you just never know about people like him. I'm more afraid of Cheese; have you noticed that one of his eyes looks in a different direction than the other?"

"He didn't have any trouble taking aim on that duffel bag with that rock, did he?"

"That had to be luck; if it wasn't, the Yankees should take a look at him." Jackie handed the duffle bag to Tommy without commenting.

They were getting closer to the hillside where the mineshaft was located and so far they had not encountered anyone else along the creek.

"I'm still curious about Bo and Cheese," said Tommy; "are they just uneducated or do they have a mental problem or something?"

"I talked to Lewis about them once. He said it's caused by inbreeding."

"What's inbreeding?"

"It's like when someone marries their cousin or sometimes even their sisters or brothers and they have children. It happens a lot in the mountains around here, sometimes the fathers have sex with their own children, and more often than not, they end up like Bo and Cheese."

"How does anyone get a name like Cheese, do you think that's his real name?" asked Tommy.

"Lewis said somebody named him that down at Louie's store; said he smelled like Limburger cheese, I guess the name just got shortened to Cheese. Mama said not to make fun of them, so quit laughing," Jackie said, straining to hold back a laugh himself.

It was apparent that they both had the same thing on their minds as they reached the entrance to the mineshaft because they wasted no time in removing the flat rock covering the cave entrance. Not a word was said as Jackie dropped the duffel bag through the hole and swiveled his slim body into the opening, searching for the rungs on the ladder with his feet. As he stepped off the ladder onto the mineshaft floor, Tommy was already pulling the rock back over the entrance and descending the rope ladder twice as fast as he had ever done before. Jackie handed Tommy a flashlight as he held up one of the lanterns.

"Hold this light while I get this thing lit," Jackie said as he struck a match on the side of a rock protruding from the cave wall.

He laughed out loud at himself as he brought the match to the small hole at the base of the lantern. "I'm shaking so hard, I almost put the damn match out."

"Why are we so scared?" asked Tommy. "I'm about to wet my pants myself."

"We're about to find out." Jackie directed the beam of the flashlight onto the duffel bag sitting of the floor of the mineshaft six inches in front of his feet.

****

The Nash Rambler had pulled to the side of the road as the balding, pear-shaped man wiped the sweat from the top of his head with the palm of his hand. He watched as the two preschool girls stood on their tiptoes peering into the one-foot square hole on top of the ice cream cart parked in the middle of the driveway. The aging Hunky Man as he became known stood patiently watching the two girls trying to decide on which flavor Popsicle they wanted.

After much deliberation and mind changing, the decision was finally made; Judy gave the old man a quarter to pay for both her and Kitty, and stuck out her hand for the nickel change. The old man put his moneybox into the hole with the ice cream, closed the lid, and stepped to the rear of his three-wheeled cart.

As he leaned into the push handle of the cart, he gave the cowbell a nudge with his pinky finger and slowly headed up the road.

The Rambler, which had been waiting for the Popsicle transaction to end and unblock the driveway, eased slowly forward and turned in. The perspiring overweight man struggled from under the steering wheel, stepped out of the car onto the sidewalk that led to Jackie Malone's small front porch.

Judy and Kitty stood at the end of the sidewalk, each with a tongue glued to the side of a cherry Popsicle, watching as the huge sweating man knocked on the screen door.

"Hello, my name is Leonard Gay, I live down on the street behind you: I hope I haven't caught you at a bad time, but I have something I need to talk to you about."

"No, no, I was just doing some ironing. Who did you say you were again?" Mrs. Malone said through the screen door.

"I'm sorry, it's Gay, Leonard Gay. I live down the street from Tommy Redden, I see him with Jackie a lot, I'm sure you know him."

"Sure, I know him; you don't see one without seeing the other: Would you like to come in?" Jackie's mother slowly pushed open the screen door.

"Is Jackie at home by any chance?" inquired Mr. Gay as he stepped into the small living room still holding onto the screen door.

"No he's not; he and Tommy have gone to the golf course over in Brainerd. They're gonna try to caddy if they can. Try to pick up a little spending money, you know." Jackie's mother smiled, holding a hand over her mouth in an effort to hide a tooth that was outlined in gold that she was self-conscious of. "He's all right isn't he; nothing has happened to him, has there?"

"No, I'm sorry. I didn't mean to frighten you, I'm sure he's OK, but something has happened and I think you need to be aware of it."

The small woman turned and walked back behind her ironing board, picked up the basket of clothes, and disappeared down the hall that led to Jackie and Judy's bedroom. After a few seconds, she returned, folded up the ironing board, and leaned it against the doorway that led to the dining room.

"Please sit down, Mr. Gay," she said as she walked over to the TV and twisted the knob that put an end to the *AS THE WORLD TURNS* daytime soap opera.

She didn't say anything; she just sat down across from the balding pear-shaped man and looked at him as if to say, "WHAT."

"Do you know about Mr. Robinson, the constable that got beat up down at Louie's store a while back?" asked Mr. Gay.

"Yes I heard about it, they think they know who did it but have never made an arrest; what about it?"

"Mrs. Malone, there's a teen over in East Ridge that everyone is positive was the kid who did it, but the boys who saw it happen are afraid of him and refuse to be a witness against him. Poor old Mr. Robinson failed to pick him out of a lineup, he still has double vision. That boy hit him so hard; he may never get his vision back like it was. Louie, who was in the back of the store when it happened, had to put a calendar over the hole in the plaster where his head hit the wall beside the Coke box. It's a damn shame; please excuse the language."

"What's that got to do with Jack?"

The overweight man unfastened the collar of his shirt and loosened his tie, stretching his neck as he turned his head from side to side.

"Earlier today on my way home for lunch, I happened to notice a person lying on the side of the road right before you get to the bridge down on Springvale Road. As I slowed down, I could see that he was in some kind of pain and was crying and squirming around. What I also saw was Jackie, Tommy, and some other kid attending to him. As I got out of the car and started across the road, it became apparent to me that the blond-headed boy lying in a fetal position on the side of the road was the boy who beat up Mr. Robinson."

"Well, what happened to the boy; did Jack have something to do with it?" Jackie's mother was pulling on the skin at the front of her neck, which she always did when she was nervous.

"I never got the full story from Jackie, but it appears that he did hit him with the golf club in the groin. I'm sure he did it in self-defense, that's sort of why I'm here. I took the boy up to the police station in East Ridge, they knew who he was, and it wasn't his first trip up there. By the way, his name is Sonny Farr, they know he's a bully but so far they haven't been able to do much about it.

"Mrs. Malone, Sonny told the police that Jackie attacked him with a golf club as he and a friend were fishing by the bridge. He said that he did it without warning, just came up and hit him for no reason."

"Did they believe him?"

"I'm sure that they didn't, but he says he has a witness."

"What happened to the other boy that you saw, did he ever

show up?"

"No he hasn't, Mrs. Malone, but I'm sure that when he does, he'll take Sonny's side."

Mr. Gay stood up and slowly walked to the door, before turning around and facing Mrs. Malone, who was still tugging at her throat.

"I don't think the police will make an issue out of this, but you never know what that Farr boy will do. I would have liked to talk to Jackie and Tommy, you know, try to find out what really happened. It's quite possible he may have taken that bully down a notch or two."

Mrs. Malone sat listening to the big man, not sure of what to make of what he was telling her. The thing that kept going through her mind was, "How will I tell Harve about this."

"I hope I haven't upset you; it's just that I would like to see that bully pay for what he did to Mr. Robinson. Maybe somebody will come forward now; the word will get around that he may not be as tough as he thinks he is."

The big man pushed open the screen door and stepped onto the small porch.

Jackie's mother watched through the screen door as he looked back up at her from the sidewalk. "Tell Jackie I came by, tell him and Tommy to stop by and see me, Tommy knows where I live. Goodbye," said Mr. Gay as he looked up into the afternoon sun on the way to his car.

Jackie's mother stood behind the screen door as she watched the Rambler back out of the driveway and drive off.

What am I going to do with that boy, it's always something, she thought as she flipped the TV back on and sat down on the edge of the sofa.

"All we need is for somebody to sue us, or better yet, Jack gets charged with some kind of assault," The now confused mother mumbled to herself. "Harve will beat that boy to death when he finds out about this."

It was getting time to get something started for supper; the house had begun to heat up from the humid southern summer as Jackie's mother stood up and put her hand to her neck pulling at the loose skin as she headed off in the direction of the kitchen.

****

"Well, don't just stand there, dump it out; if all of this is money, we've got tons of it," Jackie said, as he handed one side of the duffel bag to Tommy, who was still looking down between his feet, his eyes fixed on the dirty olive green duffel bag.

Both boys lifted the bag and turned it upside down, letting the bundles of cash pile up between their legs. It took a full minute for the duffel bag to completely empty out. The sound of the money packets hitting the floor sounded like distant thunder as it reverberated back down the abandoned mineshaft. Jackie flipped the bag upright and stuck his arm down into the bag feeling around to see if all the bundles had fallen out.

"What's that smell: it smells like mothballs," Tommy scowled as he looked at Jackie, making a face as if he had just taken a whiff of Bo Goins armpit.

"It's the Army duffel bag; don't you remember, Leonard Bean had one his dad brought back from the war, it smelled the same way."

Jackie picked up one of the bundles of twenties, and took it over to the lantern. He flipped through it watching the face of Andrew Jackson shimmer in the flickering light of the Coleman lantern.

Jackie looked across the lantern at Tommy, who had been watching the bundle of twenty-dollar bills as if it was a magic show at the Tivoli theatre before the Saturday morning matinee. Tommy's eyes came up to meet Jackie's; both boys looked at each other for several seconds before they looked back down at the bundle of money Jackie still held in his now shaking left hand.

"How, how much you think is here?" stammered Tommy.

"I'm afraid to guess;" Jackie muttered to himself, if this is real, we've got a fortune here."

"What makes you think it's not real?" Tommy asked as he examined one of the bundles of hundreds.

"I didn't say it wasn't, but if it's not counterfeit or something, we're some kind of rich. Let's count this mess." Jackie threw the bundle he was holding back into the pile beside the lantern.

As both boys stacked the bundles of currency in neat piles in front of them, the excitement grew in proportion to the height of their individual caches. After an exercise in basic arithmetic, scratching on the walls and drawing lines in the dirt on the floor, each concluded that they had a reasonable calculation of how much money they had piled before them.

Tommy leaned back, letting his head rest against one of the timbers; he brushed one hand and then the other through his flattop hair.

"A hundred and sixteen thousand," Tommy announced with a detectable quiver in his voice.

"I've got one thirty-four but it looks like one of the bundles has had some removed, but not much. I don't know if you realize it or not, Tommy, but we've got almost a quarter of a million dollars here."

"This can't be real, can it, Jackie?" Tommy had a look on his face that said, "Please tell me that it can?"

"I think that the money is the real thing, but the question is, who does it belong to? We can find out if it's real money; that's not going to be a problem. The problem will be finding out who it belongs to."

"I guess if we find out, we'll have to give it back, won't we?" Tommy asked with a hurt look.

"It depends; but one thing's for sure, we're not going to tell anybody about this until we do a lot of investigating. You take it to the police or something now and half the people in East Ridge will try to claim it."

No one said a word for several minutes as the boys sat staring at the pile of money between them. The shadow of the two stacks of money could be seen on the cave wall, and the only sound made was the steady hiss of the two Coleman lanterns.

"What do we do now?" asked Tommy, the first to emerge from the trance.

"Let's put it back in the duffel bag and store it in a dry place down here, go home, get a grip on ourselves, think about it, and come back tomorrow and see if we are dreaming." Jackie smiled as he reached for the duffel bag.

"Listen to me, Tommy, not a word you hear, not a word."

"I get it, I get it, I haven't told anybody about this cave, have I?"

"No, but this is something that could slip out, you don't talk in your sleep or anything do you?" Jackie said quietly as he began putting the bundles of cash back into the duffel bag.

"What do you think caused that hole in the duffel bag," Tommy asked, as he pushed a couple of fingers inside trying to feel for any material that could still be attached. "I wonder what the other letters are that go with this name stenciled on here. J RDUE," do you think that's the whole name, or what could the other letter or letters that go with it possibly be?" Tommy mumbled something under his breath as he began placing his bundles of money back into the bag.

"We'll have plenty of time to try to figure that out, would you please finish putting your bundles in the bag so we can get out of here?"

Jackie heaved the duffel bag onto his shoulder; he turned around, slowly scanning the small room with all the junk they had collected.

"What about hanging it on the hook where I have my hammock attached, it'll keep it off the floor?" asked Jackie.

"That would be OK, but it's not hidden very well."

"What the hell you mean, hidden; this whole place is hidden?"

"Oh yeah," Tommy said sheepishly, "I forgot about that."

Jackie eased the strap off his shoulder and placed it over the large hook that he had screwed into the one of the timbers at the entrance to the smaller shaft that led deeper into the hillside.

"Let's go," Jackie said as he picked up one of the lanterns, turning the flame off and reaching for the other one.

Tommy was already half-way up the rope ladder and had stopped to catch his breath before ascending the last few rungs; this part never seemed to get easier for Tommy.

****

As Jackie approached the back of his house, he could see that his dad had not come home from work. He was not sure what time it was since he didn't have a watch, but he was sure that it must be getting close to that time because he could see Lewis' car in his driveway; they both usually got home about the same time. It was Friday, and Friday's were becoming a day that Jackie dreaded. If his dad did not arrive home by five o'clock or a little after, that meant he would come home drunk, or perhaps he wouldn't come home at all that evening.

He decided to delay going into the house and seeing the anxiety and sadness in his mother's eyes that she tried to hide from him but couldn't. He stepped across the small drainage ditch that separated his backyard from Lewis'. He walked between the two houses and turned in the direction of the black Ford sitting at the end of the driveway. Just as he was about to step onto the porch and knock on the door, he saw Lewis come from behind the side of his house and walk toward his shiny black Ford.

"Jack Daniels," said Lewis, as his eye caught Jackie jumping down from his front porch and walking in his direction.

"Is Tomcat with you, is everything going okay for you guys?" enquired Lewis as he felt around for the hood latch in front of the Ford.

"No, he's not with me; yeah we're doing fine though. What are you gonna do; see why that thing can't keep up with the new Chevy?" Jackie grinned.

"This thing will suck the windshield out of any Chevy around here." Lewis laughed. "No, I was just checking the oil and water, Harold's getting where he don't have time; he needs some help up there at that station."

"I got a question for you, Lewis."

"Shoot."

"Do you know about all those houses they're moving out of the way for the new freeway?"

"Yeah, what about 'em?"

"Did the government just take 'em away from those people, or do they just pay for having them moved or what?"

"It's called imminent domain; they have to move but the government gives them a fair price, at least they're supposed to."

"So the people don't necessarily move with the house, they just take their furniture and buy a house somewhere else?"

"No, they very seldom go with the houses; most of them are not worth a crap after they get them to where they are going anyway. "Have you boys been over watching them move 'em," asked Lewis as he closed the hood on the Ford and looked over at Jackie, who was keeping a sharp eye out to see if his dad had come home.

"Yeah, we were over there today; they really have a mess, and people have left junk lying around everywhere."

"I know," Lewis added, "some of the things that people have thrown out are still worth something. Woodrow, down the street, found a washing machine, brought it home, hell it works fine.

"I've heard people go over there in the evening, scavenge around and find all kind of things. It said in the newspaper that whatever they left behind people could have. The only problem with that is sometimes a fight breaks out over a dispute on who saw it first." Lewis laughed.

"So what you're saying is that the people who lived there have taken everything with them that they felt had any value?"

"Yep. If you boys saw something over there that you want, just make sure it doesn't belong to the construction companies; they'll lock your ass up for that." Lewis laughed again then stepped closer to the shadow of his house, blocking the evening sun from his eyes.

Jackie started to say something when David, Lewis' son, rounded the corner of the house right behind Linda, his slightly older sister, holding out some kind of insect in front of him. She was screaming as loud as she could, but you could still hear him laughing above her screams as they both ran between Jackie and Lewis and disappeared around the other end of the house.

"That kid would rather aggravate that girl than eat," Lewis said, frowning as he fumbled in his shirt pocket for a pack of Luckies that was astonishingly missing.

"Now where did I put em this time?" He patted his pockets a second time and came up with the same results. No Luckies.

"What you keep looking down the street for, Jackie; are you expecting company or something?"

"No, it's just my dad, he's not home yet and I'm worried

he'll come in drinking again. Sometimes he's mean to Mama when he's like that."

"He's mean to you too when he's like that, isn't he, Jackie?"

"Sometimes, but I'm not worried about me, I just can't stand to see him treat Mama the way he does."

Jackie said something else as he looked down at the grass, his eyes fixed on nothing in particular, but his voice was so low Lewis couldn't make out what he had said.

Lewis was about to ask Jackie what he had said when Francis pushed open the screen door and tossed Lewis his missing pack of Luckies.

"I guess you've been looking for these; they must have fallen out of your pocket when you were in the bathroom. I just happened to see them down in the tub; heck if I know how you got 'em in there."

"Thanks," said Lewis as he caught the cigarettes with one hand, tapping the pack on his wrist. Two or three of the cigarettes protruded through the opening in the end of the pack, one of them more so than the others, which he extracted with his lips.

"Something is bothering you, Jackie, you want to tell me about it?" asked Lewis, bringing his lighter to the tip of his cigarette.

Jackie took a couple of steps closer to Lewis and answered, "Yeah, I guess so". Tommy and I decided to go over to the golf course and do a little caddying or hunt for some lost balls; you know, try to make a little spending money. Well, when we got to the bridge down on Springvale, out pops that Tush Hog, Sonny Farr, and his freckle-faced sidekick."

"Isn't he the one they think beat up Mr. Robinson down at Louie's store?" asked Lewis.

"Yeah, that's the one; we had a run in with them the other day down by the creek. We got away from them that time by hiding down in the mine shaft, but this time we had nowhere to run."

Lewis took a deep drag from his unfiltered Lucky and smiled at his young friend.

"I don't see a black eye, a fat lip, or anything, so what happened?"

"I forgot to tell you; I took my Bull's Eye putter with me. I was planning on practicing on the putting green at the golf course if I had time."

"Well?" Lewis asked as he flipped the Lucky out into the front yard.

"He came right up to me, got right in my face. I knew he had a reputation as being the sucker punch kid and if I didn't do something quick, he was going to put a hurt on me. I brought the putter up between his legs so hard the sound that it made when it hit his balls almost made us all puke. The big bully tried to scream but no sound came from his wide-open mouth. He grabbed his crotch and went to the ground, rolled up in a ball and started crying like a baby."

"What happened to Tommy and the other kid?" asked Lewis.

"Tommy and Freckle-face just stood there with a funny look on their faces. I took a step toward the tall skinny boy and he folded up like a cheap lawn chair. I still had the putter in both hands; I guess he thought he might be next. Anyway, he suddenly became one of the nicest guys you ever met. He even started calling me sir."

Jackie turned and looked down the street as a car approached and then passed on by. He looked back at Lewis, who had a grin from ear to ear.

"So what's to be upset about, it's for sure a case of self defense. It sounds like you did the community a service. I doubt if that asshole will be starting any more trouble for a while; especially with you".

"I'm not so much worried about him, I just don't know what my daddy's gonna say. You never know how he's going to react, especially if he's been drinking."

"I don't think you need to worry about Harvey; he's been in a few scrapes himself. They say he hit a colored man in the head with a shovel down there where he works. You would have more to worry about if you stood there and got your ass whipped; Harvey's not going to be mad at you for standing up for yourself."

"I hope you're right," Jackie muttered.

"Don't get your dobber down kid." Jackie turned and slowly walked across the front lawn.

He had only taken a few steps when he stopped and turned around.

"What does, get your dobber down mean?"

"The next time you get a chance to get a close look at a wasp or a dirt dobber, watch him for a minute or two, you'll get what I mean."

Jackie scratched the top of his head, trying to hold back a smile as he turned and continued across the lawn.

"Hey," hollered Lewis, as Jackie reached the barely discernible boundary between the two front lawns.

"Did you bring home a big bundle of money today…?

Jackie turned around, his face turning red as his heart skipped a beat then began to gallop.

"Wah, what, do you mean Lewis?" *How could he possibly know?* Jackie asked himself as his pulse rate began to return to normal.

"Caddying, did you hook up with any of those ten-cent millionaires out on the course today?" Lewis smiled.

"Oh no, we never made it to the course, we stopped and watched the construction on the freeway," Jackie shouted back as a drop of sweat ran down his forehead into his eye.

Lewis shook his head, pulled open the screen door, and went inside.

****

Jackie could tell that what his mother had prepared for supper contained some garlic well before he reached the screen door to his back porch. It had to be country-fried steak or maybe pork chops; either way they were always delicious.

His mother was sitting at the dining room table in front of a large glass of ice tea and reading her bible; which she did every day. Jackie knew she would be worried that his father had not come home from work, and he was correct; you could see it in her face as she looked up and smiled as he sat down at the table across from her.

"I know, Mama; he's not home yet, but cheer up maybe he'll be here in a minute."

"I just hope he doesn't do anything to hurt you and Judy."

Jackie didn't reply as he got up and walked into the living room and stood in front of the open screen door, watching in silence, trying to will his father to come driving down the street.

"It's about time for Alfred Hitchcock," Jackie said as he twisted the knob to turn on the television. "You better come on in here; you know you don't want to miss the beginning."

Jackie tried to lighten the mood and if possible try to channel his mother's thoughts away from worrying over his dad.

Hitchcock had just delivered his opening line of, "Good evening, ladies and gentlemen," when his mother got up and strolled into the living room and sat down on the corner of the couch.

"Jack, it's not just Harve that I'm worried about; someone came by to see me today and I need to talk to you about it."

"Who was it, Mama?"

"It was Mr. Gay from down on Tommy's street. He said that you got into it with that boy that beat up Mr. Robinson; he said that you hit him with your golf club and that you may have hurt him pretty bad."

Jackie got up and went over to his mother and took her hand down from her throat where she had been tugging on the loose skin. He took the other hand and held them both in his strong grip, looked her in the eyes, and grimaced at what he saw in her face.

"I was going to tell you about it, Mama; I was going to tell you and Daddy at the same time. I didn't want to worry you about it; I knew you would be upset. Well I guess Mr. Gay beat me to it.

"I had to do something, he's a big bully and if I hadn't done what I did, I'm sure he would have beaten the crap out of me," Jackie said, still holding his mother's hands in his.

"Mr. Gay said that he had it coming and you did what you did in self-defense. He said he didn't think the police or anyone else would blame you. It's just that, I don't know how your daddy is going to take this, especially if he comes home in a bad mood. You know how he is when he's been drinking."

Jackie placed his mother's hands in her lap, stood up and walked over to the TV. He pushed the button to turn off the TV, and turned to face his mother, smiling.

"Mama, you're going to have quit worrying so much; I know it's hard for you right now; Judy and I are getting older and you feel that we need things that you're unable to provide. I can't explain it right now, but I have a feeling that things may change for the better around here. You just need to stop worrying so much; I promise everything's going to be just fine; you'll see."

Jackie started to say something else when the lights from a car turning into the driveway projected the image of the Venetian blinds onto the living room wall. Judy, who had been quietly sitting in her bedroom listening to the conversation between her brother and her mother, got up and pulled the door closed. She hoped it would insulate her from most of the impending confrontation that would almost certainly take place.

"It's him," said Jackie as he watched the Plymouth proceed on up the driveway and stop beside the back porch.

"I just hope and pray if he's been drinking he'll eat his supper and go on to bed," his mother said.

This was the part that Jackie dreaded the most; the waiting was over, it was time to confront the monster.

Jackie glanced over at his mother; he could almost see her flinch at the sound of the car door slamming shut. It disheartened Jackie to watch his mother busy herself with the finishing touches of preparing the evening meal that she had been trying to keep warm for the past two hours.

Harve ascended the back steps to the small back porch two at a time; he flung open the screen door and stepped into the kitchen.

"Sorry I'm a little late," he said, "you won't believe what happened today."

"Where's Judy? Get her in here; I've got something to show everybody."

Jackie glanced at his mother, who seemed to be as confused as he was, as she headed down the hallway to Judy's room.

Everyone gathered around the kitchen table as Harve, who didn't appear to have been drinking, set a small glass bottle in the center of the table.

"What is it?" asked Judy, standing on her tiptoes in an effort to get her head closer to the object in the center of the table.

"Hell, it's a finger; what does it look like?" He picked up the bottle up and pushed it closer to Judy's face, causing her to retreat backwards, almost falling down.

"Had an accident down at the shop just as I was about to

leave. An overhead crane ran over the hand of one of the maintenance men, who happened to be in the wrong place at the wrong time. It plopped three of 'em off; they found two of 'em and took them to the hospital with him. I found this one after they left. I put it in this bottle and filled it with alcohol. They told me I shouldn't have done that, said it would make it impossible to reattach it. The nurse at the plant said that too much time had passed anyway."

Harvey picked up the bottle and held it up to the light, admiring it as if he had found a gold nugget or rare gem of some kind. He seemed to be waiting for an ovation or some kind of acknowledgement for bringing home such an unusual treasure.

"I think it'll make a great conversation piece," he said, dropping the bottle into his shirt pocket.

Everyone gave a sigh of relief that he was home and apparently had not been drinking. No one commented as the proud owner of the severed finger trudged down the hallway to the small bathroom to wash his hands. All three stood around the table not saying a word before Judy finally turned and headed back to her room.

"Has everybody already eaten?" Harvey asked as he returned and sat down at the table across from his son.

"Judy and I have, Jack wanted to wait and eat with you; he has something to tell you."

She sat a plate with two pork chops and a huge portion of mashed potatoes in front of her husband. As quickly as she finished with him, she did the same for her son. She walked into the kitchen and returned with a bowl of green beans, sitting them in the center of the table and placing a large spoon in the bowl.

"Go ahead and tell him, Jack, tell him what happened today," she said, placing a large glass of iced tea down in front of each of them.

"Dammit, son, let's hear it! You haven't fleeced anybody

else with that one-handed chin-up crap again, have you?"

Harvey stabbed one of the pork chops and started to cut off a portion with his knife but elected instead to pick it up with his hand and take a bite, holding the meat by the bone.

"No nothing like that. You heard about the boy from East Ridge that they said hit Mr. Robinson down at Louie's store, didn't you."

"Yeah I heard about it; I wish the little son of a bitch would try that with me sometime. I'd show him how tough he is," his dad said, taking a bite of potatoes and chasing it with a swig of iced tea.

"He's not little," said Jackie.

"I don't care how big he is; he'll run across somebody who'll put him in his place someday."

"That's what I wanted to talk to you about, Daddy."

Harvey stopped chewing and looked up at his son, who had also stopped eating.

"Well, what is it?" he asked with a mouthful of pork chop.

"The big bully jumped Tommy and me today down by the bridge on Springvale. He got right up in my face and I knew if I didn't do something fast, I'd have a good chance of getting hurt real bad. Everybody knows he's famous for his sucker punch and I decided I wasn't going to wait for it."

"What did you do; run?"

"No, luckily I had my putter with me; we were headed to the golf course. He glanced over at his buddy and that's when I brought the putter up between his legs. All I can say is that it took the fight out of him real quick, it also turned his buddy into a much nicer guy."

"Did it hurt him very bad?" Harvey asked, beginning to eat again.

"I think so; he was still crying like a baby the last time I saw him," Jackie said, smiling.

"Good," was all that his dad said as he got up from the table, searching his pockets for his box of Copenhagen.

Jackie looked up at his mother, who had been leaning against the doorway to the kitchen listening to the exchange between him and his father. They both just shrugged as Jackie went back to work on his second pork chop.

****

Jackie was awake before the sun came up, he had not slept well, and all he could think about was the duffel bag full of money hanging beside his hammock inside the mineshaft. Had the day before really happened or had he just experienced one of those crazy dreams? In addition to the tossing and turning from reliving the events of the previous day, a summer thunderstorm had rolled in during the night. The wind and lightning, along with periods of heavy rain, had kept him busy adjusting the windows, trying to block the rain from coming in, but also not letting the room get too warm.

Sometime during the early morning, the storm had moved on and the sound of birds chirping in the elm tree outside his window was all he needed to prod him out of bed.

It was Saturday; everyone in the house was still in bed as he snatched one of the leftover pork chops from the refrigerator, slapped it between two slices of bread and eased out the back door. He wasn't sure if Tommy was up yet, but if he were to place a bet on it, he would put a sizeable amount of his part of the money that his friend was up already. He had just crossed into Mr. Higgins backyard when Bud stepped out on his porch and tossed something to one of several beagles sitting at the bottom of the steps.

"Where you going this early?" hollered Bud, stepping around the dog at the bottom of the steps and heading in Jackie's direction. “Wait up a minute, you skinny little fart; I want to ask you something. I heard Daddy talking to Mr. Gay last night. Tell me what happened between you and Sonny Farr; it sounded like you beat the crap out of him with a golf club. Is that true?”

Jackie was silent for a moment, not knowing what to say as he marveled at how fast news traveled.

“Not exactly.”

“What you gonna do if he catches you out somewhere and you don’t have a golf club with you?” Bud asked, grinning.

“I’m going to tell him that you said that he was pussy for letting a little shrimp like me get the best of him. I’m also going to tell him that you said that you’re going to kick his ass the next time you saw him.”

Jackie turned and walked away with Bud standing with his mouth open, trying to think of what to say.

“You better not,” was all that Bud could think of as Jackie crossed the street and started down Tommy’s driveway.

“Get the hell out of the way,” Bud shouted, kicking at the beagle that was now sitting at his feet staring up at his belly.

****

It would have been a safe bet for Jackie that Tommy was out of bed; he and Linda were sitting side by side on the porch steps. Their heads were buried in a copy of *Car and Driver* magazine. Linda had her driver’s license now, but no car to drive. It bothered Tommy and Linda more than it did Mom and Dad that they didn’t own a car, even though Mr. Redden was the one who had to walk to the bus stop every day. Still it didn’t hurt to dream, and both could identify the make and model of every car on the road.

“You guys are up early to be sitting around looking at magazines.” Jackie was unable to break eye contact with his friend's sister, who looked up from the magazine and smiled.

"You're up early too, what's up?" Linda asked, standing up and brushing the back of her somewhat tight shorts to remove any dirt.

"The storm, the storm woke me up," replied Jackie, still keeping his eyes on Linda, who had not attempted to break off the staring contest. She never broke eye contact with Jackie as she slowly ascended the four steps to the porch.

"See you little boys later." Linda smiled, looking over her shoulder as she pulled open the screen door and stepped inside.

"Come on," said Tommy, "get your mind out of the gutter, let's get out of here."

It took longer than usual to get to the cave entrance; due to the storm, the creek had risen out of its banks and they had to stop periodically to investigate. Every time the creek flooded, something always changed; a foot log disappeared, or a new one was added, sometimes a log jam produced a dam that backed the water up creating a small lake.

"I don't see anything very interesting," Jackie said, "let's get on up to the cave. I can't get that duffel bag full of money out of my mind."

"Me either, I'm still not sure it wasn't a dream."

Tommy was the first one down the rope ladder; he had the duffel bag off the nail and was running his arm inside before Jackie was half way down.

"It wasn't a dream, it's here." Tommy's eyes gleamed, holding up one of the bundles in front of his flashlight for Jackie to see.

"Calm down, for crying out loud; sit down and light one of those lanterns," said Jackie, taking the duffel bag from Tommy.

"What are we gonna do first?"

"The first thing we have to do is make sure that it's real money; I'm pretty sure it is, but one thing that I noticed is that the bills that I checked were dated in the forties."

"What does that mean?" asked Tommy, looking concerned.

"Nothing really, just that it's old money."

"It'll still spend, won't it?"

"Oh yeah it'll spend all right, the only thing is you can't spend a lot of it at once or you're going to have to explain where you got it."

"Can't we just put it in the bank; you know open up a savings account?"

"What are you going to do, dumb ass, just throw the duffel bag up on the counter and tell the teller you want to open up a savings account?"

"Oh, I think I see what you mean." Tommy grinned sheepishly. "What do you suggest, Einstein?"

"It'll be easy to find out if this is real currency and not counterfeit or something; the real test is to find out who put it where we found it."

Tommy got up and walked slowly down the mineshaft. Jackie watched his friend run his hand through his flattop, knowing he was thinking about the same thing that he was. Tommy kept walking until he had disappeared into the darkness. Jackie knew shortly after he had disappeared why he had decided to make his short journey. The fart was so loud that you could hear the echo return seconds later from farther down the abandoned mineshaft.

"Thanks for your consideration." Jackie smiled as Tommy emerged back from the darkness grinning.

"OK," Tommy said as he pulled the campstool under his butt and sat down, "if we find out who it belongs to, we give it back. What do we do if we don't?"

"I told you before; we just can't put an advertisement in the paper and ask if anybody lost a quarter of a million dollars in cash. If we just turn it in, the people who will end up with it will be the lawyers; everybody from here to Atlanta will claim it was theirs."

"How are we going to find out then?"

"Do some detective work, ask around; hell I don't know, let me think about it."

"You said that it would be easy finding out if it wasn't counterfeit, how we accomplish that?" asked Tommy.

Jackie picked up the packet of twenties that had already been broken, he pulled two bills from under the paper strap and handed one to Tommy.

"Let's go shopping."

****

It was muggy and the smell of diesel fuel from the nearby freeway construction hung in the air like a wet blanket. The plan was to take the bus to town, eat as many Krystal hamburgers as they could, go to Sears and look around, then maybe take in a movie. If they found out the twenties were counterfeit; going to movies may be out. They may have to settle for throwing a leg over the Allstate Motorcycle that sat on the showroom floor at Sears instead.

"How are we going to test the twenties?" Inquired Tommy, looking around nervously as they crossed the bridge where they had the run in with Tush.

"First we'll get Harold to cash one at the service station; see how he reacts."

"Harold's no expert," said Tommy.

"I know he's not, but he handles a lot of money; there may be something he looks for that we don't know about."

Tommy ran ahead of Jackie so he could have the first try at the pinball machine that stood in the corner of the service station lobby. It was against the law to pay off when someone occasionally hit; but Harold did, as did most everyone else. The local police looked the other way since they were the ones who did most of the playing during the early hours of the morning when traffic was light and most of the town was asleep. Harold's was one of the few service stations that stayed open twenty-four hours a day and the pinball machine made enough to pay the lights and help. It wasn't unusual for Harold to toss a roll of quarters to a patrolman who had just lost his kid's lunch money in the machine. Harold considered it an insurance payment.

"Get your ass off that machine, I told you boys not to play it during the day when we're busy. What if your dad were to come in here, Tommy?" Harold scowled, tossing an oily rag at Tommy as he walked through the front door to the small lobby.

"Just wanted to try this lucky quarter," grunted Tommy as his last ball fell into a hole that unfortunately for him did not line up.

Jackie handed the twenty-dollar bill to Harold, who had retrieved his shop rag from the top of the pinball machine and began wiping his hands.

"Damn, son, did you rob a bank or something?" Harold asked, taking the twenty from Jackie.

"Chin-up money," said Jackie, "how 'bout busting it up for me. I need some silver for the bus fare too."

Harold opened the cash register, placed the bill on top of the other twenties, and started counting out Jackie's change.

So much for that test, thought Jackie, as he looked over at Tommy, who was diligently watching the transaction that was taking place before him.

"Don't spend all this on wine and women." Harold smiled as he counted the change back to Jackie.

"Have you seen the bus go down?" asked Tommy.

The bus passed in front of Harold's station and proceeded down the highway to the Georgia state line before turning around and heading back downtown. It took about fifteen minutes after the bus passed Harold's station to reach the end of the line and return to the bus stop across from the service station.

"Yeah, it went by while numb nuts here was on the pinball machine. You better hurry; it's about time for it to get here."

Both boys dodged the traffic as they ran across the highway to the bus stop in front of the Pines Motel. They had less than a minute to wait before the bus came to a stop in front of them with the smell of diesel exhaust along with the sound of the air brakes releasing. Tommy never failed to comment that the brakes sounded as if the bus had just farted.

****

Tommy grabbed the pole behind the driver's seat, swinging into the long horizontal bench seat facing across the aisle. Jackie put the exact change for them both into the coin separator that protruded from the floor of the bus then took his seat beside Tommy.

Tommy leaned over to Jackie and whispered, "I still don't understand why it says white in front and colored in the rear."

"I've never quite figured that out either, but I have a feeling that's going to change pretty soon."

The bus made its way west through the Twin Tubes and down into the city. The closer it got to downtown, the faster the back of the bus filled up.

"That sure wasn't much of a test that Harold made on that twenty, was it?" Tommy asked quietly.

"No, that didn't tell us much, but I have something else in mind, I'll tell you about it later."

The bus stopped at the entrance to a housing project where four elderly colored women struggled up the steps of the bus. As they passed by on their way to the back, the smell of fried chicken followed along, leaving little doubt as to what they were carrying in those brown paper sacks.

"Are you getting hungry?" Jackie asked, looking straight ahead without cracking a smile.

"It really doesn't smell that bad, but I think I'll still go with Krystal's," muttered Tommy.

The bus was getting nearer to downtown and the passengers entering the bus now had to resort to standing. Both boys got up and offered their seats to two ladies who quickly accepted.

"I think we're there", Tommy said quietly. The sound of the air brakes could be heard through the open windows.

The standing passengers clung to the handrails as the bus came to a stop, with both the front and the side doors opening at the same time. It took only minutes to deposit the passengers onto the sidewalk in front of Liggett's Drug Store at the corner of Market and Seventh streets in downtown Chattanooga. Tommy was the first off the bus, and had already headed up Seventh Street in the direction of the Krystal before Jackie's feet hit the sidewalk.

"Wait up a minute, Tommy, I want to tell you something," Jackie shouted, trying to catch up with his friend who was on a beeline to the Krystal one block away.

"That twenty you have; don't break it yet, I have an idea on making sure it's legit," Jackie said, catching up to Tommy, who had not slowed down any.

"What is it?" asked Tommy.

"Come on, we'll talk about it while you're stuffing yourself full of gut bombs."

Jackie didn't want to admit it, but he liked the little Krystal hamburgers as much as Tommy did. They both ordered six apiece with an order of fries and a coke. Tommy downed two and had started on his third before Jackie had eaten half of his first one.

"What plans do you have for my twenty?" mumbled Tommy with a mouth full of fries.

"I just thought of something on the way down while we were on the bus."

"What was that?

"Mae Finley, my Sunday School teacher, works at the Hamilton National Bank down on Market Street. It's the big tall building; she's the head teller there and her husband John is a coin collector. I'm sure she can tell us if it's OK."

"Where are you going to tell her you got it?" Tommy asked.

"We're gonna tell her we found it at the bus stop, and that we just wanted to make sure it wasn't a fake or something."

"What's this "we're" crap? "How about you do the telling; this is your Sunday school teacher you're about to lie to."

"Whatever." He watched Tommy stuff half a hamburger in his mouth then took a fairly large bite of his own.

Mae Finley was an attractive blond in her forties who became Jackie's Sunday school teacher over a year ago when he moved up from the junior boy's class. She looked a lot like Lucille Ball, the star of the *I Love Lucy* show, the only difference was the color of her hair. Few people knew that Lucy was a redhead, since the TV show was in black and white. It wasn't Mae Finley that inspired Jackie's almost perfect attendance at Sunday school; it was her daughter Joyce, who was also in the class. Joyce was a petite younger version of her mother, but with one stunning attribute that her mother did not possess. Although she was only in her early teens, her breasts were well developed for a girl of her age, but not to the point of absurdity. As hard as he tried, and even though he was in church, he couldn't take his eyes off of her.

Jackie had very little contact with Joyce since she went to school in Tennessee and him in Georgia. They sat together in church after Sunday school sometimes, but other than that, the relationship had yet to grow beyond seeing each other on Sunday. People at the church just assumed that they were boyfriend and girlfriend, but the truth is they never had a date, or for that matter, even held each other's hand.

"Can you tell me how to find Mae Finley?" asked Jackie, as he looked up at the huge colored man standing by the elevator at the entrance to the cavernous lobby of the Hamilton National Bank. He had on a maroon uniform with a black stripe down the trousers. The coat was held together by gold buttons that were straining to contain his immense stomach.

"Yes sir, I sure can; she be in that first door on the right after you pass that row of teller cages." The big man smiled, displaying a gold front tooth. "Is she expecting you?" enquired the porter.

"No, sir, she isn't; she's my Sunday school teacher and I just wanted to say hello."

"You boys jest go right on in, I'm sure she'll be glad to see you." The two boys walked the length of the lobby, which was a full block running from Market Street through to Broad Street. They turned right at the end of the teller cages as the colored doorman had instructed. The lettering above the open door said "MAE FINLEY - HEAD TELLER." Jackie made eye contact with his Sunday school teacher well before they got to the open doorway. When she recognized him, she stood up behind her desk and smiled.

"My goodness, it's Jackie Malone, come in here," she said, stepping from behind her desk and extending both arms. She gave Jackie a big hug then turned to Tommy and extended her hand toward him, which startled him momentarily. Tommy looked over at Jackie with a confused expression on his face before offering his hand to the smiling blond standing before him.

"And your name is?" Mae smiled, still shaking Tommy's hand.

"Tom, Tommy, Tommy Redden."

"So you're a friend of Jackie's?"

"Yes, Mam." Tommy shrugged, withdrawing his hand from Mae's grasp.

"How come Tommy has never come to Sunday school with you, Jackie? Is he new to the neighborhood or something?" asked Mrs. Finley.

"No, Mam, he's been a friend for a long time, it's just that he's Catholic," explained Jackie.

"Oh, I see," said the Sunday school teacher.

"He goes to OLPH over in East Ridge. They don't have a car, they have some friends who come and take them to Mass," Jackie added.

Tommy seemed content to let Jackie do all the talking; discussing church was something that he was uncomfortable with since he was the only kid in the neighborhood that happened to be Catholic.

"Well what brings you guys here, did you just come for a visit or is there something I can help you with?"

"You said once in Sunday school that if any of us were to come downtown, to stop by and see you; well here we are, I guess." Jackie smiled, looking around the well-kept office.

"Well I must say, I'm pleasantly surprised, I never expected any of you to ever come and see me."

"Ask her about the money," said Tommy, still standing by the open doorway.

"I'm sorry, Tommy, it is Tommy, isn't it? Come on in and have a seat" She pointed to one of the chairs that sat facing her desk.

"That's OK, Mam; I'll just stand here if that's all right."

"Sure it's all right but both of you can sit down if you like. Now what is this about the money; we do have a lot of it around here, you know?"

"We wanted to ask you about this twenty that we found near the bus stop; just wanted to make sure it was OK before we tried to spend it," Jackie said, pulling the now crumpled twenty-dollar bill from his front pocket.

"Well let me take a look," said Mae, reaching for the twenty that Jackie was holding in both hands.

"Well I'll be; it was printed in 1944, the war was still going on then. But it's in extremely good condition to be that old. The life of currency in circulation is about two years; this one definitely has been out of circulation for a while."

After studying the bill for a few seconds, Mae put the twenty to her nose. Jackie and Tommy glanced at each other as the head teller sniffed the money as if it were a fresh cut rose. She looked up at the two boys, and without saying a word, she turned and walked behind her desk and produced a magnifying glass from the top drawer of her desk. She sat down in her chair and studied the bill more closely. She picked the bill up, turned it over, and did the same with the other side.

"It's not counterfeit, but it has a funny smell, my guess is that somebody has had it stowed away for a long time, probably in a drawer near mothballs or something. Excuse me for a minute, you boys have a seat. I'm going down the hall for a minute; I'm going to do a check on this serial number."

"What kind of check?" Jackie asked, staring at the seams in the back of Mae's hose as she stepped from behind her desk and walked toward the open door.

"It may be on the lost or stolen list; it'll only take a couple of minutes, I'll be right back," Mae said over her shoulder, as she turned to the right after leaving her office.

Tommy had taken a seat beside the one Jackie now occupied. They sat facing a large walnut desk. Behind the desk hung a watercolor painting of Civil War era Chattanooga with Lookout Mountain looming in the background.

"What do you think?" asked Tommy.

"Who knows, but we'll know in a minute though."

They both sat quietly as each boy envisioned the possible outcome of Mae's investigation.

"What will we do if it's been reported stolen or missing? How in the world are we going to turn it in now?" muttered Tommy.

"Damn, Tommy, don't be so pessimistic. If it has, we'll think of something, damn."

It seemed forever but Mae finally returned, rounded the corner of her desk, eased down in the plush chair, laid the twenty down in front of her and then finally smiled.

"It looks like you boys have a little shopping to do, there's no trace of this money on any of the hot lists. It's old money but in excellent condition; you know how the story goes, don't you?" Mrs. Finley smiled.

"What's that?" they both asked at the same time.

"Finders keepers, loser's weepers."

Jackie thanked his Sunday school teacher for checking out the twenty for them. Both boys tried to hide their giddiness at finding out that the money wasn't counterfeit and that it wasn't on a stolen list or something. The Sunday school teacher picked up the twenty-dollar bill and handed it across the desk to Jackie. He grinned and looked over at Tommy, who was now standing, and running his hand through his flattop that had began to dampen from the sweat popping out from his scalp.

"Tell Joyce I said hi," Jackie said as he folded the twenty and shoved it into his front pocket.

"I sure will; she likes you a lot, you know."

"She does?"

"You know she does; otherwise she wouldn't sit with you in church every Sunday. Why don't you bring your friend to church with you sometime, we won't hold it against him because he's

Catholic," Mae said, smiling.

"I'll talk to him about it," replied Jackie as he eased closer to the open doorway.

Jackie half-waved at Mae as he ducked out the door and hurried to catch up with Tommy, who had almost reached the entrance at the other end of the bank lobby.

"Let's go down to Sears," Tommy said excitedly as Jackie caught up to him just in time for both of them to crowd into the same compartment of the revolving door.

****

Raymond Duke, a Korean War veteran who lost the sight of his right eye during the battle of the Chosin Reservoir in 1950, became the East Ridge Chief of Police after winning a bitter battle to keep his job despite refusing to stop wearing the black patch that covered his damaged right eye. The conflict had become personal when he would not drop the charges on the mayor's wife for drunk driving and assaulting a police officer. He had become well respected by his peers as well as the people in the community. He had won re-election by a landslide while the mayor was defeated soundly. Raymond Duke was known as a no-nonsense Chief, but he was fair.

"Come in," Chief Duke said quietly as he stood up, partially blocking the view of the large Marine Corps Seal that hung behind his desk. "How can I help you?"

"My name is Farr, Luther Farr, and I'm here to find out what…"

"I know who you are, Mr. Farr; you've been down here before, now have a seat," the Chief said, easing himself down in the leather chair behind his desk.

Luther Farr was an older version of Sonny, with a few exceptions; he lacked the ducktails but wore his hair in a flattop like his son. Luther was about the same size as his son, but sported an imposing beer belly, which he tried unsuccessfully to suck in as he entered the room.

"I'm here to find out what you're going to do about that boy over in Georgia that attacked my boy. He may lose one of his balls; the little bastard hit him with a damn golf club, he still won't go out of the house."

"Watch your language, Mr. Farr, I'm not going to sit here and listen to that kind of talk. Do you understand?"

"Yes sir, but…"

"We know about the incident with the golf club; the best that we can determine is that your boy, who is much larger, was about to beat up on the other kid."

"I don't care about…"

"Be quiet and let me finish," the Chief said, a hint of redness beginning to emerge from around his starched white collar. "Your boy has a reputation as a bully, and you know it. He likes to pick on boys smaller and younger than he is; and off the record, I'd call him a punk. Let me tell you something, Mr. Farr; we believe he's the one who sucker punched that old man over on Stateline road. That old man was a constable there in Georgia; he didn't get paid for what he did, which was to keep a watch on the neighborhood. You should be thankful we can't come up with a witness; if we could, I guarantee you I'd send him off for a while."

Luther squirmed around in his chair for a few seconds as he struggled to come up with a response.

"I guess I'll have to get me a lawyer then," said Tush's father. "I see you're not going to do anything about this."

"That might be a good idea," said the Chief indifferently, "not to sue somebody, but to keep that boy out of jail if he keeps headed in the direction that he's going."

Luther Farr had had enough; he stood up and sucked in his

belly, avoiding eye contact with the chief as he shuffled toward the door.

"Oh, Mr. Farr!"

"Yes," Luther said, looking over his shoulder at the police chief with the ominous black patch over his right eye.

"Tell that boy of yours that I have a friend that lost one of his nuts in the war; he's doing just fine with one."

Tush's father didn't answer; he just jerked the door open and stepped into the hallway.

Chief Duke followed Luther out the door and walked three doors down the hall to the City Judge's office. The judge had become a close friend of Duke's after he had supported him with his fight with the former mayor. Judge Hathaway was a former Marine himself and shared the same viewpoint as the chief on law enforcement.

"Good afternoon, Chief," Hathaway said over the top of his half-glasses as Duke entered the room. "You been keeping an eye out on this place while I've been on vacation?" joked the judge.

"You wish you could wear a patch, don't you, Judge? I know you do; what a pun."

"I wish I could wear one on both eyes sometimes; how you been doing?"

"Fine, fine; hey let me ask you something."

"Go for it. Chief."

"Judge, we have a bully here in East Ridge and he's been harassing some of the kids around here and we're almost sure he's the one that put that old man in the hospital over in Georgia."

"Yeah I heard about that, it's a damn shame."

"Well, Judge, he jumped on a kid the other day, and the boy who, was much smaller than him, hit him in the nuts with a golf club before he could get to him. It hurt him pretty bad, but I think he'll be all right. His father was just in here and he's pushing me to go after the kid that did it. I think the bully deserved it; I'm not sure what I should do."

"My advice is to do what you're doing, which is nothing. I don't think it's a criminal case; boys are going to get into fights. You can't arrest every teenager in town that gets into a fight, can you?"

"I know, I feel the same way, but he did use a weapon."

"You do have a right to protect yourself, especially if the aggressor is older and bigger than you," the judge said, leaning back in his chair. "The only problem, Raymond, is that the kid's father may want to bring a civil case against the boy's parents. Do you know if they have any money?"

"No, I don't thank so; they live over in Rankin Park, that's not exactly a rich neighborhood."

"I wouldn't worry about it, Chief, I don't think many lawyers would take it after they discover who the boy is that's doing the suing and the fact that the family they're going after doesn't have much. I know I wouldn't take it," said the judge, taking off his half-glasses and cleaning them with his necktie.

The police chief pulled the black eye patch away from his bad eye just far enough to run his index finger behind it so he could massage the damaged eye socket. It only took a couple of seconds and seemed to relieve some of the tension that had built up from the verbal exchange with Luther Farr.

"Well, I just wanted to get your opinion on what to do. I have a bad feeling about that Farr boy; I think he's a bad egg and he's had it coming. I believe I'll do like you said; just wait and see what happens."

The chief started to say something else when a heavyset policewoman with a trace of a mustache gave a courtesy knock on the door and stepped inside.

"Chief, you have someone in your office to see you; I think

there's a fight or something over at the freeway construction. I think one of our deputies is in the middle of it."

"Catch you later, Judge." The police chief nodded as he followed the hefty policewoman out the door.

****

The sun was already going down behind Lookout Mountain when Jackie and Tommy stepped off the bus in front of the Pines Beer Joint across from Harold's station. The days were getting shorter as the summer raced toward autumn. You could try to ignore it, but it was always in the peripheral of the mind; back to school was not far away.

After leaving the bank, both boys were elated to such a point that they decided to skip sitting on the motorcycle at Sears. Jackie suggested that they walk the four blocks up to the University of Chattanooga where the city library was located. Jackie explained to Tommy that it was nice to know that the money was legit and no one was looking for it; at least not the banks. He had a harder time convincing Tommy that they had to make an attempt to find out who put two hundred and fifty thousand dollars into an Army duffel bag and buried it.

The library stored copies on microfiche of the *Chattanooga News Free Press* that went back for years. The library had the microfiche machines to view a full year's worth of newspapers at a time.

Less than a year earlier, Jackie had gone with a friend to the library to look up a picture in the sports page of the 1952 Lookouts when they had won the Southern Association pennant. After the final game that clinched the pennant, a photograph was taken in the locker room of the celebration. One of the players was standing in the group holding a bottle of champagne above his teammates' head; what he didn't realize was that the towel that he was holding didn't cover his lower torso. Somehow, the newspaper editor missed it and the paper was published; sure enough there he stood smiling like the Cheshire cat, with everything he had swinging in the wind. His mother had to be proud of him.

Since the bank had no record of the serial number on the twenty as being missing or stolen, Jackie thought they would research the war years; after all, the money was printed in the forties. The boys were led to a machine and were given instructions on how to use it. Jackie took 1941 and 1942, Tommy 1943 and 1944. What they did was scan the headlines and front pages to see if an incident had taken place that involved that kind of money. Tommy would come over to Jackie's machine every time he came across something that needed further investigation. An armored car heist in New Jersey in August of 1943, a kidnapping in Tampa Florida of the same year where a ransom of a quarter million was asked. Nothing that took place during those years could be remotely linked to anything in the Chattanooga area. They agreed to research 1945 together; they decided to stop searching after June of 1945. It was time to catch the bus back to East Ridge; it was getting late. Not one thing could be found that they could link to the duffel bag full of cash they had hidden in their cave down by the creek behind Tommy's house. If they had continued until August 4th, they would have come across a headline that read: "**INDIANA BANK ROBBER CAUGHT IN EAST RIDGE** = SECOND SUSPECT EXCAPES = QUARTER MILLION IN CASH STILL MISSING.

"Let's stop in at Harold's for a few minutes," said Tommy, running along beside Jackie as they crossed the four-lane highway.

"It's getting late Tommy; we need to do some talking. We have to decide what we're going to do. I mean we really have to decide if we're going to keep that money or not."

"OK, OK, but just let me take a leak, I don't think I can make it to the bridge," replied Tommy, veering off in the direction of the service station.

Jackie leaned against the office door watching Harold lift the hood on a Studebaker that had just pulled in. He had made the comment many times, "You can't tell if it's coming or going; Studebakers have to be the ugliest cars on the road."

"Come on, let's go." Tommy rounded the corner from the restroom still tugging at his zipper.

Both boys waved at Harold, who was holding a can of motor oil upright as it drained into the engine of the Studebaker. Tommy stomped down on the small rubber hose that triggered the bell inside the station when a car pulled into the gas pumps. Harold looked up and shook his head as Tommy pointed at Jackie, who grinned at Harold and began to shake his head also.

"I say we keep it," Tommy said quietly, as they started walking the four blocks home.

"I kind of figured you would say that," Jackie mumbled. "I doubt if we'll ever find out how it got where we found it; I still believe it may have belonged to a soldier who got killed in the war."

"Can't we just spend a little at a time like we did today," asked Tommy, fumbling with the gold-plated rosary necklace he had purchased at Liggett's Drugstore.

"That necklace cost you ten dollars; do you know how long it would take us to spend two hundred and fifty thousand dollars ten dollars at a time? I can't get it out of my head what Mrs. Finley said down at the bank."

"What was that, she said a lot?"

"Finders keepers, loser's weepers."

"It's not against the law to spend money that you find, is it, Jackie?"

"I don't think so; we tried to find out who it belongs to. It's the ethical part that we're dealing with here; we probably should turn it in, but like I said, it'll more than likely end up with a bunch of lawyers or something."

They walked along in silence, approaching the bridge across the little creek where Jackie had introduced the putter to Tush's nuts.

"Tommy, we may have to eventually turn the money over to the authorities, but before we do, I'd like to do something good with some of it."

"What do you mean, Jackie?"

"Well, your dad needs a car, and they need to build a room for me so I don't have to sleep in the same bedroom as Judy. It's not much money out of the humongous load of cash we have down in that cave, but it's a different story for our parents. It's a ton of money for them."

"Yeah I know, I've been thinking about that; wouldn't it be great to walk in and hand them a couple of thousand, and say, 'Look what I found, let's go buy a new car.'"

"That's the problem, Tommy; we've got to figure out some way to get them the money without just saying we found it. The minute the word gets out that we've found a bag of cash, especially the amount that we have, everybody is gonna try to claim it. I promise you."

"So we've agreed to keep it for now, what do we do next?" asked Tommy, looking over at his friend beside him; Jackie didn't answer, his mind was thousands of miles away.

****

Sonny Farr was sitting sideways in the front porch swing, a pillow behind his back and another one tucked under his knees. He had just opened a copy of a pro wrestling magazine that he had pulled from the stack that piled up beside the swing. The faint smell of eucalyptus drifted with the slight early evening breeze; no doubt from the medication he was using to soothe his still swollen privates.

Sonny didn't acknowledge the presence of his father until he had reached the top step of the front porch.

"Hey," said Sonny, looking over the top of the magazine.

Luther didn't answer; he walked past his son, pulled open the screen door and went inside. Sonny flinched as the screen door slammed against the door facing, resembling the sound made by a book hitting the floor in a quiet library. Luther had made no effort to ease the door shut; he turned it loose from its full open position; the strong spring did the rest of the work.

"What's with him," Sonny wondered, turning the page on the magazine.

Luther returned in less than a minute carrying a can of Pabst Blue Ribbon. He stepped out onto the front porch, turned the can of Pabst up and gulped down half the can. He wiped his mouth with the back of his hand and sat down in a wooden rocker across from his son.

"You're still laying around nursing them balls; you've turned into a big crybaby over this, I think it' about time you got over it," Luther said, taking another pull on the can of Pabst.

"Would you like to look, Daddy, one of 'em is still almost black, the doctor said to take it easy, otherwise I might lose it."

"He said to take it easy, he didn't say you had to sit on your ass twenty-four hours a day. Where did all your friends go? I haven't seen any of them around here since this happened?"

Sonny didn't answer, he only shrugged his shoulders.

"Where's Billy?"

"Who?"

"You know who; Billy Fore, or whatever his name is. That freckle-faced scarecrow that always has his head up your ass.

Don't act like you don't know who I'm talking about."

Sonny tossed the magazine down on the floor, removed the pillow from under his knees, and sat up straight in the swing.

"Why don't you get off my back, Dad; I'm hurt real bad down here," Sonny said, pointing at his groin.

"How big of an ole boy was it that attacked you with that golf club, son?" Luther finished the can of beer and sat the empty down on the floor beside his chair.

"I don't know he was a pretty good size; big enough to scare Billy. He took off and I haven't seen him since."

Luther mumbled something under his breath, got up, and went back into the house. It took less than thirty seconds before he returned with another Pabst. He sat back down in the rocker, punched two holes in the top of his beer and slid the opener into his shirt pocket.

"I had a talk with the police chief today, son."

"You did; is he gonna arrest the little fart that did this to me?"

"I noticed you said little; why did you refer to him as little?"

Sonny didn't answer; he just grimaced as he shifted his position in the porch swing.

"After talking to the chief, I have this feeling that what you're telling me about what happened might not be exactly the way it went down. In fact, I'm beginning to wonder if maybe you are a bully and that you go around picking on boys smaller than you. It sounds to me like somebody finally stood up to you."

Sonny didn't respond; he started to say something, but decided to just grunt instead.

Luther took a long sip on his beer and set the can down on the arm of the rocking chair.

"I'll tell you what I'm going to do, Sonny. I'm gonna find out where that constable fellow lives; the chief thinks you may have been the one who sucker punched him and put him in the hospital. You and I are going to pay him a visit; I'm going to find out if it was you that did that to him. If I find out that it was you, I'm turning your ass in. If it wasn't, then I'm gonna get us a lawyer. Somebody's getting their butt sued."

Sonny the Tush sighed, leaned back in the swing, and looked up at the ceiling. "Can't this wait till I get well?" The Tush frowned.

Luther raised himself up out of the rocker, finished off the Pabst, and looked down at his son.

"How about getting a haircut, get those ducktails or whatever they are cut off. They make you look like a queer."

****

After returning home from the trip downtown, Jackie reflected on the day while he watched TV with his mother. His dad had gone to bed before the sun had set, as he did quite often. He tried hard to concentrate on the TV and carry on a conversation with his mother, but his mind kept returning to the money and what to do with it.

"You won't be watching much TV next week," his mother said.

"How come?"

"The convention starts; all three channels."

"Crap," Jackie said, not really caring one way or the other.

After a while, he gave up and went outside, sat down on the back porch steps and listened to the sounds made by the bullfrogs and crickets. It was the dog days of summer, and the nights had begun to get a little cooler; it wasn't cold but just something in the air that was different.

He had something on his mind that he had just seen on TV. "Yeah, yeah," he mumbled to himself, "that's it."

The morning came and Jackie lay staring up at the ceiling, wondering if he had even been to sleep or had he been dreaming that he was awake. He had visualized his plan, trying to come up with reasons as to why it wouldn't work. Yes, he knew a way to access the money without revealing the source, and helping others to boot. He could hardly wait to tell Tommy, although he knew that he would come up with a thousand reasons why it wouldn't work.

****

"What?"

"The millionaire?"

"But we don't have a million dollars," protested Tommy, almost laughing.

"I know that, you asshole, we'll give away a thousand or two at a time; we won't make anybody millionaires, but a thousand dollars or two sure would make a few people that I know pretty happy."

"Oh I see, you mean send money to ourselves, tell people it came from an anonymous person or something."

"You've seen the television show; John Beresford Tipton, who's never seen, sends his agent, Michael Anthony, out to give away a million dollars tax free to random people. The only requirement is that they don't tell anyone where they got it."

"Well who's gonna be our Michael Anthony?" asked Tommy. "Maybe we can hire Bud Higgins or somebody."

"No, I have a different plan; I have someone else in mind."

"Do you mind if I ask who?" Tommy grinned.

"Uncle Sam."

"Uncle Sam?"

"The United States Post Office."

Tommy ran his hand through his flattop twice before saying anything.

"You mean just put the money in the mail and send it to random people."

"Not completely random, we'll send some to people who we know could use it, some who deserve it, and to some who probably don't."

"I'm sure we're to be one of the ones who deserve it," Tommy mumbled.

Jackie kept quiet for a few seconds to let Tommy digest what he had proposed to him.

"Are we gonna give it all away?" probed Tommy calmly.

"Come on, Tommy, what I propose to do is divide up the money; each of us take a hundred thousand and hide it somewhere. We'll give away and spend the remaining fifty grand or so. It's not just my money, it's ours, that is right now, but that could change at any time. This is just something to think about, it's up to you; if you have a better idea let's hear it."

"No, no, I like it; the more I think about it, the more I like it. I'm sure we have a lot of details to iron out though."

Jackie went on to explain to Tommy more about what he had in mind.

"Before we send any money to ourselves, I think we should start with someone else; kind of see what the reaction will be. Instead of telling the person who's getting the money not to tell anyone; we put a note in with the money to let them know it's OK to say where it came from. After all, they wouldn't have a clue as to who sent them the money. I'm sure the newspapers would run with it, you know make some kind of human-interest story about it. Everyone would be wondering if they might be next; it'll be fun watching people run to the mailbox every day to see if it was their lucky day."

Tommy gazed into space trying to come up with a glitch in the plan that his friend had proposed.

"Can't the Post Office find out who mailed it?" enquired

Tommy.

"How are they going to find out? All the mail that is delivered in this area, even here in North Georgia is processed in the downtown Chattanooga Post Office. Thousands of letters go through there every day; how are they going to find out what collection box it was dropped into?"

"Can't they tell from the return address or something?" asked Tommy, not quite sure how to phrase his question.

"Sure they could, dummy, but we're not going to put one of our addresses on the envelope for crying out loud."

"So what do we do for a return address; just not put one?"

"I've given that some thought; if the letter couldn't be delivered for some reason, it would end up in a dead letter bin somewhere. It may lay there forever before someone investigated it to see what was inside."

"What do we do then?" Tommy asked.

"We get the address of some charity like the Salvation Army or a church maybe; if it is returned to them, I'm sure they'll put it to good use."

Jackie jumped down from the bottom limb of the sycamore tree he and Tommy had been perched in.

"What now?" Tommy asked, exiting the tree limb right behind Jackie.

"Let's go see if we can talk Leonard Bean out of those two-fifty caliber canisters his dad brought back from the war. They'll be perfect to put the money in. I think we should hide the canisters in the cave somewhere, just in case somebody stumbles across the entrance, you never know," said Jackie.

"I think that's a good idea too; those ammo cans; will water get in them if we bury them?"

"No, they have a rubber seal, they'll be perfect. The trick is to get Leonard to turn loose of 'em."

"He will if a few bucks are involved and I think I know

where we can come up with a few bucks or so, don't you?" answered Tommy, grinning.

Leonard Bean, who obviously had some oriental blood in his family tree, greeted the two boys outside his bedroom window with a few choice four letter words. It was almost noon and he was still in bed. Jackie liked Leonard, but always considered him to be lazy. It seemed nearly every time he talked to him, it was through his bedroom window. Tommy never said it to his face, but referred him as Eskimo, the nickname didn't stick, but everybody knew who he was talking about.

"Those two-fifty caliber ammo cans you have; how much you take for them?" asked Jackie, shrugging off the remark Leonard had made about his mother.

"Five dollars, I'll take five dollars for both of 'em," Leonard answered, lying back down on his bed, confident that they didn't have five dollars between them.

"Sold," Jackie said calmly, holding the five-spot up to the open window.

Leonard rose up in his bed, squinting at the five-dollar bill. "Wait a minute," frowned Leonard.

Jackie and Tommy grinned at each other at the sound of Leonard's heels hitting the hardwood floor of his bedroom.

"Give me that five-spot," said Leonard, pushing one of the olive drab ammo cans through the half-open window. Jackie handed up the money as Leonard handed the other can through the window.

"It's a done deal," shouted Leonard, "now you punks get the hell out of here, I have things to do."

"Sure," said Jackie under his breath, "like sleep."

Jackie handed Tommy one of the ammo cans, turned and started walking away from the open bedroom window.

"Let's get up to the cave," he said. "We've got a lot to do."

5

There are very few people who have not fantasized about finding a bag full of money, or being the recipient of a gift from some long-lost rich uncle. It does happen, but to an extremely small number of people. The situation that Jackie and Tommy now found themselves in was a moral dilemma as well as an ethical one. What would most people do? In most cases, a person would try to justify, at least in their mind, a reason for keeping the treasure that they were lucky enough to find. In some cases, keeping it would never be a consideration. In their mind, the reward would come from knowing that they were doing the right thing by turning it over to the authorities. Jackie and Tommy were convinced that they had done everything they could to find the person who buried the duffel bag full of money. In Jackie's mind, why should he turn the money over to strangers who had no more of a clue as to who the money belonged to than they did?

As they returned to the entrance to the cave, Jackie pointed out to Tommy how the vegetation had matured since the recent rains. The grass had grown taller, especially close to the large flat rock that covered the opening to the mineshaft. Discovering the entrance would be almost impossible without actually being there when the flat rock was slid away from the hole in the hillside.

Everything was just as they had left it; the duffel bag full of money still hung from the nail holding up Jackie's hammock. After getting the lanterns lit and doing a little house-keeping, it was time to get down to business. They divided the money into three stacks; a hundred thousand went into each of the ammo canisters and the remainder went back into the duffel bag.

"We've got to bring something else to put the cash in that we're going to be working out of," Jackie said, hanging the duffel bag back onto the nail.

"What are you going to do with your can?" Tommy asked quietly.

"I think I'll go back into this shaft, find a good spot and dig a hole in the side of the wall just big enough to hold the canister. I'll find me a rock just the right size to fit in front of it. You can bet your ass nobody will ever find it there. Where are you gonna put yours?"

"I've been thinking; have you thought about taking it home, maybe hiding it in the attic or something?"

"I don't think that's a very good idea, Tommy. I think we should keep it down here; we may want to move it later, but not right now. We've got to have a place to operate from and so far, this place has served us well."

"Yeah, I guess you're right; I think I'll put mine in one of those ore carts. I saw a tool compartment on one of 'em; just the right size to hold an ammo canister."

After spending the remainder of the afternoon securing their individual treasures, Tommy suddenly realized that they had not eaten lunch.

"I don't know what time it is, but my stomach says it's getting close to suppertime. Hear my guts growling?" asked Tommy, rubbing his belly.

"I don't hear 'em, but I knew you would bring it up pretty soon." Jackie smiled. "Let's call it a day."

****

The next morning, Jackie presented Tommy with a list of things that they needed to do.

1. Get some money from the cave.
2. Go to the store.
3. Buy envelopes, stamps, and writing paper.
4. Decide on who will be the first lucky recipient.
5. Decide on how much money to send.
6. Get phonebook; research mailing address.
7. Compose letter to recipient.

"Can you think of anything else?" asked Jackie.

"Let me think while we're on the way to the cave," replied Tommy.

"Where's Linda? I haven't seen her around in a while."

"Oh she's getting ready to go back to school. I don't know what excites her most, school and the boys, or cars."

"I'll bet she'll go bananas when your folks receive their "Lucky Day" money. It's for sure boys will be on the back burner for a while."

"Do you have anybody in mind as to who will be our first "Lucky Day Person?" asked Tommy, swinging his leg over the sagging wire fence separating his backyard from Willingham's cow pasture.

"I don't know; what about Mr. Robinson, the old man the Tush sucker punched?"

"I was thinking about him too; they say he still can't see very well. Yeah, let's make him the first one."

"OK, it's settled, the constable is about to have a lucky day."

As they approached the creek, several kids were standing in silence watching something that was taking place on the other side of the creek.

"What are they looking at?" Tommy asked, straining to see what was going on behind of a patch of bamboo that was obstructing their view.

"It must be something…"

"Well, hell," muttered Jackie, catching up to Tommy, who had hurried ahead of him so he could observe what was happening behind the bamboo thicket.

An old white-faced bull had singled out one of the cows and was doing his best to mount her. Tommy and Jackie had been witnesses to this several times, but it was obvious that this was a first for the young audience that stood in silence along the creek bank.

"Come on, Tommy; let's get out of here; we know how this is gonna turn out."

Jackie had to tug pretty hard on Tommy's sleeve to break his concentration and get him pointed in the direction of their cave entrance.

After going to the cave and getting the money to put into the envelope, and twenty dollars to buy the things that they needed; Tommy talked Jackie into getting a twenty-dollar bill each. He reasoned that a twenty wouldn't cause anybody to get suspicious. He also reminded him that they both had a hundred grand stashed back in their cave in those ammo boxes, and that a little spending money wouldn't have an impact on their total stash. Jackie had no reason to argue; he could use a few bucks himself. It was agreed that a thousand dollars would be the amount of the first gift, so they pulled fifty twenty-dollar bills from the already open two-thousand-dollar bundle.

After replacing the cash back into the duffel bag, Jackie commented on the need to find another container to store the remaining money. The currency had become damp while hanging in the old canvass bag; they needed something more airtight.

"I'll look around," said Tommy, as he ascended the rope ladder. "It would be nice if we had another one of those ammunition canisters."

It was almost lunchtime before they reached Harold's station, where Tommy had to take a leak. He could not pass by Harold's with going to the bathroom.

"Hey, Jackie," shouted Harold, as he lowered his grease gun from the underside of the chassis of a nineteen fifty-three Desoto.

"What?"

Harold stepped from behind the twelve-inch wide cylinder that supported the grease rack and Desoto that was perched above it.

"I have a stack of magazines three feet high in the back room. Almost a half-year of Playboys is in there. If you guys aren't going to come and get them; I'm going to give them to somebody else or throw them away."

"Hold on to 'em, Harold, we'll get 'em; we just been kind of busy lately," replied Jackie, observing the Double Cola man feed quarters into the pinball machine.

"I'll say you have; I heard about you wearing out that Farr boy's nuts with that golf club. Come to think of it; he's not been around either." Harold grinned at the Double Cola man who had no idea as to what Harold had just said. He was concentrated on working the chrome ball to the bottom of the machine and into the number twenty-three slot.

Jackie and Tommy walked the three blocks down Highway 41 to the drugstore, where they purchased a box of business size envelopes and five three cent postage stamps from the machine. Tommy insisted that he had plenty of writing paper at home. "Why spend money if you don't need to?" he asked? He may not have needed writing paper, but he did need to purchase two plastic model cars, a 1955 Chevrolet and a 1927 Coca Cola delivery truck, complete with two tubes of glue. In addition to the two model cars, he also bought a jar of *Butch Crew Cut Wax*, two *Car and Driver* magazines and a jumbo bag of Lay's potato chips.

Jackie bought a box of chocolate covered cherries for his mother; he knew she loved them, but would never waste money on them for herself.

Before leaving the drugstore, they pulled “far away” for a coke from the case of empty bottles sitting beside the coke machine by the door. Jackie won as usual; this time his bottle was from New York City, Tommy’s was from Chattanooga.

“How do you do that, I want to know, how do you do it?” mumbled Tommy, dropping a quarter into the machine that sat in the corner next to the entrance to the store.

“Just lucky, just lucky.” Jackie grinned, placing the bottle cap into the opener on the front of the coke machine.

“You must be cheating somehow,” said Tommy as they walked out into the afternoon sun in front of the drugstore. “You gotta be, I never win, never.”

****

Don Robinson was six feet four inches tall and weighed one hundred and forty-five pounds. He was fifty-two years old and what hair he had left was the color of a copper penny. He had high cheekbones and a thin pointed nose.

Don and his wife lived in the house trailer that was used by Mr. Rankin during the construction of the Rankin Park development right after the war. It sat on the Georgia side of Stateline Road, almost directly across from Louie’s store.

Don was classified as 4-F during the war; he tried to enlist twice but each time he was turned down. When he was five years old, he was kicked in the leg by a horse, destroying his right knee. He could walk, but the limp caused by the damaged knee was unacceptable to the military. Don had desperately wanted to do his part in the war effort, but the knee denied him that opportunity. Through the help of a local politician, he was allowed to join the Civil Air Patrol, a civilian organization that was organized by the Army Air Corps during the war to watch the skies for enemy aircraft.

After the war ended, he tried to get into law enforcement, but the bum knee also kept him from perusing that. It was hard for Don to hold down a job due to his limited mobility. His wife worked in a hosiery mill in Chattanooga while Jim did odd jobs in the neighborhood. The county sheriff's department awarded Don the honorary title of Constable. He went through the process of being sworn in at the courthouse and was charged with keeping an eye on the rapidly growing community that bordered the Tennessee state line. The title gave Don a sense of worth; something he had always wanted. He and his wife struggled to get by; the constable job was not a paying position and finding something that he could do wasn't easy due to his knee. He spent a lot of time keeping an eye on what was happening in the community. His eyes and ears were valuable to the sheriff, who struggled to keep a police presence in the north end of the county because of his tight budget. He had thwarted several burglary attempts, reported suspicious cars in the neighborhood, as well as breaking up fights between teenagers. Things were going pretty well for Don until one day he woke up on the floor beside the cold drink box at Louie's store. He had a splitting headache and double vision. Don had no recollection of the incident, but was told that a big blond-headed boy had hit him as he was attempting to quell a shoving match between two high school boys. Several people saw it happen, but no one could be absolutely positive who the boy was that had hit him.

It was at least an hour before Don's wife was due to get home from work. The ten-minute walk from the bus stop three blocks away had turned into fifteen, and now it was almost twenty. After eight hours standing on the concrete floor of the sock mill, getting from the bus stop to the house had become more and more difficult. Don had just returned from his backyard after feeding his Blue-tick hound when the postman pulled up to his mailbox.

"Afternoon," said Don, watching the two mail trucks pull slowly away.

It was annoying for Don. He knew only one truck was actually there, but with his double vision, it appeared to be two; one right behind the other.

After limping back into the house, Don tossed the mail onto the kitchen table. He had long ago stopped trying to read; the glasses they had given him helped a little, but the dizziness afterwards was not worth the trouble.

It was late summer but it was still hot. Don popped the cap from a Pepsi and sat down at the table to wait for his wife to return from work. He picked up the mail that he had brought in from the mailbox. *It's bad enough to get bills;* he smiled to himself, *but to get two of everything, that's just not fair.* He thumbed through the envelopes, tossing them back onto the table one by one. It was easy to distinguish between the bills and other correspondence, most of the bills had little windows in the front with his name and address typed on the paper inside.

"What's this?" he mumbled, reaching inside the bib of his overalls for his glasses.

It took a minute for him to adjust the glasses on his thin nose. It took another minute for him to get focused on the handwritten envelope that he held six inches in front of his face.

"This is getting old," Don stammered, pulling the glasses off and laying them down on the table beside the other mail.

It was easier to just close one eye; it would just take a second to see what was inside the slightly bulging handwritten envelope that was addressed to him. He flipped open his pocketknife, slipping the blade under the tightly sealed flap of the business envelope. With one eye closed, Don reached one hand inside the envelope and slowly removed a one-page, handwritten note wrapped around a quarter inch stack of almost un-circulated twenty dollar bills.

"Holy mother of Jesus," whispered Don, laying the note down and fanning the twenties out like a deck of playing cards.

He examined the bills with one eye and then the other, he put his glasses back on and counted the twenties one by one onto the kitchen table.

"Fifty! Hell, that's a thousand dollars. Where the crap did this come from?"

He grabbed the note that was wrapped around the money, closing one eye as he squinted trying to read it.

DEAR MR. ROBINSON
THIS IS YOUR LUCKY DAY. YES THE MONEY IS REAL, AND YES IT IS YOURS TO SPEND ANY WAY YOU WISH. THE BENEFACTOR OF THIS GIFT WISHES TO REMAIN ANONYMOUS, BUT FEEL FREE TO DISCLOSE TO ANYONE THE MEANS IN WHICH YOU RECEIVED IT.HAVE FUN!

Don placed the money along with the note back into the envelope. He took a drink from the Pepsi and leaned back in his chair. Don tried in vain to will the two pictures of the "Lord's Supper" that hung on the wall at the other end of the table to merge into one. After a few minutes of reflecting on the letter and the money, he closed his eyes and waited for his wife to return.

"Lucky day," he whispered.

****

After sending the thousand-dollar gift to Don Robinson, they mailed money to two other lucky recipients. It took Jackie a long time to convince Tommy that they needed to spread the gifts out into other parts of the city. He explained that the broader the area, the harder it would be to pinpoint where the sender was located. He reminded Tommy that it was getting close for one of them to be on the receiving end of a lucky day letter. After sending a gift to a policeman in North Chattanooga, and a nurse in nearby Flintstone, Georgia, both of which were people that neither Jackie nor Tommy knew personally, the news finally hit the newspapers.

CHATTANOOGA POLICEMAN RECEIVES
MYSTERIOUS GIFT IN THE MAIL.

Chattanooga policeman Gene Jefferies told reporters today that he and his wife were shocked yesterday when they received an envelope in the mail containing fifteen hundred dollars in cash. Jefferies said the envelope had a handwritten note saying it was his lucky day, and to use the money for whatever he wished. Bank officials checked out the currency; disclosing that while the bills were printed in the forties, they were in almost new condition. Patrolman Jefferies said he would like to thank whoever sent the cash. He says he'll put it to good use.

Jackie had a grin on his face as he approached Tommy in the middle of the street in front of his house.

"It's in the paper," Jackie said, withdrawing a copy of the *Chattanooga News Free Press* from his back pocket.

"What's it say?" Tommy asked, reaching for the newspaper.

"The policeman; he talked to a reporter; he wants to thank us." Jackie smiled.

"Man, this is fun," Tommy gasped, scanning the short article on the second page of the *Free Press*.

"Let's send a couple more before we send one to ourselves," Tommy said excitedly.

"Sounds fine to me; Lord knows we still got plenty. You got somebody in mind?"

Tommy considered the question, tugging on his lower lip as he stared at a puddle of melting tar in the middle of the street next to his foot.

Jackie gave his friend a light push on his shoulder, breaking his concentration.

"Let's get our asses out of the middle of the street; here comes a car. Why don't we walk up to Harold's, that'll give us something to do while we discuss it. Bud's sitting over there watching us; if we keep standing here, he'll be over here wanting to know what's going on."

"Yeah, you're right, come on," agreed Tommy.

Just as they started walking, Bud shouted at them from the steps of his front porch.

"What you little farts up to; looking for somebody's ass to whup?" Bud laughed.

"Don't even answer the fat ass," Jackie said, slapping Tommy's hand down that was about to shoot Bud a bird.

"You better keep a watch over your shoulder; I hear Sonny is still pretty pissed," Bud shouted again followed by an extended laughing session.

The pudgy antagonist finally gave up teasing the two boys, as he got up and walked back into his house, pulling at his shorts that had become wedged in his butt crack.

"I know one person that we won't be sending a lucky day letter to," Jackie said, smiling.

"You know I've been thinking we both know a bunch of people that we'd like to send a letter, and God knows, all of them could sure use it. You've told me several times that we have to send some to people other than the ones we know; otherwise somebody's going to put two and two together." Jackie reflected on what Tommy had just said for several seconds.

"OK, so what's your point?"

"Instead of just picking somebody out of the phonebook; maybe we should try to make sure it's somebody who would be deserving of it. Who knows, it's possible we could send it to a pure asshole; you know someone like Tush or something."

"Let's hear it, Tommy, you've got something on your mind; what is it? Jackie asked, reaching down to pick up an empty Camel cigarette pack.

"You remember the other day when we took the bus to town?"

"Sure, what about it?"

"You remember those signs on the bus, and how those colored people had to ride in the back and all?"

"I do."

"I think we might send a letter to couple of, you know, deserving colored folks, sometimes I just don't feel they are being treated right."

Jackie stopped walking, looked over at Tommy, and reached for his hand as if he were going to shake hands with him. Tommy extended his hand to Jackie with a puzzled look on his face. Without warning, Jackie swung down with his open left hand onto the topside of Tommy's forearm. The force of the impact was hard enough to pull Tommy's right hand from Jackie's grasp.

"Oooooo.... ooooooooooo," screamed Tommy, examining his forearm three inches above his wrist, which was already beginning to turn blood-red.

"What the crap is the matter with you?" Tommy scowled, as

tears formed in the corner of his eyes.

Jackie held up the empty Camel pack. "It's an S." He smiled, tossing the empty pack in the ditch beside the road.

"Damn, you didn't have to slap so hard."

"Quit whining, I think your idea of sending a letter to a colored person is a good one, I never thought of that. I don't know any though, do you?"

"Do you remember seeing on TV about that colored man who caught that little girl who was dropped from the second floor of an apartment house down in Highland Park? You know the house fire; they said if he hadn't caught her, it would have killed her. I heard it broke one of his arms and an ankle.

"Yeah, I remember that; the mother got burned up."

They had crossed the bridge over the creek and were almost to Harold's station, walking in silence when Jackie suddenly stopped and faced Tommy.

"Crap, have you got another Camel pack?" Tommy asked, rubbing his sore forearm.

"No, but I have an idea; let's send Harold a letter. He's been good to us; he's a hard worker and lives way over in Brainerd; he shouldn't raise any suspicion."

"That's it then, we find out who the colored guy is; send one to him and one to Harold." Tommy was beaming.

"That's right; and then you're next."

****

Jackie's parents had finished eating and were both settled in front of the TV to watch the fifteen minutes of local news that came on before the world news rounded out the thirty-minute evening newscast.

"Good evening, ladies and gentleman," the completely

bald news anchor said, staring hauntingly into the television camera.

> **"Excitement is growing as two more local residents have come forward expressing gratitude for the generous cash gift that they received in the mail from an anonymous sender. Judy Bramlett, an emergency room nurse from Erlanger hospital, and Donald Robinson, who lives across the state line in Catoosa County, are the most recent Lucky Day recipients. There are no clues as to who is mailing cash to apparently random people, or why. Each time, the money comes in a plain handwritten envelope with a return address of a local charity. Along with the cash, inside the envelope is a handwritten note informing the recipient that it's their lucky day and to spend the money any way they wish. The latest two envelopes contained a thousand dollars in twenties, although an earlier recipient claimed to have received one with fifteen hundred inside. It is impossible to trace the source of the mysterious gifts; once the envelope is put into the mail service it becomes mixed with thousands of other letters. One other side note though; all the lucky day letters were postmarked in the downtown Chattanooga Post Office.**
>
> **The news anchor looked over at his attractive co-host and smiled. "Who knows, we may be next."**

Jackie's mother took a sip from her iced tea, placing the dripping glass on top of an old copy of Field and Stream Magazine of Harvey's that was lying on the small coffee table.

"Isn't that something, we could sure use a Lucky Day, couldn't we, honey?"

"Horse shit; if there were only two people left in this town and someone was sending one of us an envelope full of cash, it would be the other guy," Harvey said, leaning over to spit a stream of Copenhagen juice into his spittoon.

"I know, but we sure could use it though."

****

Jackie and Tommy had walked the three blocks up Highway 41 to the postal collection box that stood in front of the drugstore. They had mailed a letter the previous day to Harold from a collection box ten blocks south on the same highway. Jackie was positive now that the letters were delivered the very next day after dropping them into the mail. The one that was mailed that morning was to John Rey, the Negro man who saved the five-year-old girl from certain death after her mother dropped her from the window of their burning bedroom. They hoped to be present when the postman delivered Harold's envelope to him. The letter was addressed to Harold's business address there at the Sinclair Station on the highway. The postman always stopped for a few minutes, took a leak, and talked baseball with Harold for a few minutes before continuing on his route. Tommy was sure he usually came by around eleven o'clock or so; but Tommy was always sure about everything.

As the two boys approached the station, it was quite evident that something was going on, and that Harold was not a happy camper. He and two other men were squatting down over something in front of one of the grease racks. Harold was cursing at the object that turned out to be a twelve-volt battery lying on a shop rag in front of them.

"If the son of a bitch ever comes by here again, his ass is mine; so help me I'll build a shoe shop up his phony ass," bellowed Harold.

"Calm down, it could have happened to anybody; hell you're only out twenty-five bucks for Christ's sake," grunted one of the men, standing up from his crouch in front of the battery.

"It's not so much the money; it's the thought of being had."

Jackie and Tommy skirted the action in front of the battery; easing up beside the Pepsi Cola man who was coming close to tilting the pinball machine.

"What's going on, Bony?" Tommy asked indifferently.

Everyone wondered if Bony was his real name, but that's what he had stenciled above the shirt pocket of his Pepsi Cola uniform. If it wasn't his name, it should have been; he stood over six feet tall and could stand under a clothes line without getting wet when it rained.

"It's a long story, but it's kinda funny too." The skinny Pepsi man smiled as he concentrated on the chrome ball bouncing around under the glass in front of him.

"The other day, old Dewey came by here; he's the scraggly gray-headed man who goes around selling his home-made hand soap to filling stations and garages. He stopped by here with a bunch of vials filled with chemicals that he claimed would bring dead batteries back to life. He demonstrated it to Harold with an old battery that he pulled from the trunk of his car. He let Harold put it on his tester to show him that it was truly a dead battery. Harold said he was sure that it was dead; said it wouldn't spark at all. He poured the different colored vials of liquid into the battery, put the caps back on and told Harold to give it a few minutes. Anyway, after a while the man wiped the post off real good and told Harold to hook it back up to his tester. Harold said the damn thing pegged out in the green; he even boosted off his old pickup with it.

"To make a long story short, Dewey sold Harold a batch of the colored liquid, loaded up the now good battery, and went on his way. Now this is where it gets funny; Harold was telling

Sidney over there about it. Sid started laughing so hard that he couldn't catch his breath; told Harold that he had been taken; he said the stuff was worthless, he said the same scam happened to a friend of his down in Ringgold. Harold wouldn't believe him and said that he would show him; he brought out an old battery that he had taken in a trade; he poured it full of the so-called chemicals, waited a few minutes, and put it on his tester. Well you can guess the results."

Sid went on to explain what the con artist had done. The old man had a battery with a lose post. He demonstrated that the battery was dead and after adding the chemicals, he wiped off the post with a shop rag. While he was wiping off the battery, he twisted the post back so it would make a good connection. When he hooked it back up to the tester, it showed it to be as hot as a firecracker.

"Harold often says that a sucker is born every minute; it just so happens to be him this time. You can bet old Dewey won't be back here for a while. Harold even threw the free sample of hand soap in the garbage can that he had given him. Boy is Harold pissed."

Jackie had been observing the traffic on the highway in front of the service station while listening to Bony spin the story about the magic battery restorer. Everyone but Harold had a good laugh and had gathered under the fifty-five Chevy perched on top of one of Harold's service racks. The discussion was to determine how to remove a piece of chain link fence that had become tightly wrapped around the drive shaft. Bony abandoned the pinball machine and headed to the restroom when the red, white, and blue mail truck wheeled into the parking lot and coasted to a stop by the front door, where Harold stood wiping his hands on his pants leg.

"Running a little late today, Herman; I guess it's true about what they say about you postmen. You always ring twice."

Harold stood patiently waiting for the mailman to sort through the bundle of mail he was holding.

Herman handed Harold a half-inch stack of letters and three magazines.

"Don't talk about us postmen; I've seen you looking down through the windshield when some gal drives in here in a skirt on or maybe a pair of shorts. It's not the mailman they need to watch out for; it's the damn service station man."

Harold didn't reply; his eyes were locked onto the handwritten envelope that was on top of the stack of mail that Herman had just handed him. He was aware of the lucky day gifts that folks had been getting around town. It was the hot topic of discussion he had been having with many of his customers, as well as reading about it in the newspaper and seeing it on the news.

"Could it be," he said to himself, "could this really be it?"

Jackie and Tommy struggled to keep still as they watched from the corner of the small service station lobby. Harold had tossed the magazines and other mail onto the cluttered desk and was in the process of examining the bulging business size envelope. At one point he even put it to his nose and took a whiff of the envelope as if it might have been a letter from his girlfriend back when he was in the army.

Herman had returned from the restroom and had to give Harold a tap on the shoulder to get him to move from the doorway that he was blocking.

"What's the matter, Harold, did you get a letter from some irate husband accusing you of trying to get a peek at his wife's tits while you were cleaning her windshield?"

Harold didn't answer, more than likely he never even heard Herman's question. The possibility of this being an envelope full of cash had made him unaware of anything going on around him.

"You OK, Harold?" Herman asked.

"Yeah, yeah, I'm OK; I think I just got one of those letters."

"One of what letters?"

"You know, the Lucky Day letters, the ones that are stuffed full of cash."

"Well, open the son of a bitch and let's see; what the crap you waiting for?"

"If one of you guys are pulling some kind of a joke; I'm kicking somebody's ass, this hasn't been a very good day for me anyway."

"For Christ's sake, Harold; will you open the bastard; I've got to finish this route sometime today, you know."

Jackie and Tommy had not said a word; they were leaning on the pinball machine anxiously watching Harold fool around with the envelope. The anticipation of seeing Harold's face when he opened the envelope got the best of Tommy. He walked from behind the pinball machine and picked up a screwdriver that was lying on the corner of Harold's desk, partially hidden under a copy of yesterday's *Free Press*.

"Try this," Tommy said, thrusting the screwdriver in front of Harold's face.

Harold slowly took the screwdriver from Tommy's hand and started to put the tip under the flap of the envelope, when he suddenly stopped, handing the screwdriver back to Tommy. He reached deep into his front pocket and retrieved his old Case pocketknife that his dad had given to him twenty years before. Harold had always considered it to be his lucky charm. You could hear a pin drop as the sharp blade slid along under the flap of the bloated envelope.

Herman thought to himself, *if this turns out to be a joke Harold could be dangerous with that knife.*

You could see the pulse in Harold's neck as he extracted the half-inch stack of cash from inside the folded handwritten note that he pulled from inside the envelope.

"Damn," was all that he said as he looked around at his friends. Jackie and Tommy had to try to fake being surprised; Bony and Herman didn't.

"Count it," barked Herman, stepping out of the mail truck and walking up behind Harold, who still held the envelope in one hand and the cash in the other.

Harold laid the envelope and note down on the office desk and counted out fifty twenty-dollar bills and ten one hundred dollar bills.

Harold swallowed hard and, looked up. "Two thousand dollars; I'll be damned."

Herman picked up the note, read it and tossed it back down on the desk.

"Yep, that's what it says all right; it's your lucky day, Harold. It's your lucky day."

The honk of a car horn broke up the small celebration going on inside the small service station office. With all the backslapping and laughing, no one had noticed that cars were waiting on both sides of the gas pumps, and two more had lined up behind them.

"Here," Harold said, handing the stack of cash to Bony, and then thinking better of it, he pulled it back and crammed into his uniform pocket.

"Hey, Jackie; how about you boys giving me a hand here," Harold said over his shoulder, running in the direction of the gas pumps.

"Do you think he's happy?" Tommy asked as he and Jackie followed him out to help fill up the waiting cars.

"I'd say he is; I think I would consider somewhere else to buy gas the rest of the day; maybe the rest of the week," mumbled Jackie as they walked to the gas pumps.

"You can bet your ass; everybody who comes in here is

gonna know about it," Tommy replied.

Harold had forgotten about Dewey and the bogus battery repair scam; now it was all about his Lucky Day and the two thousand dollars. Jackie and Tommy spent the rest of the afternoon helping Harold and laughing as they watched him tell his customers about his good luck. The word had gotten around and more than a few of his friends came by just to congratulate him. Jackie looked over at Tommy, trying not to laugh when Harold handed him a twenty, telling him to split it with Tommy for their help.

"I really feel good, don't you, Tommy?" Jackie said as they started their walk home, reflecting on their day.

"Yeah I do and I'm gonna feel even better soon; it's my Lucky Day next."

6

It was raining when Jim Vess stepped off the bus in downtown Chattanooga. He walked into the Greyhound Bus station between Market and Broad streets, purchased a pack of cigarettes, and sat down on a bench in front of a shoeshine stand.

Jim had been released from Brushy Mountain Prison after his sentence was commuted to time served by the governor. The governor cited his war record and the fact that he had been a model prisoner, not to mention that he had been passed over several times for parole. It came as sort of a surprise to Jim, but he had felt confident that they couldn't hold him much longer.

The prison bus had deposited him at a hotel in Knoxville where he spent the night and planned his next move. He had been looking forward to this day for over ten years; he had played it out in his mind over and over. He would go to the house in East Ridge; he would wait until no one was watching, crawl under the house on McBrien Road, and dig up the duffel bag with his money. As he sat on the bus station bench, he repeated the address he had memorized to himself. 712 McBrien Road, he could still see the black lettering beside the front door.

"Hey, boy; where can I get a cab?" Jim hollered to the balding gray-haired colored man who sat in the wooden chair beside the shoeshine stand.

"Market Street," the colored man replied, pointing down the hallway of the bus station.

Jim got up and walked down the hallway and out the double doors onto the sidewalk. It had quit raining and the sun was out. "Yes things are getting brighter." Jim smiled. A yellow cab pulled up to the curb; he grabbed his small grip, opened the back door, and slid inside.

"Where to?" asked the cabby, who looked a lot like Red Skelton.

"East Ridge; McBrien Road," Jim replied.

"Where to on McBrien road?" asked the Red Skelton look-alike?

"I'll just get out where McBrien Road comes into the highway. How much will that be?"

"Three fifty," the cabby snapped back, glancing at Jim in the mirror.

"That's a little steep, don't you think?"

"OK, three dollars," the cabby replied back.

Jim smiled. *The little red-headed fart was trying to stiff me.*

As they approached the tunnel that went through Missionary Ridge, Jim wondered if the little motel and beer joint was still down the highway. He hoped it was; it would be a good place to sit and have a beer while he planned how to get the money and get out of town. It would be a shame if he got spotted walking around with a duffel bag full of money and get caught again. *No, hell no.*

Jim peered out the side window of the cab as they exited the tunnel and headed down Highway 41, which was now referred to as Ringgold Road.

"The place hasn't changed much, a few more businesses maybe," he said to himself.

The taxi slowed and pulled off the highway into the parking lot of a drugstore that faced the highway.

The cabby looked over the seat smiling. "Three fifty, I mean three dollars."

Jim handed Red Skelton a five-dollar bill. "Keep the change," he said, pulling his grip behind him as he pushed open the rear door and climbed out onto the parking lot.

"Thanks, thanks a lot mister," said the cabby, pulling the

gearshift into low and letting out on the clutch.

Jim stepped from the taxi and looked across the four-lane highway. There it was; what he had been dreaming about all these years, MCBRIEN ROAD. Jim thought for a minute; he had enough money to buy an old car, but if he could just get that money he could get a better one, maybe even a new one.

"What am I thinking, I'll need some place to put the bag; I can't just walk around with it, I need something now."

It was only a few blocks down the highway to where the tavern was located, that is if it was still there, he thought to himself. He walked south on Ringgold Road, his eyes straining to see the Pines Motel sign that at one time sat beside the beer joint. As he got closer, it became evident that the sign was no longer there, but the tavern was, and it was still going strong; judging by the full parking lot. He stopped at a Sinclair gas station and waited for the traffic to clear before darting across the highway and up the front steps to the front door of the tavern. *Hell, this place hasn't changed a bit,* he thought as he stepped through the open front door.

Jim walked up to the bar and sat on the same stool that he had sat on when he had met Barbara Jo almost eleven years ago. The joint hadn't changed but the bartender had; it was now a female and not a bad looking one at that.

"What's your poison, stranger?" asked the attractive bartender.

It took Jim a second to get the meaning of her question. Then it came to him; she was asking him what he would like to drink.

"Beer; make it a Bud and put it in a mug," Jim finally answered, looking around the nearly full tavern.

Seconds later, she returned carrying a mug of beer in both hands. She set one in front of Jim and carried the other one on down the bar and carefully placed it in front of an overweight man in a bus driver's uniform. The bartender was a brunette in her thirties wearing a pair of white pants that reached only to a few inches below her knees. Jim had noticed several women with this style of pants since he had got on the bus in Knoxville after leaving the prison. He was sure that they had a name for them, but he wasn't going to ask. It wasn't the style of the white pants that Jim marveled over; it was the way they fit. They were so tight, it left very little for the imagination, not to mention the low cut top that exposed enough cleavage to divert his eyes from the tight pants.

With the amount of customers in the tavern, it left little time for any conversation Jim would like to have with the pretty barmaid. He downed the beer and set the empty mug down in front of him, waiting for her to spot it and inquire about a refill. She was working her butt off, but it didn't take long for her to eyeball the empty mug sitting on the bar.

She stopped in front of Jim, leaned forward slightly, looked into his eyes and asked, "Where did that beer go; I was sure I just sat one down here?"

Jim smiled, concentrating to keep eye contact and not let his eyes drift southward.

"I think there must have been a hole in the bottom of the mug; you better give me another one."

"What's your name, hun; I don't think I've seen you around here before?"

"Jim; what's yours?"

"Lucinda; but you can just call me Lucy, everyone else does."

"Nice to meet you, Lucy."

"I'll be right back with the beer," she said, turning and hurrying away, returning only moments later with a full mug.

As Jim sipped on his new beer, his mind returned to the money and how he was going to get it and get the hell out of town without anyone noticing.

I have to get something to drive; shit, I can't just walk around town with a duffel bag full of cash. The three hundred dollars they gave me when I was released won't buy much of a car, but I can trade it for a better one once I get my hands on the money. OK, here's what I'm gonna do; get hold of an old car that will run, maybe even a pick-up or panel truck if I can find one. I'll find a place to park close to the house on McBrien Road; I'll watch the comings and goings of the people who live there. When I'm sure no one's home, I'll climb under the house, get the duffel bag and be on my way. It would be better if I do it after dark, but if someone saw me, it would be hard to explain. If I go get it during the day, I could say I was looking for my missing dog or that I was at the wrong house or something.

Now where do I find a cheap car?

Jim finished his beer and decided to walk down the short hallway to the restroom; the beer had hit bottom. The restroom was still in the same place, but the window that he had spied the policeman from was now painted over. The view of the back parking lot was no longer there. As he stood in front of the urinal facing the painted windowpanes, someone stepped beside him, unzipped his pants, and farted loud enough to be heard a block away.

"Sorry about that," the man mumbled around an unlit cigar.

Jim didn't reply, he just looked over at the overweight man who looked straight ahead, chewing on the cigar.

"I need to pick up a cheap set of wheels; you wouldn't know where a man might find one around here, would you?" Jim asked, zipping up his pants.

"You might try across the street at Harold's; he usually has a couple of old cars that people have parked there to try to sell."

"Harold's, is that the service station across the highway?"

"Yeah, the Sinclair station; you must not be from around here, are you?"

"Nope, just passing through; tired of riding the bus, I think I'll try driving for a while."

"Well good luck," the chubby red-faced man said; still looking straight ahead.

"Thanks."

Jim returned to the bar; throwing his leg over the barstool just in time for Lucy to step in front of him.

"Ready for another?"

"Why the hell not."

Jim spent several hours drinking beer and talking to Lucy when she had a spare minute or two. It was hard for him to concentrate on anything except getting his hands on that duffel bag full of money.

He decided that he had waited long enough, the suspense was killing him; it was time to find a car.

****

Harold still had a spring in his step; he was still giddy about receiving the two thousand dollars in the mail. With every customer that stopped by; he had a different story as to what he was going to do with his newfound wealth.

Harold was pumping gas into a brand new fifty-six Chevy convertible when he spotted the stocky dark-complexioned man running in his direction. The man was carrying an overnight bag and could have stepped out of a Bogart movie the way he was dressed and wearing a fedora hat.

"Are you Harold?" the man asked, as he slowed to a walk a few yards from the gas pumps.

"That be me; what can I help you with? It don't look like you need any gas."

"No not yet anyway; what I need is a set of wheels. I was told you might know where I might find one. They said you may know someone who has something to sell that's not too expensive."

"I might; let me think a minute," Harold said, scratching his head.

"It don't have to be a car, a pick-up would do."

"How much do you want to spend?"

"I don't have much; around two or three hundred I guess."

"I have a customer who had a paper route that he carried in an old Willy's Jeepster. It's a fifty or fifty-one, don't look like much but it runs good."

"You know what he wants for it?"

"I'm not sure, but I'm sure it'll be in your price range. I have his number here; I'll call him if you want me to."

"Yeah I'd appreciate it if you don't mind," Jim said, watching the traffic on the highway in front of the service station.

"Let me catch this Volkswagen and I'll give him a call," Harold said as he headed in the direction of the green Bug that had just pulled in.

Jim shuffled around the small office, scoping out the pinball machine and the two-foot high stack of magazines on the floor by the cluttered desk. He noticed that the top magazine was a Playboy and wondered if the rest of the stack was the same.

Harold returned, stepped behind his desk, and flipped open a small phone directory. He ran his oil-stained finger down the list as he reached for the telephone receiver with his other hand.

Harold looked at Jim as he waited for the phone to be answered.

"What's your name?"

Jim started to answer at the same time as Harold made the connection at the other end.

"Mr. Biddy, this is Harold; do you still have that Jeepster for sale? You do; how much you want for it?" Harold held his hand over the receiver and turned toward Jim. "Two fifty."

"When can I see it?" Jim enquired anxiously.

"I have a man here at the station that may be interested; can you bring it up here?"

Harold listened to what the man was saying at the other end for a few seconds and then hung the phone up.

"He'll be here in ten minutes; he just lives a couple of blocks away."

"I really appreciate it, mister; by the way, my name's Jim, Jim Vess."

"Nice to meet you, I'm Harold Visage, I own the place."

It was less than ten minutes when the green and brown Willy's Jeepster drove up in front of the station. Jim looked over the beat-up, half-station-wagon, half-Jeep and drove it down the highway and back. He offered to buy it for two hundred dollars, but the skinny little man with an ugly mole on the side of his nose stuck to his price of two fifty. After some haggling and the skinny man conferring with Harold, Jim bought the Jeepster for two hundred and twenty-five dollars. Part of the deal was that Harold filled the tank with gas and changed the oil, which would be paid for by the seller.

Jim was now short on money, but he had wheels, even though he had no driver's license. It wouldn't be long before the short on money part would be a thing of the past.

It was still a while before sundown as Jim drove the Jeepster west on Highway 41. He turned right on McBrien Road, his heart beginning to beat faster as he drove slowly, watching the numbers on the mail boxes and houses. The one-hundred block, the two-hundred block. *Five more blocks,* he thought; *start watching close.* As he reached the five-hundred block, he saw something up ahead that caused his heart to skip a beat. An orange and white barricade stretched across the road with a large sign reading; STOP__ ROAD CLOSED.

"What the hell?" he screamed as he jumped from the Jeepster and ran up to the barricade. As he stepped around the wooden barrier, he could see that there was some kind of construction going on up ahead. *Why close the whole damn road?* "Maybe they're putting in a sewer or water main; sure that must be it," he said as he kept walking. As he got closer, what he saw almost made his knees buckle; there were no more houses ahead on either side of the street. Jim stopped at the driveway of the last house still standing. He could see it now; what used to be the six and seven-hundred block of McBrien Road was now an unfinished divided highway. In a very short time that highway would become Interstate 24.

****

Very few people in the Chattanooga Tennessee and North Georgia area were unaware of the Lucky Day letters. If the postman was late, you could be sure the local postmaster or station manager would get a call from more than one customer as to what time to expect the mail to run. A television news crew in Chattanooga did a segment on the evening news of people rushing to the mailbox after the mailman had run. Who would be the next Lucky Day recipient? How long would it go on, they asked.

Linda Redden was one of those people who rushed to the mailbox every day hoping that it would be her lucky day, but deep inside, she knew it would never be her. Two weeks before school was to start back, Linda came back from the mailbox holding a letter in her shaking hand that could possibly make a liar of her subconscious mind. *Could it possibly be?* She came bursting through the back door, screaming for her mother.

Tommy and Jackie just so happened to be sitting on the porch when the postman ran. They didn't make a move to go to the mailbox; Tommy even hollered to Linda that the postman had run. It just wouldn't be right if they were the ones to open the letter; watching was more fun even though it was hard to act surprised.

"What is it, girl; did you step on a bee again?" Mrs. Redden shouted from the back bedroom.

"Come in here, Mama, hurry, I think we have one of those letters."

"That's what you say every day, Linda; I'm tired of hearing it."

"It's addressed to Daddy and it's fat; I think this is it, Mama."

Mrs. Redden lumbered into the dining area where Linda was holding the letter up to the light. Tommy and Jackie had come inside and were standing in the doorway watching the spectacle taking place. Jackie whispered into Tommy's ear, "She's really going to have a spasm when she opens it; we may have to call an ambulance."

"Let me see that," muttered Tommy's mother, taking the envelope from Linda's hand.

"You boys playing some kind of a joke?" she asked, looking up at Tommy and then Jackie.

They both shrugged at the same time, which could be interpreted as, "Maybe."

Mrs. Redden didn't say anything else, nor did she ask for anything to open the letter. With the quickness of a cat, she ripped the end of the envelope open and peered inside. She showed no emotion as she emptied the contents of the envelope onto the kitchen table.

Linda screamed so loud she could be heard on top of Lookout Mountain. Tommy and Jackie held their hands over their ears while Linda ran around the house screaming and then ran outside and around the yard. Several dogs started barking and the neighbor's cat ran up a tree in front of Bud Higgins, standing in the driveway across the street.

"Did you step on a snake? Bud laughed, standing in his driveway picking his nose..

After Linda finally settled down and the money had been counted at least three times, it was determined that the cash totaled three thousand dollars. Mrs. Redden was praising the lord while Linda was going through the automobile magazines.

Mrs. Redden looked up at her son still standing in the doorway leading into the dining area.

"You don't seem too excited, Tommy; I'm sure you have something in mind that you would like to have, don't you?"

"I guess I'm still in shock, Mama; I think getting a car would be the thing I would like most. It's what we've all been wishing for."

"A car it will be; you get over there with your sister and pick one out. No matter what you kids pick, it's still going to be up to your daddy, you know."

Tommy glanced over at Jackie, who was leaning against the doorway; he wasn't sure but he thought he saw a tear forming in the corner of his friend's eye.

It was a tear, but not a tear of sadness; it was a tear of joy. It was great to know that Tommy's dad would be able to drive to work and not have to walk to the bus stop when it was cold or raining. Despite all the happiness that the money they had stumbled upon brought, Jackie still had that gnawing in the back of his mind; was what they were doing OK? He would always justify their actions by the fact that they tried to find out where it came from.

Linda got her way; they decided on a new Chevy Bel Air. The only concession was that it was not a convertible; she had to settle for a hardtop. Mrs. Redden wrote an editorial in the newspaper, praising God for the gift. She was convinced that the

Lord answered prayers and this was proof of that fact.

Yes, it is true; God does work in mysterious ways.

It wouldn't be until two weeks later, when school started back that Jackie's family would get their letter. It was for three thousand dollars, the same as Tommy's. The fact that three people received Lucky Day letters in the Rankin Park area drew the community into a frenzy as they anticipated the arrival of the next letter.

As summer would change to fall, so would swimming at the creek end, the end of baseball at Engle Stadium, and the closing of Lake Winne. As summer ended, so would the Lucky Day letters, but long into the winter a trip to the mailbox was still an adventure.

It would be Jackie's mother that put her foot down to Harve that another bedroom would be added. He would initially try to put it off and use the money for buying a backhoe and dump truck so he could get in on the changeover to sewers from septic tanks in East Ridge. He would eventually buy the backhoe and dump truck, but not before the much-needed room was added to their small house.

Jackie and Tommy had accomplished their mission; they were successful in getting some of the money into the hands of their families without drawing attention to themselves. In doing so, they had made several people happy in the process and still had over two hundred thousand dollars in their cave hideout. The question now would be what to do next.

****

After realizing that the house where he had buried the duffel bag under the foundation was no longer there, Jim sat down on the ground. Where he sat was not far from where Jackie and Tommy had pulled open the flaps on the dusty bag and discovered what was inside. He had grown up in a hard neighborhood, witnessed some horrible things on the battlefields of Europe, and endured the ugliness of prison life. In all these challenges, he had never shed one tear. He rested his elbows on his knees, put his head in his hands, and wept for the first time since he was a baby.

As he sat on the hillside overlooking the unfinished, divided highway, his emotion of self-pity and disappointment turned to anger. His anger turned to frustration and then back to anger. He was angry because he had no one to blame; how could he have ever guessed such a disaster?

Jim finally got up and slowly walked back to his Jeepster that he had driven for less than a mile. As he drove back down McBrien Road, he tried to put aside the shock of what he had just discovered. When he reached the highway, he turned left and drove the short distance to the Pines Tavern and turned into the parking lot. He found an empty parking spot, backed the Jeepster in, turned off the engine, and slid down in the seat.

OK, dumb ass, where do you go from here? Do you just get back on the highway and drive; try to find a job, or go on down to Florida. Should I stay around here; try to find who lived in the house after that Barbara Jo girl moved? Hell, try to find out what happened to her; she may have found the money. Find out what happened to the house; did they move it; did they tear it down? Maybe I could find out if it was moved; if so where too. If I stay around here, I'll have to find a job; and oh yeah, I'll have to find a place to stay. I have less than a hundred dollars left; I guess I could sell the Jeepster. What a damn mess. There's another option; I could hold up another bank. No, not yet; I'll try finding a job first.

Jim sat up in the seat and looked around. *Looks like those cabins are still here, but I don't see a motel sign; I wonder if they rent them out by the week or month? It looks like a couple of them are occupied; hell, they don't look like much but I don't need much. I'm sure someone in the tavern can tell me where to enquire about 'em; maybe that barmaid, Lucy, or whatever her name is. One way to find out; go in and have another beer.*

As Jim walked across the parking lot to the back door of the Pines Tavern, he took note of an East Ridge Police cruiser turning into the lot. *The police really keep an eye on this place. I guess they watch for drunks staggering out of here; wait for them to pull onto the highway and then pull them over. That reminds me, I don't have a driver's license; if I'm gonna keep that Jeep, I'll have to get one.*

It had gotten dark outside and the crowd inside the bar, who had been there since they had finished work, had become a little more vocal than they were earlier. His favorite seat at the bar was taken so he had to choose a vacant one at the other end. Jim had just settled down and was waiting for the bartender when someone tapped him on the shoulder rather forcefully, causing him to jump.

"Get your big ass out of my damn stool," sputtered a red-faced man with two day's growth of beard.

The man swayed a little as Jim stood up beside the stool, looking the man in the eyes, his blood beginning to rise.

"I'm sorry, mister, it looked vacant to me," Jim replied without blinking.

"Well, it wasn't asshole!" the drunk said, raising his hand to push Jim aside.

The red-faced man was younger than Jim, but had spent too many days sitting on a barstool drinking beer. He had a double chin and a beer gut that threatened to pop the center button off his khaki shirt.

"I'm trying to be nice to you, buddy; but if you don't get out of my face, I'm going to mop the floor up with your fat ass; do you understand?" Jim never blinked as he pushed the drunk's hand away from his chest.

The drunk stepped back, his face becoming even redder; he clenched his fist as if he were going to take a swing at Jim when a man in a pair of overalls grabbed him by the arm and led him away. As they were staggering away from the bar, the man escorting him hollered to the bartender, "Call Leon's wife; he's drunk again."

Jim watched as another man stepped in and helped the man in overalls sit the drunk down at a table. The red-faced drunk could be heard describing how he was going to whip the son of a bitch who stole his seat at the bar.

Jim returned to the barstool in time to order a beer from a skinny bartender with a sailor hat and white T-shirt.

"I guess Lucy has gone for the day," he said to the man sitting beside him.

"Yep, she works the day shift; only men work in here at night. I guess you found out the hard way; it's gets kinda rowdy around here at night sometimes," the man replied tiredly.

"Yeah I kinda get that feeling," Jim said as he glanced at the man sitting next to him.

"My name's Jim." He turned and extended his hand toward the man seated at the bar beside him.

"I'm Perry Edmondson," replied the man reaching over to shake hands.

"You from around here?"

"Yep, lived here all my life," Perry said, looking straight ahead.

Perry was a slim, dark-complexioned man in his forties, wearing a ball cap with the letters SR stenciled above the bill. It was obvious that he was part-Indian, which was the case with ninety percent of the people from this part of the country.

"What kind of work do you do?" asked Jim.

"Railroad; been at Southern since high school."

"I guess you've seen a lot of meanness in here then, haven't you?"

"They've had two shootings in here and several knife fights; no telling how many fist fights. I've been drinking beer in here since I was twenty-one, and have only witnessed one fight firsthand. The one that I saw, I was in; it was a damn brawl." Perry laughed and took a swig of his beer. "I haven't seen you around here before, mister; what did you say your name was?" asked the Indian, sneaking a peek at Jim.

"It's Jim Vess; it's been a while since I've been in here. I'm in town looking for work; they say the textile industry is picking up south of here."

"Yeah, down in Dalton, they're starting to make carpet down there now; you see fewer bedspreads on the side of the road nowadays."

Jim probed the railroad man, hoping to get any information he could about the houses in the way of the freeway construction.

"I see the new freeway's going in behind us here; what happened to the houses that were in the way? Did they just tear them down?" asked Jim, sipping on his beer.

"They moved some of them; tore some of 'em down."

"Probably didn't move them very far; I guess?"

"Nah, they're scattered all around here."

Both men turned on their barstools and watched as a beefy woman wearing a dress that was more than likely made from a Martha White flour sack stormed through the front door. She marched over to the table to the drunk that had tried to start a fight with Jim. The drunk sat with his head lying atop his folded arms.

Without saying a word, she kicked the poor slop in the side of his calf causing him to sit straight up in his chair. As he looked up, it took a second for his eyes to focus on the frowning woman standing beside him.

"Get your sorry ass up and let's go," said the angry woman in the print dress.

The red-faced man was still trying to focus on what was happening when she slapped him on the back of the head with her open hand. The sound that it made caused several heads to turn; someone at the back of the room, shouted, "Hit him again." A second passed and the whole bar erupted in laughter.

"Damn," said the Indian. "There'll be a knot on the back of his head big enough for a calf to suck on."

"I'm pretty sure I know why the poor bastard stays drunk now," Jim grinned, turning back around on his barstool.

Jim ordered another beer and another one for Perry, even though Perry still had nearly a full one sitting in front of him.

"Perry, do you remember a girl who used to come in here years ago by the name of Barbara Jo?"

"How long ago?"

"I don't know; hell it's been ten years or more. I met her right after the war; she was a looker."

"Hell, I don't know, that was probably before I started coming in here; was she a bartender?"

"No she didn't work here; she just came in here a lot. She was kind of a flirt; I think she was married though."

"I'm sorry, man; that was before my time, but if anybody would know her, it's that old man sitting over in the corner by the jukebox. I think he's been coming in here since the place was built."

"What's his name?" probed Jim.

"Bob Hodges."

"You say he comes in here a lot?"

"I've never been in here when he wasn't here; he had a boy killed in the war, his wife died not long after. They say Bob just never got over it. He blames it all on Hitler; he's convinced he's still alive and that he lives down on Sand Mountain."

"He thinks Hitler is still alive?" Jim asked, looking over at the Indian.

"He's kinda nuts, Jim; but he truly believes that Hitler is alive and that he knows people who have seen him down there. He may be a little off his rocker, but I'll bet he can tell you who hung out in here ten years ago."

Jim finished his beer and was about to order another one when he realized that Perry had not yet started on the one that he had ordered for him. He decided that he had better try to find a place to sleep; the Jeepster seat was not what he had in mind.

"One other question, Perry. I noticed that the cabins behind this place are occupied; I know this used to be a motel; who rents them out now?"

"Yeah, the motel closed years ago, but Bart, the guy who runs the tavern, still owns them. He don't come in here much, but if you're interested in renting one, see Lucy; she'll be here in the morning; she handles the cabins for him."

"Thanks," Jim said, as he got up from his barstool, extending a hand to his new friend.

"I appreciate the information, and enjoyed talking to you. I'm sure I'll see you in here again."

"Sure, mister; thanks for the beer, good luck on finding a job," the Indian said, raising his mug to Jim.

Jim paid the bartender for the second time that day, turned around on the stool and started to the front door. As he was just about to step through the door, he decided to walk over to the old man sitting in the corner by himself beside the jukebox.

"Excuse me, old-timer," Jim said quietly, pulling up an empty chair. "The man I was talking to at the bar said you've been coming in here for a long time."

"Since before the war," answered the slim man with bloodshot eyes.

"Mind if I ask you a question?"

"What's your name?" the old man asked, looking up at Jim; squinting.

"I'm sorry, it's Jim Vess," he replied, extending his hand across the small table.

"I'm Bob Hodges; what is it you want to know?" asked the old man, avoiding the handshake.

"It's been over ten years since I was in here; but do you remember a redhead who used to hang out in here by the name of Barbara Jo; I think Stephens was her last name."

The old man sat there staring at the front door, his face lost in a mask of concentration.

"Hell, that was a while ago; yeah I remember her, she wasn't bad to look at. It was a couple of years after the war was over; she came in here nearly every day. Yeah, that was her name, Barbara Jo; she liked to sit at the bar and flirt with the men who came in here. She paid for very few beers." The old man chuckled as he raised his beer up to his mouth.

"Do you know what became of her?" asked Jim, trying not to sound too anxious.

"She took up with a preacher from a tent revival that set up down the road. The word was that she left with him when the revival moved on."

"So she never came back; what about her husband, what happened to him?"

"Well, Jim; it is Jim isn't it; it seems like she wasn't married at all. The guy she was living with came in here for a while after she took off. He didn't know she was telling everybody that they were married. He seemed kinda glad she moved on; said you couldn't trust a redhead anyway."

"So his name wasn't Stephens then; I guess?"

"I don't remember what his name was, Jim; that's a long time ago. I wouldn't have remembered her, but it's hard to forget the pretty ones; even when you get to my age."

The two men exchanged small talk for a few minutes before Jim stood up and thanked the old man for his time.

"What a hell of a day," Jim mumbled, as he walked through the front door and out into the parking lot.

****

The 1956 – 1957 school year was underway with Jackie as a sophomore and Tommy becoming a freshman. The new 57 Chevy Bel Air had hit the showroom floor and were advertised as "Sweet Smooth and Sassy." Linda pleaded with Tommy's mom and dad to trade their newly purchased 56 for the new model, but failed to change their minds.

Jackie's uncle had started work on the one-room addition to their house that would become Jackie's new bedroom. Harvey took off from work to help in the construction to cut down on some of the cost. He hoped to have enough left over to put down on a used backhoe and dump truck. He was determined to quit his job at the foundry and get in on the conversion from septic tanks to sewers in East Ridge.

It was hard for Jackie and Tommy to get excited about school or anything else; including girls. The thought of the hundred thousand dollars they each had stashed away in ammo boxes inside their cave dominated their thoughts. Not only did each have a stash; they still had over thirty thousand dollars left from the fifty thousand that had not been given away or spent.

After the school bus dropped the two boys off, they would each go home, throw their schoolbooks down, say hello to their parents, and head out the door. It was usually the creek bank where they would meet; not much was going on there since school had started back. The conversation would always be about the money; they had discussed hundreds of different ways that they could legitimize having it, but none seemed to pass the smell test. Jackie was concerned about keeping the money down in the mineshaft; he worried that someone would discover the entrance and somehow get their hands on the ammo boxes that they had hidden. Both had nightmares about the place caving in and burying the money forever.

They didn't go every day they met, but at least three times a week, they couldn't resist the urge to go down and check out the cave. When they reached the floor and looked around, it was quite clear that nothing had changed since their last trip there. It was almost becoming a ritual; they would each go to their individual boxes, open the lids, and look inside. After each were satisfied that the money was just as they had left it, they would meet back at the main shaft where Jackie's hammock was strung and Tommy's campstool sat. They would inspect what remained of the fifty thousand dollars that they still kept in the old duffel bag. If they were running a little short on spending money, they would each pocket a twenty, sometimes two. No one seemed to be suspicious of them having a little spending money; after all, each of their parents had received a Lucky Day gift in the mail.

"I have an idea," Tommy said, leaning back against the cave wall of his campstool.

"I hope it's a good one; I'm out of ideas myself."

"We both get a job, you know, after school and on Saturday's kinda thing. We make a little money enough to open up a bank account. We put a little of our stash in the account along with what we make from working; I know we'll have to do it a little at a time, but before long, we'll have enough to really do something with."

Jackie didn't say anything for a few seconds.

"You know, I've been thinking along those same lines; we don't really need a whole lot right now, but the older we get, the more things we're gonna want. Soon we'll be graduating from high school; we'll probably have to go in the army for a while, but that won't be forever. When we get out, that money would sure make it a lot easier getting started."

"Yeah, and it will be easier to sneak larger amounts into the bank when we're older and have a real job," Tommy said, sitting up and bringing his stool back down on four legs. "But if we had a small job now, it would be a way to get some of the money in an account so we could write a check instead of paying cash for everything; I'm thinking cars, what about you?" grinned Tommy.

"First things first; where are we gonna find a job? We still have to go to school, you know."

"OK, the first thing is finding a part-time job; what's the second thing?" asked Tommy.

"Are we really going to leave all this damn money down here in a World War II ammo box; you know it's just a matter of time before someone stumbles across the entrance. Who knows, the place could cave in or something. We're talking years, Tommy; we've got to find a better place than down here to hide this money."

"Seems like a pretty good place to me." Tommy began, giving his flattop a workout with both hands. His unconscious habit of doing that seemed to be increasing.

They sat in silence for at least a minute before Jackie kicked the duffel bag containing the remaining thirty thousand dollars that was sitting on the cave floor beside his hammock.

"Let's take the rest of the money out of this old bag; it's going to get molded if we don't. I think I know a good place to hide it."

"Where's that?"

"That box of magazines over there; we'll put it down under a few copies of Playboys. That should keep it warm and dry; what do you think?" asked Jackie, grinning up at Tommy.

"Sounds good to me." Tommy shrugged, reaching down in the dusty duffel bag. "You know something, Jackie; I've been thinking."

"Not again, what is it this time?"

"It's Lewis; we've not given him a penny, hell, he's been like a father to us. Can't we see if we can do a little something for him?"

"I'll be damned, Tommy; you're right. Peel off a couple of those hundreds, let's give old Lewis something to talk about."

Tommy and Jackie never seemed to nail down a strategy on what to do with the remaining money, but they always came up with a way to shed a small portion of it.

They never had to have a clock to tell them when it was time to eat supper; Tommy had an internal clock telling him when it was time to eat.

"Let's get out of here, I'm getting hungry," Tommy said after an hour of discussing how to get the two hundred-dollar bills into Lewis' hands.

"Yeah, let's go, but grab that duffel bag. The next time we go up to Harold's, take it with you; if we don't pick up that stack of magazines, he's gonna throw them away. Over half of them were Playboys, you know."

Tommy picked up the dusty duffel bag and handed it to Jackie, who slung the strap over his shoulder and shook his head; it was obvious the extra weight was more than Tommy could handle as they ascended the rope ladder.

****

It was Friday, the favorite day of the week when school was in session. It was a happy time on the school bus, which meant that the driver had to make at least three unscheduled stops to either quell a disturbance or downright eject a couple of unruly passengers. Three blocks before Tommy and Jackie's stop, the bus approached Louie's store, where the largest group of kids opted to get off. The fact that many of them had to walk an extra couple of blocks didn't matter. Louie had cold drinks, and for many, it was a place to purchase a pack of cigarettes for the upcoming weekend.

The cold drinks or cigarettes weren't the reason that Tommy and Jackie decided to exit the bus three blocks early; it was because of the three police cars they saw outside the bus window. Two of them were at the store, and the other was across the street at Mr. Robinson's house. Something was going down and they had to see for themselves what it was.

There was an East Ridge Police sergeant talking to Louie and two uniformed Catoosa County Sheriff deputies speaking with Mr. Robinson and his wife. The reason for the two different agencies was because Louis's store was in Tennessee, while Mr. Robinson lived across Stateline Road, which was in Georgia.

It didn't take very long to find out what was going on. The East Ridge Police had just left with Sonny Farr; the Tush Hog himself. Mr. Robinson had called the police; he had been able to afford an operation on his eyes since he had received the Lucky Day gift. The doctors had been able to correct his double vision problem.

It took only two seconds for him to positively identify Tush Hog Sonny Farr as the person who had hit him back in the early summer. There were several people there when the police put him in the squad car and took him off. It was humorous to Jackie as he listened to different people describe the scene as they were taking him away. What was most interesting was what happened as they were placing him in the rear of the police cruiser. His dad, who had always supported him up to that point, was now on his ass like a manager of a baseball team on an umpire after a bad call. As his son bent over to crawl into the backseat, his dad kicked him squarely in the ass. A few people commented that a splattering of applause could be heard in the background.

Tush was headed for a world that consisted of bigger and meaner Tushes than him.

Jackie said to no one in particular, "Well, hell; it couldn't happen to a nicer guy."

****

Jim decided to hang around for a while, it was hard for him to accept the fact that the duffel bag full of money that he had been dreaming about for such a long time was really gone. He was in luck in one respect; one of the cabins behind the tavern was vacant and he made arrangements to rent it by the week. It was only one room with a small bathroom, but it was larger than what he had been living in for the past ten years.

He spent a lot of time drinking beer and talking to the locals, trying not to raise too many eyebrows with his questions. He sold the Jeepster to help pay his rent and buy food and beer. The Sinclair service station across the street had a pinball machine, which occupied a lot of his time during the day. It was when he came to the realization that he had to get a job or do a robbery that he decided to ask Harold for a job. Harold and Jim seemed to get along OK; Jim would run errands and help out when he needed a roll of quarters to feed the pinball. The two men had both been in the war and enjoyed talking about the places they had been and things they had done. Jim decided to tell Harold about his past, and that he had done time for robbery. He left out a lot of the details, which Harold seemed to be satisfied with. Harold had decided to let bygones be bygones.

Jim had just dropped his last quarter in the pinball when Harold returned to the small office and flopped down in the chair behind his cluttered desk. He had just replaced a windshield wiper on a nineteen fifty-four Cadillac that was headed for Florida.

"Damn, Jim, you went through that roll fast. You need to lay off that son of a bitch; it's raping you."

"You got that right, Harold, it got my last ten. I've either got to get a job or find a woman with a lot of money."

"What are you gonna do, Jim? You've been hanging around here, drinking beer over at the Pines, playing this damn pinball. You must be fixin' to hit the road, I guess."

"I don't know what to do, Harold. I don't have a family so I thought about going down to Dalton and getting on at one of those carpet mills, but I don't think I could be cramped up in something like that."

"How about working for me?" Harold asked, looking between his shoes that he had propped up on top of his desk.

"I've been thinking about asking you about that; but I don't know much about cars; I could probably learn though."

"I'm gonna hire you, Jim; I don't know much about you and I'm probably taking a big risk, but I think everybody deserves a second chance. I don't give a damn how much beer you drink or how much you put into that pinball. The only thing I ask is that you don't steal from me. Now what do you say?"

"You got a deal, now how much are you going to pay me, and when do I start?"

****

It didn't take Jim long to catch on to the filling station business. In addition to pumping gas and cleaning windshields, he caught on quickly on how to change a tire and do a grease job and oil change. Harold was pleased at how Jim took to the business; his new helper was a hard worker even though he spent his down time leaning over the pinball machine, and his nights across the highway at the tavern. Jim worked the beer joint at night, talking to his new friends and asking questions about the houses on McBrien Road and the people who had lived in them. He did the same at the service station during the day; but no one that he had talked to could shed any light on his bag full of money.

It was obvious to Jim that his quarter of a million dollars was gone, and finding it was more than likely never going to happen. He made enough to buy beer and play the pinball, but it was getting old. He had robbed a bank and killed a man; he had done ten years in prison, and for what, to work for a dollar an hour pumping gas.

Jim decided that it was time for him to get out of life what he had been waiting for since 1946. This time, he would do it himself; do a little more planning. He told himself nothing had changed. *Just give 'em a good look down the barrel and what they have is yours.*

It was just after Bony the Pepsi Cola man had abandoned the pinball when Jim dropped two dollars' worth of quarters into the slot and pulled back the spring-loaded plunger. He didn't risk tilting the machine; he just flipped the chrome balls down the chute as they popped out. The first three lined up, which would be a winner and recover Jim's two-dollar investment; however, it was the fourth ball that got his attention. It worked its way to the bottom and settled into the twenty slot, which lined up four across. Jim's pulse increased somewhat as he looked down and realized that he still had one ball in the chute. If he could somehow maneuver the fifth ball into the eleven hole it would make it five in a line. The payout would be close to two hundred and fifty dollars.

The eleven was thought to be the easiest number to hit; it was almost automatic for Jim. He pulled the plunger back slowly, stopping at just the right spot, turned the knob loose and let the ball fly. It made two bounces of the rubber bumpers and dived straight into the number eleven hole as if it had a mind of its own.

"Yes, yes; hey, Harold, get your ass in here, I've finally hit the bastard."

Harold walked into the office from the service bay where he had been changing the oil in Mr. Gay's Rambler. He walked over to the machine where Jim stood hunched over the glass, listening to the counter rack up the one thousand games at twenty-five cents each.

"Well I'll be a son of a gun," Harold said. "I hope I have that much cash, that's two fifty."

"It's about damn time; this son of a bitch has eaten my lunch ever since I've been coming in here. I'm still behind the bastard," snarled Jim.

The machine finally quit clicking off the games and stopped at one thousand and five. Harold flipped a switch on the back causing the accumulated games to start descending back to zero. He opened the cash drawer taking all the bills out except the ones. He counted out the two hundred and fifty dollars onto his desk. When he had finished, he only had one twenty and two fives left.

Harold counted the money out to Jim on top of the pinball machine, and without saying a word, turned and walked back out into the service bay.

It wasn't anything that you could put your finger on, but Jim had a gut feeling that his luck had changed, or was about to change. He had a place to stay, a job, and a nice place to drink beer that was close enough to walk from his job. He had given up on trying to find out what had happened to his bag of money, but he was confident that he could do it again; just with more planning and a hell of a lot more luck.

****

"I hit the bastard for two fifty yesterday," Jim told Perry, the Indian who worked at the railroad and had become sort of a drinking buddy at the Tavern.

"If you hit it a couple more times like that, you might get even," Perry said, looking straight ahead as he set his empty mug back down on the bar.

"Well I have enough to buy beer for a week or two; what else could a man ask for?"

"You have a point; I'll have a Falstaff." The Indian smiled, still looking straight ahead.

"Two more;" Jim shouted to Lucy, who had just came on duty.

Perry turned to face Jim; he pushed his Southern Railway ball cap back on his head and smiled.

"You did hit the son of a bitch, didn't you?"

"What, do you think I would lie to you, asshole?"

Jim looked around the room then back at Perry. "I'm looking to find me a pistol; you know where I might find me one? I think somebody has been prowling around my cabin out back here. You never know what people will do these days; I'd feel a lot better if I had some kind of protection."

"I might be able to help you; how big a gun do you want?"

"I don't know, at least a thirty-eight; if you're going to shoot somebody, you want to make sure you do some damage," Jim said, watching Lucy as she placed the two mugs of beer down on the bar.

"I have a M1911 forty-five; is that more than what you're looking for?"

"Is it a Colt?"

"You know damn well it is; the Army wouldn't have anything else."

"How much?"

"Fifty bucks."

"Damn; is the son of a bitch gold-plated or something?"

"It's like new; my brother brought it back from Korea. He said it's only been fired one time on the range. I've been offered seventy-five for it."

"How did he get it out of Korea?"

"Don't ask so many dumb ass questions; are you interested or not?"

"Bring it down here; if it's what you say it is, I'm interested," Jim said, turning up his mug until it was empty.

It was almost midnight when Jim walked back across the parking lot to his cabin. The first part of his plan was coming together; he would have a gun by tomorrow night. The next step would be getting a set of wheels.

Jim opened the door to his one-room cabin, which was located right next door to the one he had hastily vacated over ten years before. Each time he entered the cabin, it brought back the bad memory of giving up his duffel bag containing the money from the bank heist. It also triggered the memory of having to shoot Jerry so he could keep all of the money for himself. Not once did he feel any pain of remorse for killing him; he had a way of quickly pushing it out of his mind. Jim had shed any resemblance of a conscious a long time ago.

The sound of the traffic on the highway in front of the cabins was much heavier than it was ten years ago; but that was soon to change. When the Interstate system opened for traffic; old Highway 41 would become just another side road. That was still a while in the future; right now the lights and noise from the passing traffic made it hard for him to fall asleep. He kicked his shoes off and fell back on his pillow, the nights were getting cooler; maybe he would just go to sleep with his clothes on tonight, he thought.

After I find me a car, I'll be able to drive around and take a look at the bank situation around here. They're putting up branches everywhere these days. I wonder how much cash they keep in them. I guess I could do like last time; find out when the armored trucks make their deliveries. This time I won't need anyone to help me; I'll do it by myself; maybe do like I did before; shoot some poor son of a bitch right up front. It'll scare the drawers off of those little pissy-ass women they have working behind those cages nowadays. I'll be back at Harold's pumping gas before they get up enough guts to get up off the floor.

Jim tossed around on the bed, went and took a piss, peeked out between the blinds, then lay back down.

Why in the hell did they have to build a freeway right across where I hid my stash? If my luck was ink, I couldn't dot an "I." Damn, maybe they do need a freeway, it sounds like a racetrack out there; how the hell do they expect you to get any sleep around here with all those diesels changing gears? Well, maybe my luck is changing; who knows, I might hit the damn pinball again tomorrow.

****

It had been a while since the two boys had talked to Lewis. Jackie had spoken to him a few times when he came over to critique the work as it progressed on his new bedroom. He also had a short conversation with him when he found out that Harvey had received the Lucky Day gift in the mail. Lewis told Jackie's mom and dad that if everyone in the neighborhood received a Lucky Day letter; he would be the last person to get one. Harvey said that was the way he used to feel, but now he was sure that his luck had changed. He told Lewis that two days after he received the letter, he had spotted a box on the side of the highway. He turned around and went back and retrieved the box, but if he hadn't received the letter; he would probably have just kept on driving. Harvey smiled, which was unusual for him, when he described what was inside. He acted like he was more proud of the box that contained four canned hams than he was of the Lucky Day envelope.

"The damn thing must have fallen off a truck or something." He laughed.

Jackie and Tommy had talked for hours on how they were going to get the two hundred-dollar bills into Lewis' hands without him knowing where it came from.

"I've been thinking, Tommy; you know Lewis is a creature of habit. Nearly everything that he does is sort of a ritual, right down to the way he lights his cigarette. I've watched him since I was little; I think I can predict just about everything that he does."

"So what does that have to do with anything?" inquired Tommy.

"Every Sunday after he returns from taking Francis and the kids to church, he performs maintenance on that Ford of his. He takes his little whisk broom and sweeps out the floorboards front and back. He pulls out the dipstick and checks his oil. I've never witnessed him having to add any oil although I know he keeps a case in his garage. He checks the water in the radiator as well as the water in the batteries. He unscrews the wing-nut from the cover of the air filter atop the carburetor. He takes the filter out and inspects it; holding it up to the sun and banging it on the driveway to remove any bug or grime that it may have collected."

"OK, OK, I get the picture; how does that have anything to do with giving him the two hundred dollars?" shrugged Tommy, beginning to get bored.

"What if we opened the hood, took off the air filter cover, and wrapped the two bills around the filter. It is possible that they could have been sucked inside, although not very likely. No way would he miss them when he did his weekly inspection. We can't be there when he finds them; I know he would try to connect us to it, but we could hide across the street in the woods and watch," Jackie said, starting to get excited.

"I can hear him telling us all about it; I wonder how much color he'll add to the story?" said Tommy. "Wait a minute, we have a little problem here," Tommy continued frowning.

"What's that?"

"How do we get access to his car; he keeps it locked up in his garage at night."

"Who said anything about night?"

"Well, when do we do it then; we can't just walk over and pop the hood and start taking the top off the air filter in broad daylight."

"I think we can, and I know just how and when," Jackie said calmly.

Not only was Lewis easy to predict; his wife, Francis, also was. Every Friday after they had eaten their evening meal, she would go to the M&J to buy the groceries for the following week. About half the time, Jackie's mother would accompany her; it depended on whether his dad came home in time. Fridays was always an iffy day for Harvey. On the way back from the grocery store, Francis always stopped at Harold's to get the Ford filled up. That would be when Harold would get some unexpected help from Jackie and Tommy.

The two boys were watching Harold's new helper feed the pinball when Francis pulled the black Ford in front of the gas pumps and turned off the engine. There was no argument from Jim when Tommy turned and ran out the door, saying that he would get this one for him, because the lady driving the Ford was a friend of his.

"I guess you want to fill her up with high-test?' Tommy

asked smiling, placing the nozzle of the hose into the gas tank. He kept a close eye on Jackie as he turned the small crank to start the pump.

Tommy walked back to the open window and initiated a conversation while the gas was being pumped into the tank. The car had been stopped for only a second when Jackie had the hood raised, searching for the oil dipstick. It took him less than ten seconds to unscrew the wing-nut on top of the air filter and take the cover off. He placed the two hundred-dollar bills around the outside of the cardboard filter and replaced the cover before closing the hood. He had forgotten about the dipstick and checking the oil. It was only for show anyway; he knew Lewis would check it himself Sunday morning. The whole episode was finished before the tank was half-filled with gas.

"Looks fine under the hood," Jackie said, pushing Tommy out of the way as he leaned down to speak to his next-door neighbor.

"When did you boys start working here? I thought Harold hired a new man to help him out?" inquired Francis.

"Oh, no we don't really work here, we just help out when somebody we know comes in here," Jackie replied.

"Well, you're both doing a fine job; now how much is the gas? I have stuff in the trunk that needs to get into the freezer."

"That's gonna be four seventy-five," Tommy said.

"Here, keep the change," Francis said, handing him a five-dollar bill.

"Mama didn't get to come with you, I guess?" Jackie asked.

"Not today, son; I asked her though. She said she would get someone else to take her this week."

"Come over and see Lewis; he's been wondering what's happened to you two," she said, as the Ford pulled away from the gas pumps.

"There goes a Ford that's worth two hundred dollars more

than when it pulled in here," Jackie said, slapping Tommy on the back as they walked back into the station.

Tommy placed the five-dollar bill down on the cash register and looked over at Jim, who was still in deep concentration behind the pinball machine.

"The gas was four seventy-five, there's a five on the register," Tommy said over his shoulder as they walked out the door.

Jim never looked up, he just kinda grunted; saying something under his breath that neither boy could hear.

"What if somehow the money comes loose and gets blown away while the car is going down the street or something?" Tommy asked, hurrying to catch up to Jackie as they started home.

"I don't think it could; but if it did, it's not like we don't have more where that came from. I doubt if we would ever miss a measly two hundred dollars. Anyway, if somebody finds it; it might make their day a little brighter. You worry too much." Jackie laughed, punching Tommy in the shoulder hard enough to make him lose his balance, almost stumbling into the ditch beside the road.

"Damn, that hurts," Tommy complained, rubbing his shoulder. "You seem to be in a good mood; what's up?"

"Nothing, I've just been thinking about Lewis. I can't wait to see what he does when he discovers the two bills clinging to his air filter."

"I doubt if he'll start running around the yard, jumping up and down and whooping and hollering; he has seen a hundred-dollar bill before, you know."

"Yeah, I guess you're right; but I'm sure he'll put some kind of drama into his story when he tells us about it. You can be sure of that."

Neither boy said a word as they crossed the bridge where

Tush had received his Nut Job, but you could be sure that the memory crossed both their minds.

****

Perry was leaning against his pick-up truck parked in the rear of the Pines Tavern. The red-coated metal was still hot to touch from the afternoon sun. Sweat was wicking through the Southern Railway ball cap and would leave a salt stain at the base of the brim when it dried. The two-thirds Cherokee Indian didn't mind the heat as much as having to wait in the sun for Jim to get off from work and walk across the highway to the back of the tavern where they had agreed to meet. He had the 45 automatic behind the seat of the pick-up, which he was afraid to leave unattended due to the fact that the driver door would not lock.

Where is the bastard; it's five-thirty. He should have been here thirty minutes ago. I'll bet the asshole is on that damn pinball again. I'll give him another...

"Sorry I'm a little late; I had to finish up a grease job; can't just walk off and leave a car on the rack," Jim said, stepping around the corner of the Tavern. "Well let's see it," Jim continued, turning his back to the truck and leaning back. His elbow touched the fender prompting him to jerk upright with a grimace on his face.

"Damn, you could fry an egg on that son of a bitch; what happened to fall, let alone winter?"

The Indian smiled as he reached for the door handle of the truck. "I guess summer is still not over around here."

Perry snaked the pistol out from under the truck seat, wrapped inside a white towel. He carefully unfolded the towel and placed it on the floorboard of the truck. Jim looked the 45 over making sure not to point it at Perry, who stood watching with sweat dripping from the tip of his nose. Jim ejected the clip from the hand grip, pulled back the slide and looked inside the chamber. After making sure that it was empty, he slid the slide forward and pulled the trigger.

"You're right the damn thing is tight; hasn't been shot much, but could use a little oil on these slides. How much you say you want for it?"

"Fifty," said Perry, wiping the sweat from his face with the back of his hand.

"I'll give you forty."

"The price is fifty; I told you I've been offered seventy-five already."

"Well then you need to sell it for seventy-five. "He handing the gun back to the Indian as if he had discovered something wrong with it.

"It's practically a brand new gun," Perry said, without attempting to take the pistol from Jim's hand.

"I'll give you forty-five if you'll throw in that box of shells I saw under the seat there."

Perry took the pistol from Jim's hand and placed it on the towel on the floorboard of the pick-up.

"Give me forty-five, I'll throw in the shells if you buy the beer tonight," Perry said, taking off the ball cap and rubbing his hand through his damp hair.

Jim picked the pistol back up and slid the slide back again.

"Deal; now give me that box of shells and let's go get a beer."

Jim handed Perry two twenties and promised to pay him the other five on Friday; explaining that he needed the five to pay for the beer. The Indian seemed confused, but accepted the arrangement, scratching his head as he waited for Jim to take the gun inside his cabin.

"Go on in and find us a stool; I'll be over in a minute. Order me a cool one; I'll be right there," shouted Jim, over his shoulder as he walked toward his cabin door.

Well I've got half of what I need; now to find me another set of wheels. I'll start on that tomorrow. I wonder where I can go to fire this thing a few times. It's been a while since I had one of these babies in my hand. If I remember correctly; this little son of a bitch will bark. If I were a bank teller, you'd have my attention if I had the business end of this bastard stuck in my face.

Jim placed the pistol that was still wrapped in the dingy white towel between the mattress and box springs of his bed. He took a piss and headed out the door across the parking lot to the tavern.

****

Very seldom had Jackie missed Sunday school and church since he was elected president of the Young Adults Sunday school class. It wasn't so much as that he was the class president that improved his attendance record; it was because he looked forward to seeing Joyce, the Sunday school teacher's daughter.

Harvey peeked over his Sunday paper at Jackie, who darted through the living room and out the front door, stating that he and Tommy had some important business to attend to and that he would not be going to church this morning. His mother had a look of shock on her face as she hurried to try to catch up to him, but it was too late. He was already out of sight before she reached the front door.

"Now I wonder what in the world is so important that he would pass up the chance to see that little Finley girl in his Sunday school class. I'll bet she'll ask me where he is, and I haven't a clue," she said to Harvey, who had resumed reading the paper.

For some unknown reason, when old Mr. Rankin developed

Rankin Park, he built houses on the west side of the street half-way down and on the east side the rest of the way to the end. It was still fairly thick woods across the street from Jackie's house as well as across from Lewis, who lived next door. Jackie and Tommy could hardly wait to see what Lewis would do when he discovered the two hundred-dollar bills they had hidden inside the air filter on his car. They had picked out a place in the woods that gave them a good view of him as he did his weekly maintenance of his Ford. In addition to the many trees, both large and small, there was dense foliage that offered a natural camouflage for them to spy from. The plan was to go into the woods off of Stateline Road and work their way up in front of Lewis's driveway where he would be servicing his car. The question now was would he do what he did nearly every Sunday morning after taking Francis and the kids to church?

The two boys had met at the end of the street and started into the woods in plenty of time to get situated before Lewis was due to return from his short trip to the church and back.

Jackie came to a sudden stop and turned around to face Tommy, who was only a few feet behind him.

"Do you smell that?" Jackie asked, almost whispering.

Tommy stopped and sniffed the air, turning his head from side to side and up in the air.

"It's cigarette smoke and it's pretty close," Tommy whispered back.

"I have this feeling that somebody is nearby and they're watching us," Jackie said, doing some sniffing of his own. "Just keep your eyes open," he added as he started walking; this time a little more slowly.

They hadn't gone ten feet when Jackie stopped again. He put his index finger up to his lips as he turned around to face Tommy. He turned back around and pointed at a large oak tree twenty feet ahead and slightly to their left.

"I saw something move; it's behind that big oak up ahead," whispered Jackie, as he squatted down and motioned for Tommy to do the same.

"Are you sure it's not a squirrel of something?"

"I'm not sure, but I think it's a person."

"What do you want to do?" whispered Tommy.

"We find out who in the hell it is; come on," Jackie said, as he took off in the direction of the large oak tree.

When they had almost reached the big oak, a tall skinny freckle-faced boy with bright red hair stepped from behind the tree. He had a goofy grin on his face with half of a Pall Mall stuck behind his ear.

"Well I'll be; look who's hiding out in the woods smoking. It's Tush Hog's sidekick," Jackie said, looking up at the skinny freckle-faced boy.

"I'm not his sidekick anymore."

"I guess you're not; I don't see him around here anywhere; come to think of it, the last time I saw him he was getting into the back of a police car."

Tommy had not said a word, it was apparent that he was still a little intimidated by the tall red-headed boy.

"What are you doing out here in the woods on Sunday morning besides smoking?" asked Jackie.

The redhead reached behind his ear and retrieved the half-smoked cigarette and placed it in his mouth. Jackie and Tommy eyed each other as they watched the skinny kid fumble with the box of matches he finally extracted from his front pocket. His hands were shaking so bad that he could hardly hold the match to the tip of the cigarette he was trying to light.

"I'm supposed to be in church, but I guess I sort of took a little detour. I sort of keep to myself now that they have sent Sonny off to jail."

"I didn't know he was in jail; I thought his trial was supposed to take place next month? Are you sure about that?" asked Jackie.

"Yeah I'm sure. He's not going to' trial, he confessed; especially after I talked to the judge. I told them about everything; I told them about how he bullied everybody, even told them about what happened down at the bridge that day when you hit him in the nuts with that golf club. I told the judge you did it in self-defense. I said if you hadn't done something, he might have killed you. Between me and Mr. Robinson, he didn't have a chance. I think I did him a favor; the way he was going he would have killed somebody sooner or later. I know he would have."

Jackie took a step toward the redhead, who immediately took a step backwards around the tree.

"Why are you so nervous?"

"I don't know; you're not going to hit me or anything, are you?"

"Why of course not; what's your name anyway?"

"Billy Fore."

"Well Billy, I'm Jackie Malone and this is Tommy Redden. I don't see why we can't be friends, do you?"

"I know who you are; I heard that you could do a one-handed chin-up. Is that true?"

"I guess I'm famous now; I swing a pretty good putter and can do a one-handed chin-up. What a legacy."

"Guess I'll be seeing you guys around," said Billy, stepping from beside the huge oak tree.

"Yeah, we'll be seeing you around," said Tommy, speaking for the first time.

"Hey, Billy," muttered Jackie.

The skinny boy stopped and looked back over his shoulder.

"What?"

"You should consider laying off those weeds; they could

stunt your growth."

Both boys struggled to keep from laughing out loud while they watched the skinny freckled-face boy walk straight through a huge knee-high patch of poison ivy as he made his way back in the direction of Stateline Road.

"What do you think?" Tommy asked. "He seems like he might not be so bad after all."

"Yeah, he's okay; sometimes people just get mixed up with the wrong crowd. They like to be associated with people like Tush. I think it's called peer pressure or something."

After the encounter with Billy, they had to hurry to get to the place they had picked out across the street from Lewis' house.

"Hey, Jackie," grunted Tommy as he stumbled along behind his friend, trying to keep the small branches that Jackie seemed to let go of just at the right time from hitting him in the face. "I've been thinking about something. Just what in the hell do you think Lewis is going to do when he finds the money? Do you think he's going to run around the house doing cartwheels or something? Lewis is a grown man and I'm sure he's seen a couple of hundred dollar bills before."

"I don't expect him to get too excited, butt-hole, I just want to make sure he finds them. I'm sure he'll have a wonderful story to tell us the next time we go by to visit with him. You know how he likes to add color to his stories; he'll probably tell us that his Ford sucked the money out the window of a Chevy as he passed him on the highway."

Both boys had a good laugh while Jackie searched for a good location to watch Lewis when and if he returned and started his weekly maintenance.

"Here comes a car; I think it's him," Tommy said, stooping down behind a small cedar tree.

"Yeah, it's him all right; you can set your watch by him. I'll bet you a thousand dollars he goes straight to the garage and gets his whisk broom, rag, anti-freeze, and the quart of oil that he never uses."

"I would say that you didn't have a thousand dollars, but I guess you do," Tommy replied.

"Do you want the bet or not?"

"Nah, I don't need the money and neither do you," replied Tommy with a grin.

It was a good thing that Tommy refused to take the bet. Lewis did exactly as Jackie described, right down to the un-opened can of Quaker State.

Tommy stood in silence as Jackie softly whispered the sequence of events that was taking place in the exact order seconds before they took place.

"Here he goes, Tommy; it's time for him to un-screw the wing-nut from the top of the air filter."

"Dammit, I can't see for the hood; I need to move down a little. I want to see his face when he takes the filter out." Tommy frowned.

They both had to move about fifteen feet, which took only a few seconds. They settled down in the midst of a thicket of waist-high grass just as Lewis was lifting the cover from the top of the huge air filter.

He sat the cover on top of the radiator, reached inside and extracted the filter with the two hundred-dollar bills that were clinging to the outside. He took the filter out and held it up to the sunlight just as Jackie said that he would do. He slowly turned the filter around so he could get a good look at what was blocking the light on the other side. Jackie punched Tommy in the ribs with his elbow as they watched their friend peel one of the bills from the paper filter. He placed the dirty hundred-dollar bill on top of the filter cover and very slowly peeled the second bill from the outside of the filter. He blew some of the dirt off the second bill and placed it beside the first one on top of the cover. Lewis was not going to inspect the money until he had finished his routine; he beat the filter against the concrete driveway as he always did. He put the filter back inside its housing and reached for the cover and wing-nut.

"What did he do with the money?" gasped Tommy.

"I think he still has them in his hand; I didn't see him lay them down."

"He certainly doesn't seem to be excited," said Tommy, flicking a spider from his forearm.

Lewis closed the hood on his Ford and walked over to his lawn chair and sat down. Sure enough, he still had the two bills in his hand. He held the bills up to the light and studied both sides of each bill two or three times and even smelled them. It was almost like this was something that he did every day. He folded the two bills in half and placed them in his shirt pocket. At the same time, he produced his pack of Luckies, extracted a cigarette and placed the pack back inside his pocket beside the two bills.

"I guess the show is over," mumbled Tommy, as they watched Lewis enjoy his smoke.

They stayed in their hiding place and watched their friend until he left to return to the church to pick up Francis and his kids. Not once did he retrieve the bills from his pocket to re-inspect them, or just to take another look.

Jackie insisted on waiting a while before they visited Lewis. He convinced Tommy that if they came around too soon, Lewis might think that they had something to do with him finding the money. He explained to Tommy that Lewis needed time to come up with a real good story anyway.

The next Sunday, Jackie attended Sunday school and church. He was sitting beside his friend Joyce with his arm stretched over the back of the pew with his hand resting lightly on her shoulder when the preacher made an announcement that caused him to say "Shit." He said it loud enough for Joyce to turn and look at him, as well as her mother sitting on the other side of her. Someone in the pew behind him cleared their throat along with a muffled giggle. The preacher had stepped from behind the pulpit and addressed the congregation from the second step of the altar.

"BRETHERN, I'M HAPPY TO ANOUNCE THAT OUR PRAYERS HAVE BEEN ANSWERED. WE NO LONGER HAVE TO WORRY ABOUT THE REPAIR THAT IS NEEDED ON OUR STEEPLE OR THE ROOF THAT NEEDS REPLACING.

THIS MORNING, I RECEIVED AN ANONYMOUS GIFT OF TWO HUNDRED DOLLARS. IT WAS IN THE FORM OF TWO, DIRTY ONE-HUNDRED DOLLAR BILLS. THEY REEKED OF OIL AND HAD A FAINT ODOR OF GASOLINE, BUT I CAN ASSURE YOU THAT THEY ARE LEGITIMATE.

PRAISE THE LORD. ASK AND YOU SHALL RECEIVE. AMEN.

Lewis Bolt had never attended Rankin Park Baptist Church and didn't mention the money the next week when the two boys paid him a visit. He may not have told a funny story about the two hundred-dollar bills but he had made Jackie say the S word out loud in church. It was easier for Jackie to do a one-handed chin-up than trying to explain his outburst to Joyce and her mother.

7

The days were getting shorter and shadows were getting longer as Tommy and Jackie made their way up Springvale Road to Harold's service station .They stumbled into the small office and started filling their dusty duffel bag with the stack of magazines from atop the cluttered desk. They could hear muffled cursing from Harold and Jim coming from the doorway to the service bay. The 1953 DeSoto sitting on top of the grease rack was being called a son of a bitch over and over, as well as other unflattering names. The cursing could be heard above the radio that was playing I hear you knocking but you can't come in by Smiley Lewis.

Tommy didn't answer when Jackie asked him for the second time what was going on out in the service bay. He was holding the magazine up long ways admiring the full-length picture of the April centerfold of Playboy.

Tommy's concentration was broken by a wrench hitting the concrete floor, accompanied by a loud, "Dammit."

After they had finished filling the duffel bag with the magazines, they walked out into the bay to see what was causing Harold and Jim such heartache.

The long black DeSoto had been left with Jim to put a new tube inside the right front tire that was going flat. The inner tube had been patched so many times that it was decided the time had come to replace the tube. In 1953 the DeSoto had lug bolts instead of lug nuts; when Jim removed the hub cap he discovered that one of the bolts was missing and another one was completely stripped of its threads. Harold had instructed Jim to re-tap the holes and use slightly larger bolts. Jim had done what Harold had instructed, but when he finished they were unable to locate larger bolts to finish the job. This is what started the cursing and the verbal abuse of the long black car sitting atop the grease rack. What Jim did next would be talked about for years to come. The war veteran and ex-convict found two large sheet metal screws, and using brute strength, he forced them into drum along with the three good bolts. After saying to himself quietly, "I pity the poor son of a bitch who has to take these bastards out," he popped the hub cap back on and started lowering the rack. Harold just shook his head and walked back into his office, where Tommy was looking over Jackie's shoulder as he thumbed through one of the magazines.

"It's about damn time you boys came and picked those up; I was gonna trash 'em if you hadn't come this week," Harold said as he watched Jim back the DeSoto off the grease rack.

"We've been kinda busy, now that we're back in school. You know how it is, you just don't have time for shsssss…" said Jackie.

"You like to use that word a lot, don't you? I heard you even said it in church the other Sunday." Harold grinned.

"Why did you say you subscribe to Playboy, Harold; was it for the jokes, or was it to read the articles?" asked Jackie, trying to change the subject.

"Neither one, it's the cartoons, smartass."

Jim parked the DeSoto beside the service station office and walked back into the service bay, where he started picking up his tools and cleaning up around where he was working on the DeSoto. He joined the others in the office, walking by Jackie and nudging Tommy out of in front of the pinball machine.

"This little bastard is about ready to be hit again," Jim said, tearing the paper off of a half roll of quarters.

Jim pulled the plunger back as far as it would go and let the first ball fly out of the chute. He didn't have the usual vulgar comment that he usually did on the first ball. In fact, he had no idea which hole the little chrome coated steel ball had settled into. His focus was on something that was sitting on the corner of Harold's cluttered desk.

"What's the matter Jim; do you have a fart caught sideways or something? You still have four more balls to go before you start getting pissed. Man, you look like you've seen a ghost," said Harold.

Jim fired the four remaining balls, one after the other as fast as he could. Without answering Harold, he turned and walked into the restroom. Harold looked at Jackie then Tommy and just sort of shrugged. Just as he started to say something, a maroon Mercury pulled up in front, breaking his train of thought.

Jim turned the cold water on in the small wash basin. He splashed his face with water then pulled down a fresh section of towel from the dispenser and dried himself off.

It's Jerry's damn duffel bag, hell it's got the bullet hole right through the first two letters of his name. Well I'll be damned; where in the hell did those two little assholes get that duffel bag. Could they have somehow found my money? Could they still have it... did they just find the empty bag after somebody else got the money? Hell I've got to get a grip on myself... I hope I didn't freak everybody out standing there staring like some retard or something.

Jim stepped out of the bathroom at the same time Harold returned from the gas pumps.

"You okay, big boy?" asked Harold.

"Yeah, yeah, must have been that can of sardines I had earlier; I think I'm fine now."

"Well I'm glad; for a minute it looked like somebody threw a bucket of slop in your face."

Another car pulled up to the pumps and Jim started to go out the door when Harold jumped in front of him.

"I'll get it, you take a break for a while; you still don't look exactly right."

Jackie and Tommy had resumed thumbing through their newly acquired stash of magazines. Jackie looked over the top of the August centerfold and met the eyes of Jim, who was standing behind the cash register. The eye contact lasted for only a second, but it was quite evident that Jim was sizing up the two boys. It was all he could do to keep from grabbing the two squirts by the neck and demanding they tell him where they got the duffel bag.

"What you two boys gonna do with all those magazines? I'm sure your parents don't think too much of you reading that kind of stuff," Jim said, unable to take his eyes of the dusty duffel bag.

"We're not taking them home, we have a place we can keep em," Tommy said, regretting that he had offered too much information.

"He don't read them, he just looks at the pictures. He passes them on to his friends after he memorizes the centerfolds," Jackie laughed, folding up the August issue and putting it back into the duffel bag.

"Looks like you guys have just about worn out that old duffle bag hauling that junk around," Jim said, watching for their reaction.

"Yeah, I guess so," said Tommy, looking over at Jackie.

"I used to have one just like that, carried it all over Europe and half of Africa. I wish I could remember whatever happened to that damn thing."

Harold had been on the phone arguing with the Sinclair man.

"I'm going to have to pay another penny a gallon for gas starting tomorrow. Before you know it, I'll be paying a quarter a gallon. Don't guess I can do anything about it though."

Jackie closed up the duffel bag, slung the strap over his

shoulder and rendered a half-ass salute toward Jim as he walked toward the door.

"We're out of here, thanks for the books, Harold. Sorry we took so long to pick 'em up." "Come on, Tommy, it's already dark."

After the two boys left the service station, Jim wasted no time in finding out from Harold as much as he could about the two boys that had just left with Jerry's duffel bag. Jim tried hard to hide his excitement from Harold. He knew that Harold was very fond of his two young pals, and he didn't want to arouse any suspicion with his questioning. He had to be careful, but he was determined to get his money from them if they had it. Age didn't mean anything to Jim; he had his mind made up. He would do whatever it took.

His plans to rob another bank was now on the back burner; maybe just maybe, his bad luck was about to change.

****

Jim tried his best, but no matter what he did, he couldn't go to sleep. Since Harold had changed his work schedule, the friends that he had made at the tavern had already left by the time he got off. After work he went directly to his cabin behind the tavern to plan his next move and try to catch some sleep. The discovery of Jerry's duffel bag was so unexpected that he became totally consumed with the thought of finding out what happened to its contents.

I wonder if that old fart that thinks that Hitler is still alive could tell me anything about Harold's two teenage buddies. The old drunk may be a little off his rocker but he seems to know everybody in town. I don't know where he gets his information, but he also knows quite a bit about everybody's business. I wonder if he's still over at the tavern; nah, it's too late, I'll look for him tomorrow. Now how in the hell did those boys get their hands on that duffle bag?

Jim finally drifted off to sleep thinking about Jerry's dusty old duffel bag sitting on top of Harold's desk.

It was hard for him to keep his mind on his job the next day. It wasn't just the lack of sleep from the night before, but also the overpowering urge to ask customers about Jackie and Tommy. He had acquired their names and where they lived and a little bit about their parents. One or two of the customers from their neighborhood had made a comment about Jackie being able to do a one-handed chin-up; as if that was supposed to impress Jim.

Jim had talked Harold into letting him off early. He told Harold that he didn't feel well and that having a few beers and going to bed early might make him feel better. The real reason was that he wanted to visit the tavern when some of his old drinking buddies would be there. He had found out during his life that people seemed to talk more and sometimes remember more when they had a few drinks under their belt. He was determined to find out where those two boys got hold of that duffel bag. He was sure that he would, but he wanted to do a little detective work first. He would do his homework but when it got right down to it; he might have to get nasty. *Hell the money could be long gone and the boys may have just picked up the old bag after someone else took the money and discarded it. I'm sure anything could have happened, but somehow I think those two punks know something.*

"Well look who's here; did you guys run out of gas or something over at Harold's? Still have the same, Bud in a cold mug?" Lucy asked, smiling at Jim as he eased onto the empty barstool.

Jim nodded his head yes, glancing up and down the bar.

"No we still have plenty of gas; I just need a fill-up, I've been running on about empty lately," Jim answered tiredly.

"Well you just sit down there and we'll see if we can fix that." Lucy smiled as she turned and walked in the direction of a man holding up his empty beer mug.

Jim looked around the smoke-filled room, his eyes searching for the Indian or any of his friends that he had met, either at the tavern or at the service station. He didn't see Perry, but he did recognize several of the other patrons scattered around the room. Most of them either nodded or threw up a hand when eye contact was made. Jim had made several friends, most of whom were customers of Harold's, but a few who he had drank beer with. The one that he was searching for was Bob Hodges; and sure enough there he was sitting in the same seat by the front door where he had first met him.

When Lucy returned with his beer, Jim swallowed it down with two swigs. Lucy shook her head and smiled.

"I guess you're ready for another," she queried.

"Yep, but bring it over to the table where old Bob's sitting if you don't mind. I want to talk to him for a few minutes," Jim said, getting up from the bar stool.

"Sure thing, sweetie; I'll be right over."

Bob had no expression on his face as the large dark-complexioned man slid the empty chair back from his table and sat down.

"How's it going, old-timer? I see you're still vertical, you must be doing something right," Jim said, smiling across the table.

"What does vertical mean?" Bob asked, without smiling.

"Hell, it means you're still standing; you know, not horizontal like when they put you in the ground." Jim laughed, unsure if old Bob had caught on to the jest.

"Yeah, I guess I'm doing okay, but I stay constipated. I don't get it. What are you trying to find out now? I never talk to you unless you're trying to find out something about somebody."

"Well Bob, when you need to know something, you go the person who knows something. The rest of these peckerwoods around here can't find their way out of the bathroom." He watched Bob's eyes follow Lucy working her way in their direction with his beer.

"It's been a while since I've seen you in here; where in the hell have you been? I guess you must have got hooked up with one of those flirty women needing their tanks filled up. That's okay you don't have to answer, it's none of my business," Bob said indifferently, without cracking a smile.

"I'm sorry, Bob, it's just these two boys that hang out sometimes over at the service station. I was wondering if you could tell me anything about them; they seem like good kids and they always seem to have a little money to spend. The thing is, I don't think they have a job, I'm sort of concerned that they may be dipping into the cash drawer when we're not looking," Jim lied.

"You know their names?"

"Jackie Malone and Tommy Redden," Jim said, watching Bob's eyes for a reaction.

"As far as I know they're good kids; Jackie, the smaller one, is the boy who put a hurt on that bully who sucker punched that old man over on Stateline Road. The bully and one of his buddies jumped him and Tommy right down there by that bridge." Bob pointed in the direction of Springvale Road across the street.

"Jackie hit him in the balls with a golf club; must have taken the fight out of him, I don't think he's bothered anybody else since. The last I heard, he'd been arrested for hitting the old man. The word is that his buddy turned on him; told the police all about him."

"What about Tommy; the pudgy one?" Jim asked.

"That's Max Redden's boy, that's his sister Linda who sports the new Chevy around. You know, the one they bought with the Lucky Day money. Max purchased the car so he wouldn't have to ride the bus to work. I think every minute the car is at home she's in it."

Jim stopped listening after he heard the words "Lucky Day." He had heard that term several times, but never inquired as to what it meant.

"What is Lucky Day money?" Jim asked, interrupting Bob, who was rambling on about the new car.

"You never heard about the Lucky Day gifts? Where have you been, under a rock or something?" Bob asked, then took a long sip of his beer.

"I guess you could say I was under a rock of sorts; must have happened before I got in town. Tell me about it, Bob."

"People started getting cash in the mail along with a note telling them it was their lucky day. Hell, people all over town were getting them, anywhere from a thousand up to two or three thousand. You could follow the postman around the route just by watching folks run to the mailbox after he went by. Then it stopped just as mysteriously as it started. Anyway, Mr. Redden got one of those letters, damn, Harold got one too, come to think of it. Surely you should have known that, he told everybody he saw."

Jim sat staring down at his beer for several seconds.

"I heard him mention it a couple of times, but didn't know what it was all about. Bob, did the Malone boy's dad receive one of those letters also?"

"Hell, he could have, I know several people around here that got one. But I'm not sure about him."

Jim could feel his face getting flushed at the thought of those two little bastards giving his money away to strangers.

"So they never found out who was sending out the letters then?" asked Jim.

"Nope, not a clue; people compared it to the millionaire show that comes on TV. Folks seem to think it was some rich person that had more than he knew what to do with."

Bob settled back in his chair and stared off into space.

"I would have liked to have gotten one myself, but it still wouldn't have brought my boy back. I don't understand why somebody can't spend a little money and catch that murdering bastard that's still living down on Sand Mountain." Bob's his eyes fixed on something off in the distance.

"Maybe they will, maybe they will," Jim said as he stood up digging into his pocket.

He tossed a five-dollar bill on the table in front of Bob, who was still staring at something on the far wall.

"Let me buy you a beer, and thanks for your time, old-timer. I got to go, but I'll be seeing you around,"

Jim walked back to the bar but the stool he was sitting on earlier was now occupied. He placed another five on the bar, waved at Lucy, and strolled out the back door.

As he marched across the parking lot to his cabin, he was already working on a plan to get what was left of his money back from those two punks. *"Simmer down and do it right,"* he mumbled quietly to himself as he turned the key in the lock, pushed open the front door, and stepped inside.

****

It took less than five minutes for Mr. Simpson, the manager of the Red Food Store, to interview Jackie for the bagboy job that was listed in the paper. It took him another minute to tell him that he would keep him in mind and would let him know the next day if he had the job, explaining that he had several more boys to interview. It took only ten seconds for him to tell Tommy that he was too young.

"Think he'll hire me?" Jackie asked, as they started their

twelve-block walk back down Ringgold Road in the direction of Harold's station.

"Who knows, but one thing's for sure, he's not going to hire me," answered Tommy.

"I think you should take that job up at the Cascades Motel, the kid in my Sunday school class is giving it up. He says the motel doesn't pay him, that he just works for tips. He told me that sometimes he makes up to ten or fifteen dollars a night. That's pretty good for three or four hours' work."

"I've been thinking about that; what do you do as a bellhop?" asked Tommy, scanning the side of the highway for empty cigarette packs.

"You show the guests to their rooms, take their bags in, turn on the air or heat, go get them ice. I think the more you can do for them, the bigger tip you get."

"I think I could do that; I need to find something."

They walked silently for several minutes as each set of eyes searched desperately for an empty Camel pack.

"You know something, Jackie?"

"Know what?"

"I'm worried about all that money down in that mine shaft. Something could happen, any day somebody could discover it somehow and they could come and seal it up or it could just cave in own its own. I think I'm gonna take my canister and hide it in my house somewhere; maybe under the floor or something."

"Yeah, I'm worried about that too. The thing that we need to do is find a job so we can open up a bank account and start putting some of it in the bank."

"Something else is bothering me, too."

"Does it have anything to do with all those Playboy magazines we took down in the cave the other day?"

"Not exactly, butt-hole; I'm serious."

"Okay, I'm sorry; what is it?"

Tommy didn't say anything; he darted into the ditch and retrieved an empty pack of Camels. He ran back up onto the pavement and stopped in front of Jackie holding up the empty pack as if it were made of gold. He looked at his friend and smiled as he started to pull the blue tax stamp up to reveal the letter underneath.

"Wait, numb-nuts, hold on for just a second. It's already been pulled! "He slapped the empty pack from Tommy's fingertips.

"How about giving me a break sometime, "hawk-eye,"" Tommy grunted, kicking the empty package back into the ditch.

"Okay what was it that is bothering you, little buddy?"

"Do you remember the other day when we were up at Harold's getting the magazines?"

"Yeah, what about it?"

"It's that Jim guy, you know the new man that Harold hired to help him. He sort of gives me the creeps. He kept staring at the duffel bag like he knew something about it or something. If I didn't know better, I think it was the reason that he suddenly got sick and had to go to the bathroom."

"You been reading too many comic books; how the hell could he know what was in the duffel bag. He's only been in town a few weeks. From what I can tell, all he wants to do is play the pinball and go over to the Pines and drink beer." Jackie smiled, running a hand through Tommy's flattop.

"I guess it's just me, but I had a funny feeling about him even before he started working for Harold. I heard Daddy telling my mother the new man up at Harold's was an ex-con. I didn't know what an ex-con was, so I asked Linda what it was. She told me that it meant that it was a person that had been in prison. Like I said, he just gives me the willies."

"He does talk different than people around here, and does look like one of those gangsters in the movies, but if Harold saw fit to hire him, he must be okay," said Jackie, grinning.

"Anything else bothering you? Hell, most people with your kind of money are worried how they're going to spend it all."

****

After Jim returned to his cabin, he dug down in the small dresser in the corner of his room and pulled a half-empty bottle of Jack Daniels from the bottom drawer. He went into the bathroom and returned with a drinking glass converted from a jar of strawberry jam. He poured the glass half full of the Tennessee whiskey and turned it up and drained it with one gulp.

I don't know how much is left but no question about it; somehow those two boys have got their hands on that duffel bag with my money. I have to plan this right; I know who they are and where they live. I'll get me a car first; I'll have to have a way to get out of here when I do get the money. It may get messy, but by God, that's my money and I'm getting it back. I'll bet the little farts have it hidden somewhere; the trick is to find out where. The only way to do that is to watch 'em. It may take a while, but I've done this kind of stuff before, it shouldn't be hard tracking these two. Catch them in the right place, let' em get a good look my automatic, Jap slap 'em a couple of times, they will probably piss in their pants and beg me to take the money. Yep, my luck has changed.

Jim was up early and excited as he stood in front of the Pines Tavern, waiting on the cab to pick him up. He had been talking to a customer at the service station that had 54 Mercury for sale and he had made up his mind to buy it. The man operated a small used car lot on Rossville Boulevard located in Chattanooga, just through the tunnel from East Ridge. He had been saving up some money to obtain a car to use in his planned bank job. He no longer needed the car for a bank job now; that was before he had spotted the dusty duffel bag on top of Harold's desk.

"Forty-five eleven, Rossville Boulevard," Jim said, sliding into the backseat of the cab, almost before it came to a complete stop.

"Don't guess you'll need a ride back; that's a car lot," the cabby said, raising the flag on his meter.

"Probably not if I can make a deal."

"What you looking at?" asked the cabby.

"A fifty-four Merc, new tires with low miles."

"Well good luck, some of those folks down on the boulevard have a pretty bad reputation if you know what I mean."

"Yeah, I know, I'll keep my eyes open," Jim said.

Jim watched in amazement at the number of dump truck coming and going on their way to the construction of the nearby interstate.

How in the world could those boys have gotten their hands on that duffel bag with all that construction going on? I just don't get it.

Jim sat staring out the window of the cab, wondering what to do next after he got a car. He fought the urge to just chase the two boys down and make an example out of one of them and demand the money.

"I've been out of town for a while; what's the deal about this Lucky Day letter?" Jim asked the cabby.

"That was something; I didn't get one myself, but I checked my mailbox every day."

"Who do you think was giving the money away; I understand they never found out."

The cabby scratched his head and looked at Jim in the rearview mirror.

"Beats the crap out of me, I guess they must have run out, people stopped getting them." The cab driver smiled as he turned on his headlights approaching the twin tunnels.

Jim sat mostly in silence for the remainder of the trip down

Missionary Ridge to Rossville Boulevard. He paid the cab driver and stepped across a chain that bordered the sidewalk, making his way to the one-room office. "This is going to be one of the easiest sales this fool has ever made," he said to himself as he spotted the Mercury between a pickup truck and a 1950 Ford.

Jim made a modest attempt of haggling over the price, but came to an agreement fifty dollars less than the asking price. He paid two hundred dollars down and agreed to pay ten dollars a week until it was paid off.

Jim smiled at the salesman and waved as he drove off the parking lot, knowing if things went the way he expected, another ten dollars would be all that he would ever see. If he got lucky, he may never even see that first ten.

****

Jim continued working at the service station. He said little about his new ride, even parking it behind the station as if he were ashamed of it. If he had to leave town in a hurry, maybe a few folks wouldn't know what he was driving. He came to work at 2:00 P.M. and worked until they closed up at around eleven o'clock. Since school started early in the morning and didn't let out until around three, it was hard for him to find out much about the coming and goings of his two subjects. He did, however, find out that they spent a lot of their time down on the creek that ran behind Tommy's house. This information was gathered from none other than Tommy's older sister Linda, who stopped by to gas up the new Chevy the family had bought from some of his money. Jim had casually asked where her brother had been, that he hasn't seen him and Jackie for a while. She told him that they were both looking for a job, but would probably not find one since they spent most of their time down by the creek doing God knows what.

Jim put that information in his memory bank, making a mental note as a place to start. He also made a mental note that Linda was a real knockout; wishing that he were a few years younger.

Harold had finished putting a new muffler on an old Plymouth when Jim approached him beside the Coca Cola machine.

"Harold, I hate to ask you this, but would it be possible for me to work days for a couple of weeks. I'd like to be off in the evenings to tend to some personal business. I don't mean permanent, just until I get a few things taken care of?"

"Do those things you have to take care of have blond hair or brown hair?" Harold asked, smiling as he tossed an oily rag at Jim, who caught it in front of his stomach. "Yeah, yeah, that'll be fine, I need to see what's going on around here in the evenings anyway. I miss seeing some of my old customers that I don't see anymore. You come in early in the morning; I'll work in the evenings for a while. I don't know what's going to happen when they get the freeway going. I hope we have enough local people to keep us open. That highway out there is never going to be the same," Harold said retrieving the rag from Jim's hand.

Jim smiled at how things were going his way.

"It's about time," he said under his breath, walking in the direction of a powder blue 55 Chevy that just pulled up at the pumps.

****

Jackie got off the school bus one block past his street to walk the half block with Tommy to his house, before turning up and going through Bud Higgins' back yard. He wanted to see what it was that Tommy was so eager to tell him. He said that he couldn't tell him until they got off the bus.

"Okay, Humphrey Bogart, what is it that is so important that you couldn't talk to me about on the bus?" asked Jackie, as they separated from the other kids who had just exited the bus with them.

"Don't look now, but see that car parked in the driveway at the empty house down on Springvale?" Tommy whispered, looking straight ahead.

Jackie couldn't help it; as soon as Tommy had finished, he turned and looked.

"I said don't look, now asshole." Tommy frowned.

"Okay, I'm sorry, but yes I see it. What about it?"

"Do you know whose car that is?"

"I don't have a clue; do you?"

They both walked on for a few seconds before Tommy turned around. At the exact moment that they both looked back up the street, the shiny Mercury backed out of the driveway and headed north.

"Well who is it, Sherlock?" asked Jackie.

"It's Jim's, the guy who works for Harold; he just bought it the other day."

"How do you know; we haven't been up at Harold's since we got those magazines?"

"Linda told me."

Jackie was silent for a minute as they stopped in front of Tommy's mailbox.

"Well, so what if it was him, Tommy? He has a right to look at a vacant house if he wants too. What's the big deal?"

Tommy opened the lid of the mailbox and peered inside, knowing that it would be empty.

"The big deal is that he was there Monday, Tuesday, and now again today. I think he's up to something. I don't know why, but that man just gives me the creeps. I've already told you that."

“I think it’s because of that movie, *The Man Who Knew Too Much*; you’ve been acting like this ever since you watched it.” Jackie laughed, taking a half-hearted swing at his friend’s chin, missing him by not more than a quarter of an inch. ““I’m going home; I’ll be back down here in a half hour or so. We’ll talk some more about this. I want to get home and see if I got a call from the Red Food Store.

Jackie started to walk off then turned around and walked over to Tommy’s mailbox, opened the lid and peered inside.

“I didn’t get a good look when you opened it a few minutes ago; I just wanted to see if you may have got another Lucky Day letter,” he joked, attempting another half-hearted swing at Tommy’s chin. “Quit worrying so much; remember, you’re a rich boy now.”

Jackie shook his head and headed home.

8

Jim had begun to get a little impatient. He had a pretty good idea of the coming and goings of his two little thieves, as he now thought of them. He had become obsessed with getting what was left of his money from them and getting the hell out of town. He went in to work every day, but had a hard time concentrating on what he was doing. He had no interest in the pinball machine and even less interest in the customers who he had come to know in the short time he had been working for Harold. While he was changing the oil in a customer's car, he had forgotten to replace the plug in the oil pan. He lowered the rack; poured the new oil in only to have it go straight through the engine and out the bottom onto the floor. It pissed him off so much that he kicked the hubcap hard enough to dent it. When he had finished cleaning up his mess, he approached Harold about taking a couple of hours off ; saying he was sorry but he was having trouble with his girlfriend and that he needed to get things straightened out. Harold had suspected as much and patted Jim on the back, telling him to take as much time as he needed.

Jim went to his cabin and opened the bottom drawer of his dresser, withdrawing his pistol and a half-full bottle of Jack Daniels that was wrapped in a brown paper bag. He fished around in the bottom of the drawer and located a box of the 45 shells; he put the shells in his front pocked and closed the drawer.

I have to find some place to get some practice; it's been a while since I've done any shooting. I'd be lucky if could hit the side of a barn with this thing. I hope I don't have to use it, but if

I have to; I want to make sure the son of bitch works.

He had asked around about a place to do some target practice and more than one person had suggested Willingham's farm. He was told about the creek that ran through it and the wooded hills south of Rankin Park; a lot people went there to shoot. It was part of the Willingham property but no livestock stayed in that area. Several people mentioned the old man and his son who lived in an old shack back in those woods, but not to pay any attention to them as they were sort of retarded.

Jim drove the three blocks south on Springvale Road, crossed the state line and went on south past Tommy's house on Vero Beach Avenue, stopping at the dead end. He locked the Mercury and shoved the 45 inside his pants under his belt.

The dead-end street extended several hundred feet past the last house, which made the turnaround quite secluded. As he walked away from his Mercury, he noticed that the dead-end street was frequented for reasons other than turning an automobile around. Evidence of several nights of romancing lay scattered across the gravel cul-de sac.

Jim followed the footpath west that led to the barbed-wire fence marking the boundary to Willingham's farm. He walked the two hundred yards to the shallow creek and turned south. As he followed the creek, he stopped occasionally at spots where the grass had been trampled down to the dirt from either a fishing place or a spot where the water looked deep enough for swimming. He grinned and almost chuckled out loud at the crude art that had been carved into the stump of a sycamore tree that had fallen diagonally across the creek. Some kid with a pocket knife had worked hard to express his knowledge of the human anatomy on the thin bark of the sycamore. It was quite evident that the tree, which had probably blown down some time ago by a thunderstorm, was frequently used to traverse the shallow creek. Muddy footprints could be seen both coming and going; nature had provided the only way to get from one side to the other without getting wet.

"It'll probably be gone when the next big rain comes and floods this place," Jim said to himself.

After proceeding for less than a mile, the creek turned in a more eastwardly direction and the woods became thicker with more thorns and blackberry bushes. There were several hills to the east and he decided he had reached a place to do a little target practice. No houses were in sight, and by the looks of the damage done to the base of a hundred-and-fifty-year-old oak tree; he wasn't the only one that had been shooting at that location. It appeared as if someone had been zeroing in a high-powered rifle and had used the trunk of the tree to place their target. The bark had been shredded in a spot about the size of a pie plate; sap was still oozing from around the bullet holes where the bark had been blown away. He looked about for something to attach to the tree to take aim at. Not finding anything, he removed his wallet from his back pocket and took out a crisp one-dollar bill.

If I get my money back; I'll never miss this one.- What do I mean if; I'm getting it back. Dammit I'm gonna get it back.

Jim positioned the dollar bill in the same area that the other shooter had placed his target. He broke a twig from a small sapling, punched it through the dollar bill and stuck it into one of the many holes that was made by the recent shooting. He stepped back several paces to about thirty feet; pulled the 45 from under his belt and chambered a round. It had been a while since he had fired a pistol like the one he now held, but it came back to him quickly. The model 1911 Colt 45 came into existence during the Philippine-American war due to the ineffectiveness of the .38 caliber, which failed to stop the Moro warriors. The semi-automatic pistol held a clip of eight rounds, with room for one more inside the chamber. It became the standard issue sidearm for the US Armed Forces after the Muslim uprising because of its stopping power.

Jim assumed the standard firing stance, gripping the pistol with both hands; his feet spread apart to shoulder width, and knees bent into a slight crouch. He fired two rounds and lowered his arms a few inches to see if he had hit his one-dollar bill. Slowly bringing his arms back up into firing position, he finished firing the remaining six rounds, taking dead aim. He ejected the empty magazine as he walked slowly forward, studying the target as he got closer. He grinned when he got close enough to see the results of his shooting. The dollar bill had been hit at least four times, and what looked like two hits in the same hole. The remaining shots were high and slightly to the right.

"A little rusty," he muttered to himself, reloading the magazine and walking back to his firing position, where he picked up the empty brass cartridges lying on the ground all within a few inches of each other. He re-took his firing stance and emptied the eight rounds into the base of the oak tree in less than ten seconds. When he lowered the 45, the dollar bill had disappeared and a section of bark the size of a Washington State Apple was also missing.

Jim didn't return to the tree to search for the dollar bill or even to see the results of his shooting. He bent over and retrieved the spent cartridges, putting them into his pocket before reloading his now empty magazine and popping it back into the bottom of the handgrip.

"No need to waste any more ammo," he mumbled, pushing the Colt back down inside his pants.

It was a minute or two before he started his walk back north in the direction of where he had parked his Mercury. He stood in silence with the smell of cordite still in the air; it brought back memories of the war, some good and some not so good. It also brought back other memories of the smell of gun smoke in the air. He quickly pushed the memory of Jerry from his head, as he jumped down into a shallow ravine and started climbing up a steep escarpment on the other side.

****

Jackie threw the World History book onto his bed; one of the few books that he actually brought home from school. He somehow was able to receive A's and B's in most of his classes with doing little or no homework. He walked from his bedroom into the kitchen and gave his mother a big bear hug. He opened the refrigerator and took out a ceramic pitcher of ice water that was always sitting right next to the freezer compartment. It never occurred to him that the proper thing to do was to pour it into a glass before taking a drink. He turned the pitcher of water up and swallowed down half of its contents before placing it back inside the refrigerator. After closing the door to the refrigerator, he balled up his fist and pounded himself on the forehead in an attempt to relieve the blinding headache from drinking the cold water too fast. He wiped away some of the water that had spilled down the front of his shirt when a few of the ice cubes had shifted inside the pitcher.

"What am I going to do with you; you would think that you would stop drinking out of the pitcher when you got older? I guess you'll just keep on doing it the rest of your life," his mother said, shaking her head.

Jackie just grinned and hugged her again, then turned and walked out of the kitchen back toward his bedroom.

He had picked up the history book and was thumbing through it when he was startled by the excitement in his mother's voice.

"Jack, come in here; what's going on down in front of

Tommy's house?"

Jackie went back into the kitchen where his mother was standing on her tiptoes, peering out the small window above the kitchen sink.

"What do you mean, what's going on?" Jackie asked, easing up beside her in front of the sink.

"There are two police cars down there and several people standing out in the street. I think I see Tommy and Linda standing in their driveway watching something going on across the street from them."

"I think it's at Bud Higgins' house; everybody seems to be looking in that direction. I'm going down there; I told Tommy I would be coming down there anyway."

"Don't you go down there and get in the middle of it. It's none of your business; do you hear me?"

"I won't; I'll be back in a little while." Jackie hurried out the back door and down the porch steps before his mother could offer another protest.

He was correct, there was something going on at Bud's house; he could see the police talking to Bud and his sister as he passed by on the way to Tommy's. Whatever it was, it was obviously over; some of the neighbors were leaving and slowly walking away, probably back to their own houses. He also noticed that someone was sitting in the back of one of the police cars and that someone looked a lot like Roy Higgins; Bud's dad.

"What's going on?" asked Jackie when he got close enough to Tommy and Linda to inquire without shouting.

"It's Bud's Daddy," said Linda before Tommy could answer.

"Well what did he do?"

"It's not clear what happened; so far we've just heard a lot of gossip. An ambulance came and took Mrs. Higgins away and then the police came," Linda said, stepping between Jackie and Tommy and putting her arms on both of the boys' shoulders.

"I think he must have hit her or something; she was doing a lot of hollering, you know the way she does sometimes." Tommy was finally able to get a word in.

"I could hear her screaming at him way back in my room and then it suddenly stopped. The next thing we know, we hear the sirens and here comes an ambulance and two police cars. I guess he finally took all he could take and gave her a knuckle sandwich," Tommy surmised with a goofy grin on his face.

"That's not what I heard." Linda was, still propping herself up on the boys' shoulders.

"Well, what did you hear?" probed Tommy sarcastically.

"Mrs. Nix said that Mrs. Higgins took a slap at him while they were on the back porch. She said when he raised his arm up to keep from getting hit, it deflected her blow causing her to lose her balance and she fell off the porch."

"How bad did it hurt her?" asked Jackie.

"I think it broke her arm and it must have cut her head pretty bad. They said when they put her in the ambulance she had blood all over her."

"Whatever he did, it sure shut her ass up," interjected Tommy.

"Bud called the ambulance and they called the police after she told them that Roy hit her and threw her off the porch. Now that's all I know; take it for what it's worth," Linda said, removing her arms from their shoulders.

She turned to walk away, but not before lightly brushing one of her breasts across one of Jackie's arms.

"I don't know where she gets all that information; she's been standing right here with me except for the two minutes she spent eavesdropping on the two neighbors across the street," Tommy said quietly.

"Poor old Mr. Higgins; he can't win for losing. I guess if I were him though, I'd probably be happier in jail than have to listen to the crap that she puts out," Jackie muttered almost inaudibly.

The two boys wandered off in the direction of Tommy's backyard and ending up at the fence at the rear of the lot.

"Did you hear any news about that job at the Red Food Store? Tommy asked.

"I forgot to ask when I got caught up in the commotion down here, it just slipped my mind. Are you still upset about that Jim guy that works for Harold? Do you really think he's been spying on us?" probed Jackie, trying to suppress a grin.

"I don't know, but I'm telling you, something about him just isn't right."

"I know what we should do, old buddy."

"What's that?" Tommy asked, leaning up against the fence separating his backyard from Willingham's farm.

"It's been a while since we've been to the cave. Let's go check and see if everything is in order; I need to pick up a little spending money while I'm there. Don't you think it's about time we bought ourselves something? What do you say?" Jackie held up the bottom strand of barbed wire for his friend to crawl through.

****

Jim scurried up the steep escarpment and looked around. He thought he had heard someone shouting right before he jumped down into the shallow ravine. It came from far off but he was sure that it was a person and that they had a threatening tone in what they were saying. He reached the top of the embankment and stood still trying to listen for any other sounds. Then he heard it again.

"You're on our property; you have no beeness here…Git off our land… Git off now."

Jim searched the woods in every direction; he looked up and down the creek, he scanned the top of the hills that he could make out through the pine thicket. He could see no one; the voices were from a long way off, but he was sure that the distant shouting was directed at him. Having been raised in the north, the drawl in the voice seemed somewhat amusing. It reminded him of some of the movies he had seen; Hollywood actors could never imitate that accent.

Unable to determine who and where the hillbilly shouting had come from, he decided to move on back in the direction of his car. He followed the creek, stopping occasionally to listen for more voices. He stopped at the edge of the creek bank and was in the process of emptying his bladder when he saw something out of the corner of his eye.

There were two of them and they were walking in his direction. Jim slowly zipped up his fly and took two steps backward, shielding himself from sight behind a scaly bark hickory tree. Not sure if they had spotted him or not; he stood still a full minute before peering from behind the tree. When he peeked from around the base of the large hickory tree, the two figures that he had spotted coming in his direction had disappeared.

Damn, they were right there; where in the hell did they go?

As he stood beside the tree scanning the creek bank for any kind of movement downstream, he heard it; the distant chatter of voices. It wasn't coming from the creek bank; it was coming from the base of a hill that rose out of the thorn bushes and vines a few hundred yards east of the creek. He couldn't hear what they were saying as the voices got fainter, but he was positive it was coming from the direction of the scraggy hillside.

There was something that upset him about the voices; it wasn't what they were saying, it was something else.

Well I'll be damned; that it. It's them. It's them. It's those two little farts that have my money. I don't know where the bastards are headed; but I'm sure gonna find out!

Jim slid from behind the hickory tree and darted in the direction of where he had last heard the two boys chattering. He tried to move as stealthily as possible, but he let out a few curses that were louder than he intended when he became entangled in a growth of blackberry bushes that had already shed their leaves. He gritted his teeth while he pulled the thorns from his clothes and skin, but never took his eyes off of the looming hillside. He was almost ready to give up when he saw movement halfway up the side of the hill. He only saw it for a split-second, but he was positive it was them; he cursed himself for not being able to get free from the prickly thorn bushes.

After struggling inside the briar patch for several minutes, he finally broke free and started ascending the hill. He abandoned some of his stealth techniques in exchange for speed. He was hell-bent on catching up to the boys that he believed had his money. He was breathing heavily when he stopped to catch his breath, holding onto the edge of a large rock jutting out of the hillside. While wiping the sweat from his brow with the back of his hand he heard a scraping sound coming from the other side of the boulder he was leaning against. He slowly peered around the side of the rock to see what had caused the scraping noise.

He had caught up to them quicker than he had thought; there sat the two boys beside a flat rock the size of a trash can lid. He wasn't sure what they were doing, but from where he stood, it looked like they were staring at something that was lying beside the thin flat rock.

Jim was over thirty yards away and his view of what was going on was somewhat obstructed, but what he saw next increased his pulse and brought a slight grin to his face. The slimmer of the two boys disappeared up to his armpits, and a second later, he completely vanished. The heavier boy with the flattop haircut did the same as the first one, but before completely disappearing, he struggled with the thin rock, pulling it in his direction.

Well kiss my ass; it's a damn cave. The two little punks went down in a hole that was covered with that big flat rock. This sure explains a lot of things; I'll bet this is where they keep my money hidden. I can see how they have kept it a secret; nobody would want to come up here to this spot; and if someone did, they would never suspect there would be a cave opening here.

It took Jim a few minutes to decide what to do next; he slowly walked from behind the large boulder in the direction of where the two boys had disappeared down into what was obviously a cave underneath the small hill. He approached the flat rock and marveled at how well the entrance had been concealed. The natural camouflage would have made it almost impossible to detect if he hadn't actually witnessed the boys removing the rock and going down inside.

He was excited, but at the same time he was unsure of what to do now. The unexpected discovery had caught him off-guard. He had a decision to make; should he go down there now and demand that they give him the money, or should he wait and come back after they left. He wasn't sure that the money was even down there and even if it was, they probably had it hidden and after what he had observed so far, it would probably be hidden very well. If he went down later and didn't find the money, they would know someone had found their secret hideout and if the money was down there, it wouldn't be there for long.

Jim walked back to the large boulder and sat down with his back resting against the piece of rock that had been there since the last Ice Age.

One way or the other, I'll have to get rid of the two little punks. I hate to do it but it's the only way. I can't expect them to just give me the money and promise not to tell anybody. Now's the time; I have my pistol, I'm going down there and getting my money. If I were a betting man; I would bet this is the only way down there. I'll be thousands of miles away from here when someone finds them if they ever do.

Jim removed his 45 automatic from under his belt; he pulled the receiver back and slid it forward, pushing a round into the firing chamber. He extracted the magazine and fed another round into the slot that was created when he chambered the round. He placed his wide thumb on the hammer and slowly eased it forward before replacing the pistol back under his belt. As he approached the cave entrance; the decision had been made; he was going to get his money. "It's about time," he mumbled to himself, reaching down and grasping the thin rock.

****

Tommy pulled the rock over the cave opening and clumsily descended the rope ladder. He reached the bottom at the same time Jackie struck the match to light one of the Coleman lanterns.

"One thing about it, this place never changes. I wonder if it's going to get cold down here when the weather changes," mumbled Tommy.

Tommy went straight to the box of magazines; he started digging down into the stack removing the first six inches or so to reveal the bundles of cash that was underneath. He grabbed up the bundle of twenties that they had already opened and placed it on top of the small stack of magazines he had just removed.

"How much you gonna get, Jackie? I think I'm going to take forty. What do you think?" Tommy asked, trying to make it sound like a statement and not a question.

"Hold your horses, butt-hole; I'm going to ease down the

track here and take a leak. We'll discuss it when I get back."

Tommy watched as the flashlight Jackie was carrying swept back and forth across the narrow tracks of the mineshaft. After a couple of minutes, the light stopped moving and the sound of the water splashing onto the mineshaft floor left little doubt as to what Jackie was doing.

While Tommy waited for Jackie to return, he peeled off four twenties from the now half-empty thousand-dollar bundle. He placed them in two piles on top of one of the empty wooden boxes that they had been using as a makeshift table. He glanced down the shaft where Jackie was walking back in his direction with the flashlight under his armpit, struggling with the zipper on the front of his jeans. Just as he was going to make a comment, something startled him from above his head. His heart raced as he looked up to see the rock being slid back from the cave entrance. A beam of light almost blinded him as he stared at the opening, still holding his breath. The light dimmed as he saw the silhouette of someone leaning over the opening gazing down at him. Jackie had almost made it back to where Tommy was sitting when he saw the beam of light beam down from the entrance hole. He stopped in his tracks and dropped his flashlight, which landed on one of the steel rails and went out just as he picked it back up.

Not a word was said from the intruder or the two boys as the entrance opening was filled by the large figure that now had made his way onto the second rung of the rope ladder. The huge man snaked one of his hairy arms through the small opening and slowly maneuvered the thin rock back over the entrance. Jackie had eased up beside Tommy, who was gaping at the huge man descending down the ladder. While Tommy sat with his mouth open, Jackie picked up one of the magazines and placed it on top of the packets of money that was still lying exposed inside the box on the floor of the cave. He scooped up the four twenties that Tommy had extracted from the half-empty bundle and shoved them down inside the back-pocket of his jeans.

As the large man came closer to the bottom, it became very clear to the two boys who the uninvited guest was. They looked into each other's eyes at the same time with an expression of shock and fear. They didn't have to say it; the big man was Jim and they both knew that it was really bad.

Jim reached the floor of the cave with his back to the two boys; he turned around and smiled. Still not a word had been spoken by anyone. He stood by the ladder for a few seconds looking around, adjusting his eyes to the dim light. With the two lanterns going it illuminated the small room fairly well. With only one lantern it took a while before the eyes adjusted. It didn't take the other lantern for the two boys to see what Jim had pushed down inside the front of his pants with the grip looped over his wide belt. Jim smiled a little wider when he saw that both boys were staring at the 45. It wasn't the first time he had witnessed that expression; and he knew it got worse if you were looking down the business end.

"Well, I guess you boys weren't expecting company. In fact, I doubt you have ever had any company down here," Jim said still grinning.

"How did you find us?" asked Jackie, trying to keep the fear out of his voice.

"It doesn't matter; what matters is that you boys have something that belongs to me and I'm here to get it."

"We don't have anything of yours…"

"Okay, now let's stop the bullshit, Jackie; it is Jackie, isn't it? I know you guys somehow got your hands on my duffel bag. I know you're the ones that have been giving my money away with that Lucky Day crap. Now I don't know how much you have left, but I want it, and I want it right now."

"You must be crazy, we don't have any money," said

Tommy with a quiver in his voice.

The little dumbass has guts Jackie thought to himself. But he needs to keep his mouth shut.

Jim snatched the 45 from under his belt and pulled the hammer back.

"You're damn right I'm crazy, and I think that I'm getting mad to go with it."

He pointed the pistol at Tommy and then over at Jackie.

"If I have to tear this place apart, I will. If I have to shoot one of you, I will. If it comes down to it, hell, I'll shoot both of you."

"Can I ask a question?" asked Jackie.

"What?"

"Why are you so sure that we have your money? Why us?"

Jim looked around the small room searching for something.

"There's how I know," he said, pointing at the dusty duffle bag lying beside a Coleman fuel can. "That duffle bag belonged to a friend of mine. He gave his life for me to have that money. Now is the money down here, or am I going to have to wait down here with one of you while the other one goes and gets it."

No one said a word.

"Before I shoot one of you; I want to know something else. Is there an easier way out of this place?"

"No sir, this mine has been sealed up; this is the only way in or out," Tommy stammered, knowing that he had made a mistake as he watched Jackie shake his head in disgust.

Jim grinned; he knew that the heavy-set boy was telling the truth. Jackie's body language couldn't be disguised; he could have punched his friend right in the nose right there.

He now knew that once he got the money, he would not have to be in a hurry to get out of town. "It may be a while before they find out what happened to these two. They may never find out," Jim mumbled under his breath. "I'm only going to say this one more time. GET… ME… THE … DAMN… MONEY!"

Tommy looked up at his friend with tears forming in the corner of his eyes. Their eyes met for a second as Tommy waited for Jackie to do or say something.

Jim, who was facing Jackie, turned toward Tommy and brought the 45 up slowly and stopped with the muzzle inches away from the side of his head.

"WAIT," shouted Jackie.

He picked up the box containing the money and the remainder of the magazines. He sat it on the floor of the cave and pushed it in front of Jim with his foot. Jim lowered the pistol slightly and peered down at the box that sat on the floor in front of him.

"What the hell is this?" he asked, staring at the cover of the December issue of Playboy.

"Under the magazines; it's under the magazines," explained Jackie calmly. "Would you please quit pointing the gun at Tommy?" he said quietly.

Jim didn't answer or move the pistol away from Tommy. He kicked over the box, spilling the remainder of the magazines and the bundles of currency onto the cave floor.

Not a word was said as he placed the 45 back into his waistband behind his belt and got down on one knee. Tommy stole a glance at Jackie as they watched the big man sift through the contents of the overturned box. He extracted the bundles of cash, placing them in a stack beside his knee. He tossed the magazines in every direction, not unlike a small child opening a Christmas present and disposing of the wrapping paper.

After he was satisfied that he had extracted all the bundles, he stood up and did a quick calculation of the amount of money that was stacked at his feet. He walked around the small room, occasionally stopping and looking over at the pile of money. He was not very good at math, but he was damn sure that the stack of cash that was in that box came way short of what Jerry and he had taken from the bank years before.

He put his hand on the grip of the pistol and looked down at the two boys. Jackie sat on his hammock with his arms folded across his chest, while Tommy sat on his camping stool staring down at his feet.

"You two punks know what I'm thinking, don't you? You have two seconds to tell me where the…"

"Lucky Day letters," Jackie shouted, before Jim could finish.

"I heard about those stupid-ass lucky day letters. You're going to tell me you gave away all the rest of my money to some poor son of a bitch you didn't even know?"

Both boys were now staring down at the floor as Jackie nodded his head slightly.

"Damn; I just do not believe what's happening here." Jim ran a hand through his thick black hair as he started pacing around the small room again. "What's down that tunnel?" he asked, pointing down the dark mineshaft.

"Just an old mineshaft," replied Jackie.

"How far back does it go?"

"I don't know, maybe half a mile or so," Jackie said, not mentioning that it split.

Jackie was watching his friend; he knew that Tommy was getting jumpy. He hoped that he wasn't about to do something stupid. He knew Tommy was contemplating something, but he had no idea what. He wasn't sure how much Jim knew about the Lucky Day letters. They had stopped sending them before he showed up at Harold's. He may not have any idea how many letters were actually sent out. He hoped that the big man would take the money they had given him and go away before Tommy threw in the towel.

Jim pulled the 45 back out, the hammer still back in its firing position. He squatted down in front of the two boys and placed the pistol on top of the stack of cash.

"It's come down to this, boys. I think there's more money than this and I think it's down here somewhere. Now here's the deal. I want the rest of the money that you haven't given away."

"Where did you get the money?" Jackie asked.

"Dammit to hell; I'm done arguing with you two."

It happened almost in slow motion; Tommy kicked over the lantern that was sitting on the cave floor between Jim and Jackie. It knocked over the bundles of cash, smashing the glass lamp on Jim's pistol that had been resting on top. The lantern rolled across the floor of the cave and went out just as Jim grabbed the pistol lying beside a large sliver of glass from the shattered lantern. Tommy was off his campstool and had bolted down the mineshaft. Jackie was still holding the flashlight that he had used while taking a piss earlier. While Jim scrambled to retrieve his gun, he slid from his perch on the hammock and followed Tommy down the dark tunnel.

Jim secured the 45 and stood up cursing in the total darkness that surrounded him. Jackie could hear his friend running down the mineshaft ahead of him; he knew that he couldn't see in the pitch black darkness.

He also knew that it would be risky, but he switched on the flashlight, hoping that Jim hadn't been able to follow them. He wanted to know how far Tommy had gotten down the mineshaft. He needed to catch up to him in the hopes of calming him down and working out a plan to get away from this monster.

"Slow down a minute; it's me," Jackie shouted, shining the light down the dark shaft. "Slow down man, the asshole is in the dark; he can't see us now."

Jackie had been turning the light on and off so that if Jim was following them, it would be hard for him to get off a good shot. He was wondering if the big man would even shoot at them anyway. He flicked on the flashlight to see his friend leaning against a timber twenty yards in front of where the shaft split.

He switched on the light for only a second or two and then turned it off.

The shots were deafening. Blam blam. It sounded as if he were standing right behind him and firing over his shoulder. Jackie saw sparks fly from up ahead and the sickening thud of what was undoubtedly Tommy falling onto the damp floor of the mineshaft.

Jim could hear the two boys running down the shaft, but the darkness was absolute. He assumed that they had more flashlights and lanterns; but had no clue as to where they were. He cursed himself for not carrying a match or cigarette lighter. The only thing he could do was to follow the sounds of the footsteps that were getting farther and farther away. He felt his way around to the opening of the shaft and stumbled, almost falling down when his toe caught one of the crossties that supported the track of the narrow gauge railroad.

Just as he regained his balance and was reaching for the mineshaft wall, he saw it. A dim light, a flashlight flicked on and then flicked off.

"The little pricks," he mumbled as he got into a firing position and waited for the light to come back on.

He didn't have to wait long; the light came back on and was shining onto the back of the boy with the flattop who had kicked over the lantern.

He squeezed the trigger at the exact time that the light went back out. He saw the sparks as the second round ricocheted off the mineshaft wall. It wasn't the sound of the bullet hitting the rock wall that got his attention; it was the sound of something heavy slamming onto the floor of the mineshaft floor.

"Noooooooooooooo, nooooooooooo," screamed Jackie, running up beside his friend.

Tommy was lying between the track and the mineshaft wall. Jackie flicked on the flashlight just long enough to see the blood that was beginning to pool beside his friend's head. He didn't want to leave Tommy, but he knew if he stayed it would be him next. He turned the light on for a second, shining it up the tunnel trying to make his mind up as to which shaft to take. He had his mind made up for him when he heard the buzz of the bullet fly past his ear followed by the loud blast from the 45. He was up and running before the echo from the gunshot made its way back down the shaft.

Jim stood in the darkness waiting for the light to reappear. He had never experienced the kind of darkness he was experiencing now. He waited and waited, five minutes passed, then ten.

As Jim stood inside the mineshaft in total darkness, he knew that he had a decision to make. He put the pistol back under his belt and felt his way around the wall of the mineshaft, cursing each time he bumped his head or stubbed his toe.

What in the hell do I do now? I'll never find that little prick without a light; .for all I know he may know another way out of here. The little bastards might have been lying about this place having just one entrance. Screw 'em; I guess I'll just get what's left and get the hell out of here... I'm in Georgia here; if that little punk up there is dead, it's the electric chair. Yeah; guess I better get the hell out of Dodge.

Jim crept slowly back out of the shaft entrance into the larger room where they had been when Tommy kicked over the lantern, hurling the bundles of cash across the cave floor. He stumbled over Tommy's campstool, falling face down onto the floor, cutting his hand on the broken glass as he tried to break his fall. He let out a loud, "Son of a bitch," grabbed the stool and flung it against the cave wall. He rose to his knees and extracted a sliver of broken glass from the palm of his hand.

The fall was not a total loss; his other hand landed on top of one of the packets of cash. While he knelt on the cave floor, he began feeling around for the remaining bundles. He unfastened a button on the front of his shirt, placing the bundles inside when he located one. While he expanded his search for the packets that had been kicked farther away, his hand caught the side of a large piece of the broken glass. It opened up a larger wound than the first; he cursed as he felt the stickiness of the blood between his fingers.

After slicing his hand, he stood up and used his foot, trying to locate any remaining bundles. After several minutes of searching with his feet with no results, he gave up and started feeling for the rope ladder.

After several minutes of groping for the ladder and unable to locate it, he let out another loud, "Son of a bitch." He put his hands on his hips and started to turn around when he felt something touch his right elbow. He flinched and jumped back before realizing he had just brushed the edge of the scratchy hemp of the ladder.

"Well I'll be damned," he said, reaching over and securing the ladder in his sticky blood-soaked hand.

He made sure his pistol was secure and fastened the button on his shirt before starting up the ladder, ignoring the pain from the cuts on his hands. He ascended the twenty-five feet to the top with little effort and slid the flat rock to the side before crawling out. The shadows were getting longer and the light was fading, but he could see good enough to examine the cuts on his hands and determine that it was little more than a scratch.

While still on his hands and knees, he scooted around in a circle marveling at the almost total concealment of the cave entrance. Jim peered back down into the blackness of the shaft and settled back on his heels. He wiped some blood that had oozed from the cut on his shirt and reached into his front pocket of his trousers. Grimacing as he extracted the three-and-a-half-inch Barlow jack-knife from his dirty khaki pants, he opened the larger of the two blades with his teeth while reaching down and pulling up one side of the rope ladder. He cut the ladder from the steel rods the boys had driven into the side of the entrance wall. The ladder dropped to the floor of the cave, making almost no sound as it landed inches away from the broken lantern. With one hand, he slid the large flat rock over the opening to the entrance and stood upright.

"Now to get the hell out of this place," he mumbled, checking to see that the front button of his shirt was secured where he had placed the bundles of cash.

After several attempts of descending the hill and running into thick thorns and blackberry vines, he retreated to the base of the large boulder where he had first observed the boys at the cave entrance. He ran his blood-stained fingers through his thick black hair, trying to remember the direction where he had ascended the hill earlier. Not being able to distinguish any discernable path or trail, he decided to just go straight down the sloping hillside, thorn bushes or not. He knew the general direction of the creek; if he could just get down to it, he could easily find his way back to his car.

"To hell with it," he mumbled, turning to face the direction of the creek and stomping through a tangle of honeysuckle vines and briars. He had traveled no more than ten feet when he slipped on a loose stone and fell flat on his ass.

9

Jackie sat on the floor of one of the ore carts they had left parked at the end of the shaft, where the track ended under the massive cave-in. His eyes were closed and his head rested against the cold steel of the slightly reclining front or back of the cart, depending on which direction the cart was headed. He made a valiant effort not to cry as he pushed away the image of his friend lying in a pool of blood. He waited for his pursuer to emerge from the darkness at any second even though he had not heard a sound for at least twenty minutes. He cursed himself for his predicament and asked God to forgive him and Tommy for keeping the money. He promised God at least fifty things he would do or stop doing if he would just get him out of this, and make sure that Tommy would be okay. His ears were hyper-sensitive to any noise, real or imagined, as he sat in the bottom of the ore cart. His eyes were shut tight, but it wouldn't have mattered if they were wide open; it was total darkness either way.

Ten more minutes passed, then thirty; still no sound.

Maybe he's gone; maybe he just took what money there was and just left. That's got to be it; he must have just climbed up the ladder and took off.

It had been over an hour since the shots rang out and his friend crumpled to the floor of the mineshaft. He could not put aside the image of Tommy lying beside the track with blood oozing from his head any longer.

"I can't sit here forever; I have to do something if it's wrong," he said out loud.

He blinked his eyes several times as the flashlight flicked on in front of him. He had been holding it with both hands in front of him, not realizing the lens was pointed directly at him when he slid the switch forward. Quickly pointing the beam down the shaft, he stood up inside the ore cart. His heart was pumping hard while he traversed the beam back and forth down the shaft, expecting to see the large monster of a man step into view at any minute.

"So far so good," he whispered, throwing his leg over the side of the ore cart and searching for the top of the track with his toe. Hugging the wall of the mineshaft, he inched forward, stopping every ten feet or so as he turned off his light, took a deep breath, and listened for any sound or movement. Satisfied that he had heard nothing, he made his way back down the dark shaft in the direction of where he had left his friend lying in a pool of blood. He made more promises to God if he would just let him find him still all right. He even promised not to look at any more Playboys if he would grant his prayer. Somehow, he wasn't sure that God was listening as a tear leaked from the inside corner of his eye and ran down into his mouth.

****

Jim half-fell and half-climbed down the rugged hillside in the direction of the creek. He was soaked from head to toe with sweat from working his way through the tangle of vines and blackberry bushes. He had accumulated numerous cuts and scratches and torn his shirt and pants in several places. One of the thorns had torn a hole in his shirt large enough for the bundles of cash to fall through. He was constantly stopping to shift the bundles to the opposite side to keep from losing what was left of his bounty. He let out a constant barrage of curses; threatening to not eat another blackberry for the rest of his life. At one point, a rabbit jumped up in front of him and disappeared into a thicket of vines. Jim pulled the 45 from under his belt and would have shot it if it were not for one of the packets of twenties falling through the tear in his shirt.

The hill finally flattened out and he could make out the line of trees that bordered the creek two hundred yards to the west. He stepped up his pace and traversed the short distance to the path running parallel to the shallow stream. Reaching the path, he turned north heading in the direction of where he had crossed the fence into the pasture. He hoped that his car was still parked at the end of the dead-end street.

"All I need is for something else to go wrong," he mumbled to himself.

Jim followed the path that ran alongside the creek; his thoughts focused on what to do next. He paid little attention to his surroundings; his eyes were on the trail in front of him, occasionally glancing to the east in an attempt to locate where he should veer to the right and cross the fence in the vicinity of where he had parked his Mercury. He spotted the fallen sycamore tree up ahead that had quickly become known as the foot-log. It was the reference point he had been looking for; just a little farther and he would head east across the two hundred or so yards of pasture to where he had crossed the fence.

Something moved up ahead at the edge of the creek where the fallen sycamore was lodged against a tall sweet-gum tree. At first he thought it was a bird or a squirrel, but it wasn't; it was a funny looking little man with a dirty brown fedora hat that dropped down covering most of his face. He could not have been more than five feet tall and was what most people from the north visualized when they thought of mountain people from the south. Aka Snuffy Smith. Jim would have laughed except for one thing; the goofy little troll was holding a rifle and it was pointed straight at his chest.

"Hold it right there, mister; you is trespassing and I'm pretty sure you was the one that was shooting that pistol a little while ago. I watch out for this property for Mr. Willingham; he don't want people shooting guns down here. You might hit one of his cattle, you know."

"Well I guess you're going to just shoot me then; is that right, little man?" Jim said, walking slowly, closing the distance between him and the comical-looking hillbilly.

Bo Goins pulled the hammer back on the single-shot twenty-two rifle.

"Don't you get smart with me, City Boy. It aint nothing for me to shoot your Yankee ass," Bo snarled through his three tobacco-stained teeth.

Jim stopped ten feet from where Bo stood atop the end of the foot-log, holding the antique twenty-two. He had heard about this kind of people that existed in this part of the country. He knew most of them were half-crazy and trying to reason with them was out of the question. He was sure that the dirty cartoon character standing on the fallen sycamore tree hadn't spotted his 45 tucked under his belt. If he could just get the little bastard to take that peashooter off of him for a second, he would end this conversation once and for all.

"How about I just give you twenty bucks and we call it even?" Jim said, reaching behind him and withdrawing his wallet from his back pocket.

He pulled a twenty from the wallet and tossed it on the ground between him and the hillbilly troll. It was what he had hoped would happen; Bo jumped down from the foot-log and went to reach down to pick up the twenty-dollar bill that lay in the center of the dirt path.

Jim had the 45 out of his belt in a split-second; he shot Bo behind the left ear and put another round through the center of his back before the little man hit the ground. Bo's outstretched hand landed six inches away from the twenty, the index finger twitched twice and then relaxed. Jim kicked the old twenty-two rifle away, leaned over, picked up the twenty, and shoved it inside his front pocket before standing up. He was smiling as he took a deep breath, enjoying the smell of gun smoke in the autumn air, when he heard it. It would be the last thing that Jim Vess would ever hear. Cheese, Bo's son, had been watching from behind a stand of small cedar trees directly across and slightly above the fallen sycamore. The cross-eyed teenager pulled both hammers back on the double-barreled Winchester twelve-gauge shotgun.

Jim slowly looked to his right just in time to see the blast from the left and then the right barrel of the Winchester. The first round of the high velocity buckshot hit Jim square in the midsection, lifting him up off his feet and propelling him backward toward the creek. As he was falling backward, the second blast tore into his thighs and groin. Before he lost consciousness, he felt the effect of the second blast rip through his lower body. He was dead before he hit the water.

Jim's shattered body fell into the creek landing on his back; the shotgun blast tearing through his shirt and exploding the packets of money like confetti at a New Year's Eve party. The few bills that were left intact floated downstream, along with pieces of his shirt and trousers. Jim's body floated face up under the foot-log and got caught up in a tangle of water lilies fifty yards downstream.

Cheese dropped the shotgun at his feet and walked to where his dad lay dead in the center of the path that ran beside the creek. He sat down on the ground beside his father's head and began to rock from front to back. He wrapped his arms around himself and was still in that position when he was found the next day by a man walking the creek looking for turtles. Cheese Goins would never stop rocking, nor would he utter another word for the remainder of his life.

10

Jackie slowly made his way back in the direction where Tommy had fallen. The beam from the flashlight landed on what looked to be a fifty-pound sack of potatoes, or maybe a discarded trash bag lying beside the track thirty yards in front of him. He turned off the light and leaned against one of the mineshaft timbers; his heart skipped a beat and the urge to vomit consumed him as he tasted the bile in the back of his throat. He knew it wasn't a sack of potatoes or a bag of garbage, it was the body of his friend, and it was still in the same position as when he had last seen him.

It seemed like an eternity before he reached his friend and squatted down beside him. Tears flooded his eyes, making it impossible to see clearly as he reached out to touch Tommy's arm. He tried not to look at the blood that had now dried on the ground under his head. It was hard to tell the color of Tommy's skin from the gradually weakening flashlight, but he noted that it looked pretty normal to him. He moved his hand down and searched for a pulse in Tommy's limp wrist, trying to remember the proper way that he had been taught in health class. "Use your fingers not your thumb," he mumbled to himself, remembering that your thumb had a pulse of its own. He tried to will the feeling of the faint heartbeat that could be felt in the wrist, but could not make it happen. He was about to try feeling for a pulse in the neck when he heard something that startled him. He turned the light off and held his breath. *Something is down here with me; is it an animal or is it Jim?* His heart felt like it was going to explode in his chest.

What in the hell is it? His mind screamed for an answer.

After several minutes of holding his breath and straining his ears to make out where the strange noise was coming from, it finally hit him.

It was the sound of snoring and it was coming from right in front of him. It was Tommy and the shit-ass was asleep.

Jackie put his ear right up to Tommy's mouth just to make sure it was him that he heard. Sure enough it was him, and he was definitely alive. It was too soon to be overjoyed; Jackie knew that his friend could be in real trouble, but at least he was alive. He knew that anytime you had a head wound, it could be real bad, especially if you were shot.

Jackie sat in silence trying to think of what he should do. He had paid attention in first-aid training, but he never dreamed he would have to deal with anything like this. "Should I sit him up, should I just let him stay like he is; what should I do, God? Tell me what to do," Jackie said out loud.

After several minutes of talking to himself, he decided that he would not risk moving his friend and that the best thing to do was to go get help. He jumped to his feet and took off down the shaft toward the entrance. *If Jim is still down here and I run into him; it's gonna take more than a one-handed chin-up to help me.* He had to get help. The batteries were almost gone in the flashlight when he reached the end of the shaft where the entrance was located. He had just enough light to examine the mess that Jim had left and to locate another light with better batteries. He found another light that he had placed on the floor beside his hammock. The batteries were stronger and he was able to get a better look at the mess that had been made in what had been referred to as their living room. The broken globe of the lantern was strewn across the floor as well as the magazines and a busted bundle of twenty-dollar bills. As he stood by his hammock examining the mess, what he saw lying in the center of the room made his heart skip a beat. Almost right on top of what was left of the Coleman lantern was the rope ladder piled up like a bundle of snakes. Jackie felt the lump grow in his throat while he watched the beam from his flashlight settle on the bottom of the flat rock covering the entrance of the cave. He could see where Jim had cut the rope from the steel rods they had driven into the wall. He dropped the flashlight onto the floor between his feet and put both hands to his face.

"Jesus, help us, we're trapped."

****

It was mid-morning when the East Ridge and Catoosa County Georgia Police descended on Rankin Park and the adjacent dairy farm. The bodies of Jim Vess and Bo Goins were placed into body bags and transported across the pasture from the creek, through the back yards to the street in front of Tommy's house. They were loaded into awaiting ambulances and taken to the morgue in downtown Chattanooga, Tennessee. By lunchtime, the FBI and the Georgia and Tennessee Bureaus of investigation were on the scene. The FBI took over the investigation and dismissed the Georgia authorities, but solicited the help of Raymond Duke, the East Ridge chief of police with the patch on his right eye. The street was crowded with neighbors and curious onlookers as well as newspaper reporters as far away as Atlanta. All three television stations were on the scene trying to interview anyone that would stand still. No one was sure of what had happened, but the rumors were flying. The only thing anyone was sure of was that old Bo Goins had been shot dead and that and an ex-convict from up north had done it, and Bo's son had shot the Yankee. The fact that two teenagers were missing was not even mentioned in the afternoon newscast.

Special Agent Buck Shadrick met Chief Duke in his office at in East Ridge. The Korean War veteran remained in his chair when the young FBI Agent entered his office. Agent Shadrick had heard of the chief with the patch on his eye. He was well respected and known for his no-nonsense approach to law enforcement.

"Have a seat," the chief said when Buck Shadrick walked in and shut the door behind him.

"That's okay, Chief; I think I'll just stand if it's the same to you,"

"It's fine with me, but I'm gonna keep my butt in my chair; I think maybe I might be getting a little soft in my old age." Duke grinned up at the FBI agent.

"What the hell's going on down here?" Buck asked, staring at the Marine Corps seal on the wall behind the chief's head.

"Not real sure, but from what I can find out it looks like old Bo finally did what he's been threatening to do for a long time."

"I'm sorry, I don't follow you."

"Well, old Bo was not exactly all here, if you know what I mean. He's probably a product of the family tree not branching out the way it's supposed too."

"You mean like marrying your cousin and stuff like that?" asked the young agent.

"You got it, but more like marrying your sister. Some of the people around here are pretty messed up."

"What did you mean when you said he's been threatening to do something?

"He and his son stay in an old shack out on Willingham's farm. Mr. Willingham lets him stay there for free; it has no electricity but it does have water. Old Bo sort of took it on himself to be the caretaker of the farm for letting him stay out there in that old house. We've had folks come in here and report that Bo had threatened to shoot them if they didn't get off his property. We always thought he was harmless, but I guess we were wrong."

"What about his son, the one they call Cheese? I guess he's messed up also?"

"Yep, even worse, they tried to get him in school, but it was no use. He just wouldn't go."

"Are we positive that Cheese is the one that unloaded the shotgun on the ex-con?"

"That's what it looks like; the con shot his daddy and the boy unloaded on him. Nearly blew him in two."

"Who is this Jim Vess?" Agent Shadrick asked, flipping open his notepad.

"He served over ten years up at Petros for bank robbery. He's been working at a service station here in East Ridge since his release a few months ago. Harold, the station owner, says he has been a good employee, hasn't had any problem with him so far. He knew he had been in prison, thought he would take a chance on him. The problem we have is that we don't know what in the hell he was doing down on that creek. He had a 45 automatic with him; the one he shot Bo with. We think he may have been down there taking target practice; a couple of the neighbors said they heard shots being fired down there. I think he might have come across Bo and they got into it, but that's just a guess," Chief Duke said, fiddling with the patch on his eye.

"I understand Bo's son Cheese hasn't spoken a word about what happened. Do you think he's just in shock or has he gone completely of his rocker?"

"No one can remember hearing him say that much to begin with; I'd say he has completely lost it."

Chief Duke stood up and walked around the corner of his desk and extended his hand to the FBI agent.

"That's about all we have right now, Agent Shadrick. I hate to cut you short but I have a bunch of people to talk too. I've got your number, if we come up with anything, you'll be the first to know. Have a good day, Agent Shadrick."

Chief Duke opened the door and they both stepped out into the hallway.

****

Jackie stood in the center of the small room inside the abandoned mine, staring at the flashlight lying on the floor between his feet. The magnitude of his predicament came crashing down upon him like a bolt of lightning.

What am I going to do about Tommy? his mind screamed.

Picking up the flashlight, he scrambled back down the shaft where Tommy lay unconscious and bleeding. He had decided that he would do whatever he could to make Tommy comfortable and, if possible, help him regain consciousness. As he approached the spot where Tommy had been lying unconscious in a pool of blood, he stopped and dropped to his knees. Up ahead, the beam of his flashlight caught his friend leaning back against the cave wall, running his hand through his flattop. At first he thought he was just imagining the vision of Tommy sitting up against the wall, rubbing his head. While he stood on his knees shining the flashlight beam down the shaft, it became apparent that what he was witnessing was real. He watched Tommy shield his eyes from the flashlight beam with his hand.

"I'll be damned; I guess I'll live a dull life keeping all those promises I made to God. It looks like he's gonna live."

When Jackie finally made his way up beside his friend, it was almost as if nothing had happened. Tommy only asked where he had been; he had no memory of what had happened. Jackie had to bring him up to speed on what had taken place. The last thing Tommy remembered was kicking over the Coleman lantern. As it turned out, the 45 hollow point struck the mineshaft wall inches away from Tommy's head. The bullet exploded into small fragments, one of which slammed into the side of his head. A piece of lead the size of a pencil eraser punched a hole above his right ear all the way down to his skull. The impact knocked Tommy out cold and he lost quite a bit of blood, but otherwise he was fine, except for a scar on his scalp that would be there the rest of his life.

Jackie was so thrilled that his friend was alive and appeared to be okay that he forgot the dire predicament they were in. He wanted to give him a big hug, but refrained from doing so for fear of sending the wrong kind of message. Men just didn't hug other men; and after all, they were just a couple of years away from being a man, he reasoned.

"What happened to that crazy bastard; did you beat him up, Jackie, did you hit him in the nuts or something? Where is he?" Tommy asked, still rubbing his head.

"I have some good news and some bad news," Jackie answered, breaking eye contact with his friend.

Tommy stopped massaging his scalp; the small hole left by the bullet fragment began to well up with blood and started to trickle down the side of his neck.

"I'll give you the good news first; the asshole is not down here anymore. The bad news is that he cut the rope ladder; our asses are trapped down here. That is unless you know of a way out of here that you haven't told me about."

Tommy sat staring down the dark shaft, trying to grasp what Jackie had just told him.

"So he cut the rope ladder from the top when he left; did he cover the entrance back up with the flat rock?" Tommy asked indifferently.

"Yep," he did, but guess what?"

"What?'

"The scumbag left without getting the rest of our money; he just took what was hidden under the Playboys. When you kicked over the lantern, he couldn't see in the dark and couldn't find a flashlight. He even missed a bundle of twenties lying on the floor."

"He may come back, you know," Tommy muttered sheepishly.

"Yeah, he could, but if he does, he better bring a rope. He did away with the only way down here when he cut the ladder down."

Neither boy said a word as each was lost in their own little world that had turned into a nightmare. Jackie thanked God for letting Tommy be okay. Tommy gave thanks for Jim leaving them the hundred thousand dollars that they each had hidden away. Tommy was the first to speak.

"How long do you think we'll have to wait before someone comes to let us out?"

"I was wondering the same thing. Tommy, how many people know about this place? Let me ask it another way, how many people know where the entrance is and how to get to it?"

Tommy didn't hesitate.

"ONE."

Jackie smiled at his friend. "You see why I wanted to show this place to Lewis; he'll be here as soon as he finds out I didn't come home. All we have to do is just sit back and wait. He'll be here."

They both returned to silence for several minutes before Tommy broke it again.

"What about the money; what are we going to do about the money. Are we just going to leave it down here?"

"I've been thinking about that. I still don't understand how Big Jim knew we had the money. He says that it was his, but it just doesn't add up. Where in the hell did he get it and damn, we found it buried in the ground inside a duffle bag."

"It's the duffel bag; it's that stupid duffel bag. He freaked out when we brought it up to Harold's to pick up those magazines.

Don't you remember, he looked like somebody threw a bucket of puke in his face when he saw it?"

"Yeah I do remember, the asshole almost threw up; had to go in the restroom and clean up. I'll bet the bastard wet his pants," Jackie said, without smiling.

Tommy was bleeding again from the small hole in his scalp. His white T-shirt was almost completely red down the right side, front and back. He hadn't lost a lot of blood, but enough to make it look like he had been in an ax fight, with everybody but him having an ax.

"Do you feel like walking, buddy; we need to get back down to the living room and see what we have as far as water and food? We need to get prepared just in case it's not Lewis that slides that rock away from the opening up there. That monster may come back, you know. If he does, we need to be ready."

Tommy stood up slowly, holding onto the side of the mineshaft wall for support. He was a little wobbly, but otherwise okay.

"I'm fine, let's go," he said, shuffling along the track in front of Jackie.

After returning to the larger room that had been their living room, Jackie took inventory of what remained of the provisions that they had accumulated, while Tommy rested.

They soon cleaned up the mess; picking up the pieces of broken lantern and scattered magazines. Jackie lit the other lantern and set it in the center of the room. He placed the things that he considered essential on the floor beside the flickering light.

One full gallon of water and two full canteens, two coca-colas, one Doctor Pepper, one 7UP and one can of Falstaff Beer that they had been hoarding for a special occasion. As for food, they had one unopened packages of Ritz crackers, three Moon pies, and six Zero candy bars.

"Well I guess that's it; but I don't think it really makes a difference. Lewis will be down here tomorrow anyway. We have enough water to last us several days; we can do without food for a lot longer. Hell, you could probably go for a month without starving," Jackie said, with a sly grin.

"What about the money? If Lewis comes to get us, I'm sure he'll have the police with him, wouldn't you think?" Tommy asked.

"He may and he may not; what do you think we should do? You think we should just hand it to the police when they come, and tell them that it belonged to Jim, the big bastard that tried to kill us?" Jackie fired back.

"I don't know what to do, I'm just asking you."

"I say we leave it where it is; let's see what's happened to Jim. It's very possible he may be in jail or something; he may have told the police where it came from. He may be long gone and we'll never know," Jackie said, knowing it wouldn't be hard to convince Tommy to keep the money.

Jackie settled back on his hammock and Tommy leaned back on his campstool and propped his feet up on an empty Coca-Cola case. Lewis would be down to get them out tomorrow; all they had to do now was to wait.

****

Two days passed and Chief Duke had no more to go on than when they had found Jim Vess floating in the creek and Cheese Goins sitting beside his dad bobbing back and forth like an Orthodox Jew at the wailing wall.

Agent Shadrick did a full background check on Jim, but came to a dead end from when he was sent to prison in 1945. He had been a model citizen since his release. The case was unusual, but it seemed that he was just at the wrong place at the wrong time. The chief and the FBI, along with Catoosa County Georgia Sheriff, came to the consensus it was a case of dim-witted hillbilly ignorance up against a hardened criminal. Bo Goins would have probably lived out the rest of his life threatening the locals, who knew that he was a little screwed up, and he would have continued to get away with it. The problem was that he came across someone who didn't know about this sort of people and the result was just what it was. There was a showdown and both men lost.

The other part of the puzzle may or may not have been related, but the FBI handed it over to the local police.

Two teenagers were still missing and the last place they were seen was heading in the direction of where they had found Jim Vess and Bo Goins dead beside the shallow creek.

****

"I thought you said that Lewis would be here by now; we're down to our canteens now and we've eaten all of our food except one Zero. Why hasn't he come, you know he must have heard we're not home; do you think he's forgotten about us showing him this place?" Tommy asked.

Jackie stood up and paced around the small room at the bottom of the mineshaft entrance.

"All right, Tommy, stop the whining; I don't have answers to your questions. You've asked me fifty times already; now stop it for Christ's sake. I think it's time we started thinking about getting ourselves out of this mess."

"Getting out; just how in the hell do you propose to do that? Its twenty-five feet at least to the ceiling of this place, what do you plan to do, climb the side of these walls like Spiderman or something?" Tommy asked, almost crying.

Jackie grabbed Tommy by both shoulders and turned him

around to face him.

"Listen to me, little buddy, I don't know why Lewis hasn't come to get us out of here, but we have to come up with something or we're going to be down here forever no matter how rich we are."

"Think of something, Jackie, you always do," Tommy said, his eyes welling up with tears.

****

2:45 PM Minneapolis, Minnesota

"Mr. Bolt, I hate to interrupt you but your wife just called; she needs you to call her when you get a break," the pretty redhead shouted above the noise of the machine Lewis was watching perform its final test before approving of its purchase.

Lewis looked back over his shoulder and nodded. He stood upright and removed his safety goggles. One more week and he would have made up his mind on the purchase of the multi-million-dollar machine to help build the nuclear reactor his company was engaged in.

He walked the five-hundred-foot hallway back to his makeshift office and sat down behind his temporary desk. The four weeks of watching the tests and re-tests of the huge machine had taken its toll. Not only was he tired, but his hearing was about gone as well. He wore hearing protection most of the time, but had to remove the earplugs if he were to get the questions answered that he needed to know. He picked up the phone, placed the receiver to his ear and dialed nine for an outside line.

"What is it, Francis; is everything all right? You know I'm down to the nitty gritty on this project, another couple of days and I'll be home," Lewis barked into the phone as soon as his wife answered.

"Honey, I hate to bother you and I know you're busy, but Mrs. Malone next door wanted me to call you. Jackie and that boy Tommy from the street behind us are still missing. She knows that you and those boys were good friends and that they confided in you; she was hoping that you might have some idea as to where they might be."

Lewis said nothing for several seconds; his ears were still ringing from the machine shop he had just come from.

"How long have they been missing?" he asked, remembering that she had mentioned it to him the night before.

"Going on four days now," she replied.

"I'll be home in the morning," Lewis said calmly, hanging up the phone.

****

They had shared the Zero candy bar long ago and drank the last of the water. Jackie remembered a place in the mineshaft that branched off from the main track that had water standing in a few spots. He insisted that they try to find it and see if it was still there. Tommy had not moved in over five or six hours and refused to go; he had decided to just give up.

"Get your ass up, fart-face; I'm sorry I haven't figured out a way to get out of this place, but I'm telling you we're gonna get out of here, but right now we need water," Jackie pleaded.

Tommy picked up one of the canteens and threw it against the wall of the shaft.

"Screw you, Jackie, screw you; we're done, do you understand, we're done. I thought Lewis could be trusted, how could he let us die down here, how could he?"

"Well you can lay here and die if you wish, but I'm going after that water and I'm gonna live. When I make it out of here,

I'm coming back and getting my ammo box full of cash. Now if you'll just tell me where you have yours hidden, I'll get yours too. I'll give it to Linda, I'm sure she'll find some place to spend it."

"Kiss my rosy ass," Tommy said, raising himself up into a sitting position. "I'm not telling you where my ammo box is; what's the difference, we're not getting out of here anyway."

Jackie picked up the empty canteen and slowly headed down the dark mineshaft taking the lantern with him and leaving his friend in the dark. The batteries in the flashlights had given out days ago; the only light was the lantern, which would be out of fuel soon.

"Hold up, Dammit, I'm going with you," Tommy said, pulling his shrinking body upright.

Tommy had taken no more than two steps when the sound of the flat rock being slid away from the opening up above stopped both boys in their tracks.

"Shuuuuuh, Shuuuuuh," Jackie whispered, holding his finger to his lips.

As the big rock slid from the opening, a beam of sunlight illuminated a two-foot section of the cave floor three feet in front of where the boys were standing.

"Hey… hey… Jackie, are you and Tomcat down there? It's me, Lewis."

11

Lewis finally showed up along with the Catoosa County sheriff, the East Ridge chief of police and the Chattanooga resident agent of the FBI. Also with him were Jackie's mother, Tommy's mom and dad, along with Tommy's sister Linda and Jackie's sister Judy. Harvey decided not to join the entourage; he concluded that the boys had skipped school and would come back when they ran out of money.

Jackie and Tommy were dumbfounded to discover that Jim and Bo Goins had had a shootout and that both were dead. They were even more surprised to find out that no trace of the money that he had taken up from the cave was recovered. They read everything about the incident, and not one word was mentioned about the money. Neither could anyone determine the reason Jim had followed the boys to the cave and trapped them inside.

Two weeks after they were rescued, the boys got permission from the County Sheriff's department to go down inside the mineshaft to retrieve some of their stuff as they called it. The sheriff granted their request, but assured them that the cave would be permanently sealed when they were finished.

After the boys brought up the things that they had decided to keep from the mineshaft, they sat down on top of their ammo boxes full of cash and stared at each other. After several minutes, Jackie started to smile, watching for Tommy's reaction. That was all that it took; Tommy face broke open in a wide grin and then into laughter. The decision was made to keep the money for now; after all they were still not sure where it came from. No, they were not sure about anything; anything at all.

****

June 1 1961

Jackie and Tommy attended a weekly drill with one of their friends who had a brother in the Tennessee National Guard. Though they had agreed to visit the armory just to see what it was all about, they were talked into joining under the buddy plan, which guaranteed them to be together through basic training and their Advanced Individual Training. Tommy was still in school, but the recruiter let Jackie drill with the unit while he waited for Tommy to graduate. Although they didn't know it then, it was either a stroke of fate or just plain luck, but that decision may have been one of the most important ones in their life. In just a couple of short years, most of the boys they grew up with would be sent half-way around the world to a place where many would not return. Vietnam was a place neither had ever heard of; but it would not be long before everyone would know where it was.

The Greyhound Bus pulled out of the station on a rainy Saturday morning two days after Tommy was handed his diploma from Lakeview High school. The bus skirted the Tennessee River around Moccasin Bend and headed north on Highway 41 on its way to Fort Knox Kentucky.

"How much did you get out of your box?" Tommy asked Jackie, staring out the window at the raindrops peppering the bus window.

"Just a thousand; I don't think we'll need much for a while. What about you?"

"I just got a hundred; from what I hear, we're not going to have time to spend that much."

The bus slowed down at Haletown and started onto the bridge south of Hales Bar Dam.

"I hear they're going to blow up that old dam," Jackie said, pointing out the bus window.

"Why?" Tommy asked.

"They're building a newer and bigger one down river; it's going to be named Nick-a-Jack. Don't ask me where they came up with that name though. Hey, Tommy, I read in the paper that some of the divers that are setting the dynamite down by the old powerhouse there have refused to go back down."

"Why?"

"The catfish; they said some of them are big enough to swallow them whole."

"You're pulling my leg, aren't you, Jackie?"

"No, it's the truth,"

Tommy stared out the window at the partly demolished dam as the bus crept along behind the one-lane traffic.

The bus came slowly to a stop just as they started up the gradual incline of the old truss bridge. Traffic had grown to more than the two-lane highway could bear as they approached the small town of South Pittsburgh.

"Look, they're pulling an old car from the river," Tommy said, pointing out the bus window.

"Yeah, it looks like an old Ford, I bet it's been down there for a while," replied Jackie, watching the water pour from the grill of the twenty-five year old coupe. "I'll bet that old river holds a lot of secrets; no telling what they will find down there," Jackie added, settling back in his seat as the bus slowly started moving again.

"Yeah, no telling what." Tommy sighed.

THE AUTHOR

Jack Brisendine, born in Harlingen, Texas in 1944, grew up in the Chattanooga, Tennessee area where he still resides. He is a retired Postmaster and retired Master Sergeant from the U.S. Army Reserve. He is widowed and has two children and two grandchildren. "Old Money," his first fictional work, reflects the flavor and events of his own 1950s childhood.

Made in the USA
Columbia, SC
05 February 2025

53330771R00181